Brittany's hand swung back, and Paul realized that she intended to slap him.

He reacted automatically. First, he sidestepped swiftly, so that he no longer stood in the spot where he'd been just a moment ago. Next, as Brittany's hand whistled past him, he reached out and seized it. Then, before she could recover her balance, he captured and imprisoned her other hand, as well, jerking her hard against him.

For a couple of seconds they swayed, struggling together.

Even Paul didn't know what he intended to do until he found himself kissing her, crushing her petal-soft mouth beneath his own.

Only then, as his senses started swimming in sheer delight, did he understand that this was exactly what he'd wanted to do from the very first moment he'd seen her....

Dear Reader,

Once again, six Silhouette **Special Edition** authors present six dramatic new titles aimed at offering you moving, memorable romantic reading. Lindsay McKenna adds another piece to the puzzling, heart-tugging portrait of the noble Trayherns; Joan Hohl revives a classic couple; Linda Shaw weaves a thread of intrigue into a continental affair; Anne Lacey leads us into the "forest primeval"; and Nikki Benjamin probes one man's tortured conscience. Last, but certainly not least, award-winning Karen Keast blends agony and ecstasy into *A Tender Silence*.

What do their books have in common? Each presents men and women you can care about, root for, befriend for life. As Karen Keast puts it:

"What instantly comes to mind when someone mentions *Gone with the Wind*? Rhett and Scarlett. Characterization is the heart of any story; it's what makes you *care* what's happening. In *A Tender Silence*, I strived to portray two people struggling to survive in an imperfect world, a world that doesn't present convenient black-and-white choices. For a writer, the ultimate challenge is to create complex, unique, subtly structured individuals who are, at one and the same time, universally representative."

At Silhouette **Special Edition**, we believe that *people* are at the heart of every satisfying romantic novel, and we hope they find their way into *your* heart. Why not write and let us know?

Best wishes,

Leslie Kazanjian, Senior Editor
Silhouette Books
300 East 42nd Street
New York, N.Y. 10017

ANNE LACEY
Light for Another Night

Silhouette Special Edition

Published by Silhouette Books New York

America's Publisher of Contemporary Romance

ANNE LACEY

hails from Baton Rouge, Louisiana, an ideal jumping-off point for her ardent explorations of antebellum homes up and down the Mississippi River and her frequent visits to two favorite cities, Natchez and New Orleans. Having lived in Arkansas, Oklahoma, Arizona, Mississippi and several places in Texas and having traveled extensively in the United States, Europe and Canada, she admits to being a rolling stone. Even when she's busy writing, Anne keeps a bag packed at all times; after all, she never knows when a chance to travel might pop up.

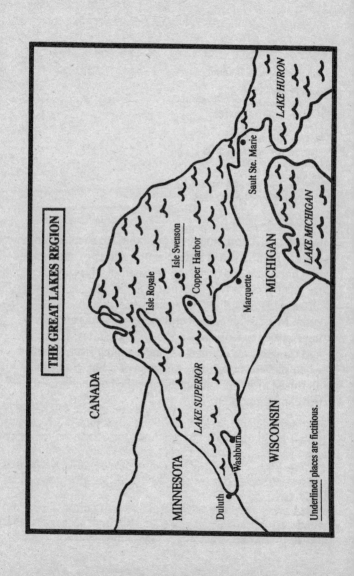

THE GREAT LAKES REGION

CANADA

MINNESOTA

Duluth

Washburn

WISCONSIN

LAKE SUPERIOR

Isle Royale

Isle Svenson

Copper Harbor

Marquette

MICHIGAN

Sault Ste. Marie

LAKE HURON

LAKE MICHIGAN

Underlined places are fictitious.

Prologue

Last Year, November 8

He hated to admit it but maybe they were right.

As the earnest, concerned voices, one after another, battered so relentlessly on Paul Johnson's ears he had to concede that they had built quite a case against him.

Clearly he was more messed up than he'd thought.

"We know how you felt about Peg. But, Paul, you've got to straighten up now and accept the reality of her death." That was Paul's mother, Gina Olszewski, strident and abrasive as always.

"Peg wouldn't have wanted you to act like this, Paul." That was the softer voice of Paul's mother-in-law, Ruth Foster. A less assertive woman than Gina, Ruth turned away to grope for the hand of her husband, Griff.

"We know what you're feeling, Paul, and how much you've missed Peg since she...left. After all, we lost her, too," Griff chimed in.

Did every single one of them have to mention Peg? Paul wondered resentfully. Each time they did he felt another stab from that knife already lodged in his heart.

But apparently they were bent on stabbing him more. For now Vicky, Peg's older sister by a year, was going on—and not only about Paul's recent misdeeds but about the grief that *she* felt, too, at the loss of her sister. But *she* hadn't caved in. *Her* behavior hadn't turned erratic. Vicky, with her red hair and freckled face, was another painful reminder of Peg.

What was being staged here, with all the family members ringed around his chair like so many accusing judges, was a classic "intervention," Paul realized. Obviously it had been set up in advance and all of its participants rehearsed by that smug-looking psychologist they'd called in. He was leaning back now against the Fosters' living room wall.

What Paul hadn't realized was exactly how much such an intervention could hurt.

Usually, of course, this was a method of confronting people with a substance addiction, but no one in this group would dare to call Paul alcohol- or drug-dependent. Because he wasn't. Still, his "sporadic abuse" of booze had already got a going-over, as well as every other thing he'd done wrong in the past several weeks.

The list they'd raked up was considerable. Paul felt jolted both by its length and severity.

"Mood swings," "hostility" and "sudden explosive anger" were just the beginning. That led to "arguments and fights in bars," "all those traffic tickets," and "that night you *almost* spent in jail after you shot off your mouth to the cop."

They still hadn't touched on the worst one. Paul tried to brace himself and be ready for its coming. He knew they were going to bring up the time he'd run off to Canada for three days with his young son, Chad.

Now it was Steve's turn. Steve Olszewski, the stepfather Paul had always detested, usually knew better than to tick Paul off. But tonight Steve was primed. Responsive to Gina's nod he hitched up his pants—Steve employed lots of macho gestures—and began. "Look, Paul, we've all noticed that you aren't acting like yourself—"

At last Paul felt goaded to respond. "How the hell do *you* know when I'm acting like myself?" he said icily to Steve.

Steve fixed Paul with a steel-eyed gaze. "Look, I know you don't like me, Paul. You never have. And I guess I know why. You think your mother and I married too quickly. Well, these things happen—"

"Flaming passion on the oncology ward?" Paul cut in, his words flippant but his voice still bitingly chill. "Why, even the nurses found your particular love affair unique. Of course, it might have been *nicer* if you'd waited till those two people in oxygen tents had finally quit breathing!"

"Now, just a minute, Paul!" Gina cut in angrily. "Your father and Steve's first wife died quite a long time ago. Steve and I have been married for years so I'd say we're doing something right. Which is certainly more than I can say for you! Why, you've never—"

"Just a minute, Gina." Griff Foster, who had the coolest, calmest head in the group, took charge before Gina could add something really devastating. Not that Paul was ignorant of what his mother, with her dollars-and-cents mentality and her cutting tongue, had intended to say.

"Paul, it's not only what you've done—it's what you haven't done as well," Griff continued. "Steve meant to say that even your mood swings are damaging. Obviously you've been uncertain about what to do next. And, God knows, *that's* certainly not like you! You've always charged full steam ahead. You haven't written a page of your novel since Peg died. I can understand why, of course. Still, I hate to see you abandon it after working on it for so long and being so close to the end. Why, that New York editor who read the first half was really interested in it."

The mention of his novel made Paul ache inside, too. It was another loss—and a substantial one at that—to add to the loss of Peg.

"Instead, you keep threatening to do this—or, no, it's that. Rent an apartment or try to find a house. Take a job with the Michigan tourist bureau or be a reporter on the newspaper...."

I lost my rudder when I lost Peg, that's what it amounts to, Paul thought bleakly.

"Next day, of course, you've lost all interest in whatever you were planning to do yesterday," Griff went on. "Or else you decide to buy a car...."

Oh God, Paul thought, and felt his fingers dig into the upholstery of the armchair where he sat, surrounded and confronted by the family. Here it comes.

"That's right!" Vicky said. "I didn't mind loaning you my car, Paul, but I surely didn't know you were going to take it *and* Chad off to the wilds of Canada."

This was Paul's latest offense and the one they were least understanding of. At Vicky's reminder, the other women chimed in shrilly.

"Don't you know we were out of our minds with worry, Paul?"

"That's right! I didn't sleep a wink for two nights, not until the Canadian Mounties called us from Thunder Bay and said you and Chad were all right—"

"We know you love Chad and I don't think he was *damaged* by your—adventure—but it sure didn't help him, either."

Chad. The last living link to Peg. How could I ever have done anything to worry or frighten Chad? Paul wondered. But he also knew he probably had.

Unbidden Paul heard the anxious echo of his young son's voice as it had sounded on the great locks at Sault Ste. Marie. "Daddy, if today's Tuesday shouldn't I be in school?"

Exuberantly and expansively Paul had replied, "Oh, Chad, we're not worrying about dreary things like school today. We're off to see some pretty ice sculptures in Canada and then we'll rent skates and find a pond...."

"Okay, Daddy. But can I go back home tomorrow for show-and-tell?" As Paul listened to the young voice in his head it grew more anxious. "And can I go to Dickie's birthday party on Friday—*please*?"

Now the people ringing Paul all spoke in unison, tripping over their tongues, contradicting themselves and each other. Only Paul's stepfather, Steve, remained silent, lacing his thick fingers together then bending them backward as he stared off uncomfortably. Of course, Steve was never really happy unless he was out in the pens with those damned dogs he'd bred, fussing over them and putting them through their paces. Briefly Paul wondered what a psychiatrist would make of Steve's canine fixation.

Then that thought, too, died away as Griff started to sum things up. "Paul, since Peg died you've done some reckless things and you apparently haven't been able to make any major decisions about the future. But you've got to get your act together now. Before you hurt yourself. Before you wind up really hurting Chad."

"Yes, I know." Slowly Paul allowed the huge and enormously painful realization to spring forth from deep inside him: Chad will really be better off if I'm not around.

"I guess you're right," Paul added reluctantly. Although he kept looking at Griff, he heard the group's collective sigh of relief.

It was for Chad's sake that he'd just made this agonizing admission. For himself, Paul didn't really care much one way or the other.

But he had to agree that Chad had been through enough. He was just a little boy who had already lost his mother, and he surely didn't need to be with a screwed-up father whose feelings were still too close to the surface and far too volatile to predict.

Yes, I have to pull myself together for Chad's sake, Paul realized. Fortunately, his son hadn't seen ol' Dad at his worst. Not yet, anyway. But the boy had definitely been confused by their rash trip to Canada.

Since an avalanche had upended Chad's small world all he wanted now was the comfortable sameness of school and show-and-tell. He wanted to be back at Aunt Vicky's house where he shared a room with her two young sons. And he certainly didn't want to miss his cousin Dickie's eighth birthday party.

As a relieved silence fell over the family, the psychologist stepped into the breach. "Well, Paul, now that you admit you've been having problems, the next logical step is to decide what you're going to do about them. Listen, there are some fine treatment programs available," he said heartily. "You might be interested in those designed for Vietnam veterans since—"

"No," Paul interrupted. The typical veteran's problems were far different from his. Nor did Paul have any interest in plumbing his darker motives for this or that. He turned to look back at his father-in-law instead. "Is my old caretaker's job on Isle Svenson still open?"

Griff's weathered face drew into a frown. "Yes, it is, Paul, but you shouldn't—"

"Then let me tell you what I'll do. I'll go back to that island where I lived for so long with Peg and Chad. I'll sit there at my typewriter until I can figure out how to write once again. After that, I'll try to finish my novel."

For my wife, Paul thought, but he didn't say the words aloud.

Peg had really cared about his book and had believed in its worth. She'd read all its pages enthusiastically and had always encouraged Paul to keep going, even during a couple of creatively dry periods when Paul himself had decided his novel was just plain no good.

Of course, Peg might have been biased. She'd loved him, after all. That was why she'd made so many sacrifices, both for Paul and for the novel he'd wanted to write.

Since going back to live alone on the island was perhaps the hardest thing Paul could possibly think of to do, maybe that was why he had to do it.

Wasn't that what he'd really been running away from ever since Peg had died? An entire island that was saturated with memories of her and their marriage, memories both poignant and sweet? As well as an unfinished novel that seemed as much Peg's as it was his?

If he could just manage to do these hard, *hard* things, then maybe he'd recover his interest in life again and find his way back to being the father Chad deserved. Paul knew he had always settled down when he was writing in the big lantern room at the top of the Isle Svenson lighthouse. He'd also kept his nose clean and his brain clear, the better to look out and appreciate the island's scenic glories. So, of course, he had to go back. Why had it taken him so long to understand that?

He barely heard the women's shocked outcries. "Not that cold lonely island!"

"Not right now, before Thanksgiving and Christmas!"

"You'll be so depressed without Peg!"

"That's enough, Ruth, Gina, Vicky. Paul's a grown man and he can decide what he wants to do," Griff reminded them.

"But what about Chad?" Vicky blurted.

Chad! Just thinking about leaving his son behind made Paul feel chilled. His spirits, all revved up just a second ago, plunged just as quickly. But there was no choice, of course. The boy's education and his other considerable needs must be met. Peg, an elementary teacher, had tutored Chad when they lived on the island and he was now a bright, inquisitive little boy.

Paul turned back to Vicky. "I think Chad should stay here with you—temporarily," he emphasized. "He's been enjoying school in a regular classroom, and he seems to fit right in with your two boys. He and Dickie are especially close. And I think he needs to keep on seeing that child psychologist, too—to work through his own feelings of grief and loss."

Vicky's anxious face eased. "Good."

Perhaps Vicky still needed to do something, Paul thought. She'd taken Peg's death very hard. Also, as the wife of a Great Lakes' seaman who was frequently away, Vicky had lots of time on her hands.

But, God Almighty, what about his life without Chad as well as Peg? It hardly seemed worth bothering with....

Then Paul took himself in hand and looked squarely across at Vicky. "Make no mistake. Just as soon as I'm coping better I want Chad back!"

Five days later, on a morning as gray and overcast as any he'd ever seen, Paul prepared to return alone to Isle

Svenson. As he waited on the dock for the supply boat to finish taking on its provisions, he was startled to see his stepfather, Steve, come running down the dock. Steve looked bluff and hearty in his jogging suit, his face reddened by the wind. As usual he had one of his German shepherds on a leash and it bounded along beside him.

"Glad we got here before you left," Steve panted as Paul stared at him wordlessly. Then Paul felt the dog's leash pressed into his cold gloved hand while an alert, curious animal reared up on its hind legs to study him. Its erect ears twitched; its black nose sniffed. Then a long length of wet pink tongue unfurled and the next thing Paul knew his face was receiving a cold damp lick.

"My God, Steve, get this damned dog off—" he began.

"Paul, this is Ivy. She's still young and frisky but she'll be a good friend to you."

And just like that Steve *gave* him the damned dog!

Chapter One

This Year, April 20

Are Yellowstone's famous grizzly bears in danger of starving?''

That provocative opening line in a newspaper article seized Brittany Hagen's attention immediately. Her long legs and booted feet, stretched out lazily before her, hit the bottom of the supply boat with a resounding thud. She sat up to read in earnest the morning newspaper whose pages she'd just been idly skimming. Another passenger, a man who had gotten off the supply boat at its first stop on Catt Island, had left the paper behind.

According to the article, legislators in Cheyenne were listening to arguments for and against reintroducing wolves into their state. Ranchers and wool growers objected, but wildlife experts argued that without wolves as natural predators the balance of nature had become upset. That, they said, breaks a natural food chain in the American West and imperils grizzly bears, such as those at Yellowstone Park.

How amazing! Brittany thought. This story tied right in with her own research study on Isle Svenson. Maybe some-

day her work would sway Western legislators to vote in favor of the much-maligned and misunderstood wolf. She
might even be asked to testify on matters of species preser-
vation and ecological integrity.

It was a heady notion, and Brittany would have happily
read the newspaper article on to its end. But, as she bent
back over it, the supply boat heading toward the lighthouse
on Isle Svenson entered rougher waters. As the boat began
to rock from side to side, Brittany's stomach took a similar
lift and plunge.

Quickly she pushed the newspaper aside and leaned her
head back against the side of the boat. I am not going to get
seasick, she vowed.

She closed her eyes and tried to think of something besides that steadily sinking sensation in her midsection.
Promptly her mind fleshed out her earlier fantasy.

"Ladies and gentlemen, the next scientist to testify before this committee will be Dr. Brittany Hagen, distin-
guished wildlife biologist from the University of—"

It was no good. As the supply boat continued to rock
Brittany's daydream evaporated. She was not a distin-
guished scientist, not yet, anyway. She was a mere graduate
student on her way to a long and probably grungy study on
an almost deserted island, and if she didn't get something
into her stomach quickly she was going to be very seasick
indeed! Swiftly she fumbled in a pocket of her parka for a
granola bar.

Lake Superior was really churning today, its blue waves
rough and high. Brittany finished her first granola bar and
bit into a second one just as quickly as she could get it un-
wrapped. With further reading clearly out of the question
she carefully folded up the newspaper article that debated
the rights of wolves to exist and jammed it into the box
closest to her feet.

That article with all its implications might impel her to go
on, once she was alone in the wild and mired deep in snow,
searching for moose carcasses or wolf dens with newborn
pups.

Gradually the granola bars helped quell Brittany's churning stomach even though she lamented their four hundred calories. She sat up straight and stared directly out at the horizon to avoid seeing the rocky, roiling, icy water and wished desperately that she'd never, ever heard of seasickness.

Since Brittany was already a little edgy about her forthcoming meeting with Paul Zachary Johnson she definitely didn't want to greet him with a green face.

What would he be like, she wondered, this guy she couldn't get any kind of fix on? Ask ten different people, as Brittany had done recently, and you wound up hearing ten different answers.

"Paul? He's a great guy!" said Brittany's former college roommate, Amber Villet.

Ordinarily that would have settled matters as far as Brittany was concerned. But on that particular day when she'd met Amber for lunch, two of her friend's male coworkers had tagged along.

They hadn't shared Amber's opinion. "Paul Johnson—*great*?" exclaimed one in surprise. "Why, that guy's a real bastard. Right, Tony?"

Tony had hesitated. "'Bastard' is kind of strong, though he was sure obnoxious that night we saw him at The Velvet Glove."

"*Paul?*" Amber had cried, whirling around in astonishment. "Hey, are we even talking about the same person? The writer? Dark-haired guy in his midthirties?"

"That's the one. He's lucky I didn't punch his lights out!"

This lack of consensus about someone she would soon meet and have to coexist with on an otherwise deserted island had naturally intrigued Brittany. Since Nash, Michigan, was a fairly small college town in the state's Upper Peninsula most people who lived there either knew or had heard of Paul Johnson. Apparently all of them had an opinion, too.

"Paul's a bit eccentric, like most artists."

"Frankly I always thought the best thing about Paul was Peg, his wife."

"Hey, haven't you heard? That poor guy nearly went around the bend after his wife died."

Even Brittany's hairdresser had ventured an opinion. "Honey, I knew Paul back in high school, before he got really serious about Peg Foster. Take it from me, *he's* the biggest wolf you're going to meet on that island!" Then with a grin and a final snip she had finished cutting Brittany's thick, straight blond hair.

So who was he, really? Brittany couldn't help wondering, especially since everyone usually added that Paul was also intelligent, gifted and attractive.

He sounded disturbingly like a certain man Brittany had tried very hard to forgive and now just wanted to forget forever.

But for eight weeks—no, make that nearly nine—she would be all alone except for Paul Johnson, published author, fairly recent widower and modern-day lighthouse keeper.

Of course, she could certainly look after herself on Isle Svenson, Brittany thought as she propped her feet back up on the camping gear that was piled all around her. At five foot eight, Brittany had always found little to fear from either mashers or muggers.

Anyway, she and this Johnson guy didn't exactly have to rub elbows, although a little friendly contact might be nice since they would be alone together in the middle of huge Lake Superior. And since Brittany had never met a published author before, she was just plain curious about Paul.

Later, as summer neared, various professors and their graduate students from the College of the Upper Peninsula would also arrive. Although the island was noted primarily for its famous old lighthouse, it was a popular place for researchers since it had been carefully preserved in its natural state.

The picturesque lighthouse stood only as a nostalgic sentinel now. Its light that had once flashed rhythmically across this, the largest and most dangerous of the vast Great Lakes, had been removed several years ago when newer navigational aids began to replace lighthouses. At that time the college had also converted the lighthouse into a dwelling of sorts.

"Paul has always kept his office in the lighthouse," Dr. Griffin Foster, Brittany's thesis adviser and, coincidentally, the young widower's former father-in-law, had told her. "Now he lives there, too. He says he finds it too depressing to be alone in the cottage where he lived with Peg and Chad. So you can stay there, Brittany, until the weather warms up enough for you to do fieldwork from a tent. You'll be more comfortable at the cottage, and I'm sure you won't mind sharing a kitchen with Paul."

Brittany wasn't entirely sure about that. She'd always been something of a kitchen nut, wanting dishes and silverware, pots, pans and other utensils kept sparkling clean and in their proper place.

"No, you're not a nut," Amber had told Brittany fondly when she'd shared this concern. "You're a bloomin' *fanatic*!"

On Isle Svenson, though, Brittany wouldn't have any choice. Oh well, it wouldn't kill her to share a kitchen for nine weeks. As a matter of fact, it might even come in handy since she hadn't known exactly how many groceries to bring for her first two-week stint. Since the supply boat wouldn't return for a fortnight it might help to have someone from whom she could borrow bread, butter or milk if she ran out.

Was Paul generous? No one had discussed his having that particular attribute.

Paul Johnson. Brittany frowned, realizing that the bland name bothered her because it sounded practically generic. It offered no new clues to the guy, either. Brittany was used to the more colorful ethnic names of the many different nationalities that had settled the Great Lakes—French, Polish and Dutch; German, Italian, Irish and, of course, all varieties of Scandinavian. Brittany herself was of Swedish and Norwegian descent.

But "Paul Johnson" sounded even more banal than "Howard Pierson."

Now why on earth was she thinking of that jerk again? She probably had Howard on her mind because when she'd seen Dr. Ingrid Jensen yesterday, that forthright woman had made immediate reference to Brittany's dashed plans. "Say, weren't you going to get married, Brittany? What happened?"

Discussing what happened was still far from Brittany's favorite topic.

Think about something else! she commanded herself now as she jammed the granola wrappers down into a pocket of her parka since littering here in the Great Lakes area was, in Brittany's opinion, tantamount to sacrilege.

Again she scanned the horizon, then excitement gripped her. Lo and behold! There was Isle Svenson looming up now. How wonderful finally to be here and how eager she felt to begin her work!

The island looked just as it had in all the color photographs Brittany had seen. A rocky shore where waves crashed and foamed; thick inland forests, pale green with birches and dark with fir and spruce, all still overhung with snow. And, of course, that unmistakable lighthouse so tall, white and appealing. Its unusual inhabitant, living high up in the lantern room, probably enjoyed a panoramic view of the harbor and the rest of the island, Brittany thought. She realized that she was curious about Paul Johnson's unique vantage point, too.

Brittany drew a deep breath and stood up, preparing to disembark.

From the lantern room at the tip-top of the lighthouse Paul watched the gleaming red-and-white supply boat head in toward shore. "Hey, Ivy, here comes your dog food!" he called. Then he reached for the warm windbreaker hanging on the back of his chair.

Ivy, sprawled on the landing of the spiral staircase two flights down, gave a canine sound of acknowledgement and began to thump her tail. She rarely waddled all the way up to the lantern room anymore, her unborn pups having distended her sides and slowed her once springy step.

But as Paul came whipping down the staircase, Ivy lumbered up heavily. "C'mon, girl," Paul urged.

Ivy, a genial dog, followed Paul down the steps obediently. Yet he knew she was less than enthusiastic about leaving the warm tower and plunging out into the sharp April wind. Damp and chill, it cut like a knife through layers of clothes and went straight to the bone. Winter's icy breath had definitely not abated.

But overnight a small miracle had happened. Beneath the white carpet at his feet Paul saw to his amazement that several tiny green shoots had stirred and wakened. Now a full inch of green plant poked up. A crocus? Paul thought and felt a rare surge of excitement lift his heart. Was that what Peg had called these same green shoots when they'd appeared last year?

Peg. Why, oh why, hadn't he appreciated her more? And why hadn't he done just a few more things to show her he did, instead of always intending to make everything up to her "later"?

He still missed his wife desperately. But, by now, Paul supposed he was fairly far along the comeback trail. Of course, it was hard for him to measure his own progress due to his still-persistent mood swings, even though they were less extreme now.

At least he had learned to identify his emotions instead of simply feeling overwhelmed by them. For the past couple of weeks Paul knew he'd been heavily into guilt and remorse. But even these seemed a positive step up from those first dark days when all he could feel was suffering and grief.

There was another change, too. Now it was no longer solely for Chad's sake that Paul braved the island with all of its memories. Nor was it strictly to honor Peg's memory that he forced himself to his typewriter each day and faced the difficult, painful process of putting his thoughts down on paper. Now, for his own sake, too, Paul wanted to recover and write again.

Alas, he still wasn't making a lot of progress at controlling his temper. Just last week, mired down in the mishmash of Chapter Thirteen, Paul had suddenly found himself in a towering rage, trembling and holding his typewriter suspended over his head. For one perilous minute he'd been ready to pitch it through the great wide window of the lantern room and send it crashing down to smash on the rocks far below.

At least he hadn't done it. And, overall, he was starting to write pretty well once again. But that anger, always waiting to flare, still mystified Paul. He never knew exactly what would set him off. A know-it-all letter from his mother telling him what he ought to do. Or an obstreperous jar of pickles that he couldn't manage to get opened. Or the hideous, demonic howls of the local wolf pack rending the quiet night peace of the island.

The only time in five-and-a-half months that Paul had ever struck Ivy was when she'd started howling in unison with the wolves. Then it was just a quick, glancing lick and Ivy had promptly forgiven him, although Paul still hadn't quite forgiven himself. These unexpected outbursts of anger told him he still wasn't quite ready to be Chad's daddy again and an otherwise responsible citizen on the mainland. So Paul had kept his visits back to Nash, Michigan, brief and infrequent, although he stayed in near-constant touch with his son through letters and shortwave radio. Fortunately Vicky and her husband were radio buffs.

He heard the supply boat cut its motor and start to glide smoothly into shore.

"C'mon, Ivy," Paul said a trifle impatiently, as he turned back to urge his pet through the lighthouse door. Laboriously Ivy plodded out, making a sound like a doggie sigh.

At first Paul had thought Ivy might have five or six puppies, but recently horror stories of ten to twelve had begun to cross his mind. He had already decided he must have been out of it ever to have let Steve talk him into breeding Ivy and later selling the puppies. Of course, after several months alone out here Paul had needed a distraction, a new interest, something—*anything*—to think of besides Peg, Chad or the pages of his book that still refused to jell. So on his last visit to the mainland Steve had caught Paul at a weak moment and, the next thing he knew, Ivy had supposedly been bred to one of Steve's shepherds.

Paul sure hoped they weren't wrong about that!

Now, as the boat began maneuvering into position to dock and unload the supplies, Paul drew a deep breath of fresh, fir-scented air and looked all around. Each day there was less snow and more exposed brown grass that would later turn green. At the moment the wind had died down, too, and the temperature felt almost tolerable, although the waves crashing toward shore still left ice crystals glittering on the rocks. Suddenly as Paul contemplated the pleasant scene—golden sunlight sparkling on snow and a pale blue sky above the churning, sapphire-blue water—he felt that eager leap of life once again.

"C'mon, Ivy," he encouraged his dog. "Let's walk down to the dock. Why, I'll bet they've brought you crunchy Milkbones for your teeth, and dry cereal that makes its own gravy, and cans just packed with chunks of meat—"

Ivy gave a more encouraged sound. She definitely understood "meat."

Together they started down the long stone walk to the dock that jutted far out over the water. Halfway there the dog stopped, frankly panting. Uh-oh, I haven't been giving her enough exercise, Paul thought as he reached down to scratch behind Ivy's ears.

Lately he'd been letting everything slide, but at least he had finally wrestled Chapter Thirteen into acceptable shape. Now he didn't have much further to go to The End.

At just the moment when he straightened up again, Paul saw a young woman leap unaided off the supply boat. Abruptly he froze, caught utterly by surprise.

If an errant breeze hadn't blown the navy cap from her head, releasing a rippling wave of Rapunzel-like blond hair, Paul probably wouldn't have guessed her sex or age so readily.

She was quite tall—several inches taller than he preferred a woman to be—and rather solidly built as well. Of course, she was all bundled up and winter padding tended to make people look heavier. Paul, gazing at her in astonishment, saw the woman's parka gape open to reveal full breasts encased in a white sweater. From the fit of her gray wool slacks Paul could also tell that she was generously endowed in the hips department as well.

Definitely she was not the type he would have noticed back in the long-ago days before he'd been married. Although Paul used to watch women a lot then and mentally size them up, he knew he would probably not have paid Ms. Queensize any special attention. Except, perhaps, for admiring that long gorgeous hair.

It was a ripe golden blond that didn't look as if it had come from a bottle. Then, as the woman turned and Paul saw her face with its high cheekbones and striking features, the breath caught suddenly in his chest. Momentarily he forgot how to exhale.

Valkyrie.

The comparison leaped swiftly into his mind. Yes, that was exactly what this big beautiful blonde, so obviously of Scandinavian descent, reminded him of. She looked like paintings of those warrior maidens who had served Odin, the Norse god of death. Beautiful and awful, the legendary Valkyrie were described. Howling, shrieking, raging...

Of course, all this particular woman was doing was chasing after a flyaway cap.

Who was she and what on earth was she doing *here*? Paul wondered, awakening as if from a dream to the reality of his duties. Now she was scowling, an expression scarcely calculated to make a woman look appealing. But Paul felt a spontaneous chuckle rise in his throat. This woman definitely had a few drops of Valkyrie blood.

The latest gust of wind landed the navy cap right at Ivy's feet.

Ivy barked and pounced on it eagerly. Seizing the cap firmly between sharp white teeth, well-honed on a thousand doggie biscuits, Ivy began shaking it as if it were one of her favorite playthings.

"No, Ivy!" Paul yelled, moving belatedly to the dog's side. He knew some of those caps carried designer labels, although he would never pay their whopping price tags.

Swiftly he bent down to retrieve the cap but Ivy only locked her jaws tighter, grinding her teeth.

"Ivy, give that here!" Paul commanded.

But Ivy was having the first fun she'd had in days, growling and snapping and shaking the cap all around.

"*Ivy!*"

The blonde rushed up to them just as Paul applied a certain pressure-hold to the underside of Ivy's jaw. He'd learned it in Vietnam for use on night patrols. Ivy gave a surprised whine and promptly spat out the cap. Paul scooped it up, finding it well gnawed and very wet.

"Sorry," he said and extended the cap to the young woman.

Now, as Paul saw her up close for the first time, he marvelled over her large expressive eyes. They looked as clear and sapphire-blue as Lake Superior itself, and she had very fair skin that was smooth, fine-textured, and tinted rose by the wind.

She took her knitted cap and inspected it anxiously. Then as her index finger poked through a hole she groaned. "Oh, no!"

"Family heirloom?"

He knew the minute he said it that he'd sounded too flippant, too uncaring. But, after all, he was a man who kept matters in perspective. Compared to life without his wife and child, one dog-gnawed cap didn't seem like the end of the world.

"No, just brand-new. My going-away present," the tall blonde said ruefully. As she raised her head to look directly at him, Paul was struck full force by her fresh vibrant beauty.

Her face was a perfect oval; her brows and lashes a light natural brown. Of course, he was making a purely impersonal observation, Paul assured himself.

"Where are you going?" he inquired automatically.

"Why—*here!*"

For the first time, Paul noticed that the men on the supply boat were busily unloading a veritable ton of boxes. From the lettering on the sides they obviously held scientific equipment and camping gear. There were also lots of groceries. Paul's two modest grocery sacks were already dwarfed by ten or twelve others that he certainly hadn't ordered. Perplexed, he turned back to the woman, noting irrelevantly that her lips were exquisitely shaped and colored with that robust pink that denotes good health.

The perfect lips parted. "I'm Brittany Hagen," the woman announced.

She spoke to Paul as if her name ought to ring some bells. Rapidly he scanned his memory banks. Nothing.

Because she looked like a graduate student, Paul decided to assume she was. After all, he couldn't imagine anyone else who would want to come out here now, while the snow was still hip-high in the interior of the island. Of course, the college was always supposed to let him know well in advance of anyone's arrival, especially if the visitor would be on Isle Svenson for more than a day. Since Paul had received no such notification and the amount of Brittany's gear certainly indicated she'd come to stay for a while, he knew he'd better check this out.

He also found himself hoping that there had been a mistake. Brittany Hagen was absolutely the last thing a serious author needed to have hanging around. This woman was just too—too distracting!

"You don't look as if you've ever heard of me," she observed astutely. Although uncertainty flickered in her deep blue eyes there was hint of defiance in her voice.

"I guess I missed receiving the usual letter." Paul spoke rapidly, trying to sound as businesslike as possible. "There's no problem, I'm sure." Suddenly he remembered that he hadn't even introduced himself and stuck out his hand. "I'm Paul Johnson."

"Yes, I know." The blonde's blue eyes had narrowed slightly but there was real distress in her voice as she gave his gloved hand a perfunctory brush. "I can't believe—I mean, Dr. Foster made a point of telling me how he'd written you about my coming."

Son-of-a-bitch! Paul thought. Wouldn't you know she'd be Griff's graduate student!

Looking back into her eyes Paul tried to pull this situation together. What he definitely didn't need was to have Golden Girl here writing to Griff and complaining about Paul's dereliction of duty—if, indeed, this particular mix-up really was his fault. Drearily Paul suspected that it probably was, just because he'd been so preoccupied lately with Chapter Thirteen.

"No problem, Ms.—ah—Hagen," he said to her formally since he certainly didn't intend to get on a cozy, first-name basis. "I'll go—ah, verify—"

He lost his train of thought as another, far worse notion struck him suddenly.

Dubiously Paul looked at all of Ms. Hagen's gear, which was still being piled on the dock. "You'll be staying in a tent? Won't that be awfully cold this time of—"

"Dr. Foster said I could stay at the cottage until the weather warmed up. He said that you lived in the lighthouse now."

Ominous echoes intermingled with the uncertainty in her voice.

The cottage! Inwardly Paul winced. Oh God, when had he ever cleaned it? For that matter, had he even bothered to pick it up lately? Usually he did but for the past couple of weeks he'd just been over at the cottage long enough to fix something to eat. And Paul knew perfectly well that he'd dirtied every single dish, skillet, pot and pan, even using some of them more than once. He knew because they were all still there, an awesome unwashed heap piled and waiting in the sink.

Unfortunately the laundry room was in the same approximate state.

Paul longed to groan. Although he wasn't the neatest person in the best of times he didn't usually live like such an unregenerate slob.

"I'll be right back," he said aloud to Brittany Hagen. "Make yourself comfortable. Oh, I suppose you've gotten signatures on all those required forms—"

"Yes. They were all signed before I left the college."

Paul noticed that her voice had acquired a detectable chill. He was also aware that she'd interrupted him twice, because he'd always hated it when people did that.

"Health card, too?" he asked, his own voice growing clipped.

"It's being processed. I saw Dr. Ingrid Jensen yesterday, if you wish to check with her."

Paul knew that he needn't bother Dr. Jensen. Ultimately the green card—or was it the long yellow one?—would wend its way out to him. In fact, right now Paul frankly didn't care if Brittany was Typhoid Mary. All he cared about was that she not make an unfavorable report of him and his actions to Griff.

Paul certainly didn't want all the family trooping out here to confront him once again!

"I've never really figured out what those health cards are for," he said to Ms. Hagen, striving to sound friendly again. "Do they really think graduate students are going to introduce Australian fruit fly or killer bees?"

His lighthearted remark elicited no reaction, not even a faint smile, from the tall lady.

No sense of humor, Paul decided, rubbing a hand over his untidy beard. Yes, this was definitely the sort of woman who wouldn't have been a bit of fun on a date.

"I'll be back," he muttered and took off in a sprint, leaving Ivy to either stay outside or follow along at her own pace. Paul really wasn't surprised when he heard his dog padding after him. Something about Ms. Brittany Hagen, some small but definite thing, was downright chilling.

Make yourself comfortable, Paul had said but just how was she supposed to do that? Brittany wondered. Couldn't he have at least invited her inside the cottage or the lighthouse where she could sit down?

She supposed that both were probably an ungodly mess if Paul Johnson was a typical man who hadn't been expecting company. Since Brittany had grown up with three older brothers she knew well the ways of unmarried males.

She walked back down to the lake's edge and looked around curiously. The long wooden dock could accommodate good-sized ships, but, according to Dr. Foster, Paul was an indifferent sailor and content to use the small runabout for traveling between islands. Brittany supposed that Paul's craft was presently anchored inside the nearby boat house built at the end of the dock, but she wasn't curious enough to go see.

Instead, as she watched the choppy water and listened to the crash of waves Brittany thought again of all the contradictory comments she'd heard about Paul Johnson, measuring them mentally against the man she'd just met.

He had appeared sober and stable. He hadn't been flirting with her, either, although Brittany knew she had seen something ignite in the depths of his eyes. He had dark, restless, changeable eyes, she'd noticed. Still, her overall impression was of a man somewhat distracted and more than a little dismayed but determined to be businesslike.

Of course, the absolute last thing Brittany had imagined was that Paul wouldn't be expecting her.

He was attractive all right. No one had misled her about that. But Paul Johnson wasn't her type at all. The three men who had figured prominently in Brittany's past had all been of the same general build as her father and brothers: big and tall, broad-shouldered and athletic. The kind who were usually described as rugged rather than attractive or even handsome.

Paul, though, quite definitely qualified as attractive. Indeed, he bordered on handsome, even with his brush of a moustache and black, pointed, Lucifer-like beard. Even with the thick drab fisherman's sweater he wore over none-too-clean jeans.

Sighing, Brittany kicked at a stone in her path and sent it arcing out over the water. She really didn't like beards on men, and moustaches rated only a little higher in her opinion. Of course, she could also appreciate that a man wintering alone on a snow-encrusted island might have reason for growing all the hair he could.

For the rest, Paul was a dark, slender, clever-looking man. "A slight fellow," Brittany's brothers would say disparagingly. He stood less than an inch taller than Brittany herself, and she frankly suspected that Paul probably weighed only ten or fifteen pounds more than she did, too.

Not that she needed to concern herself with appearances, either his or hers. She was here solely to do a job, Brittany reminded herself. The supply boat began pulling off now, headed across the icy blue waters for its next stop, and Brittany gave the men working topside a farewell wave.

Then she swung around resolutely. She had a lot of work to do and needed to get started or she wouldn't be able to manage an hour in the woods today. She could start by hauling all this stuff up to the cottage. Wryly Brittany contemplated the crates of equipment, the boxes and piles of supplies and sacks of groceries. She had hoped that Paul Johnson might offer some muscle to help with the lifting and lugging. So much for idle hopes.

Halfway to the cottage with her first load Brittany passed Paul's dog who had stopped to rest. Ivy—wasn't that what he had called her? "You mutt," Brittany began accusingly, thinking of the smart new wool knit cap that Amber had given her only yesterday and that Ivy had riddled today.

Ivy looked up with a hopeful whine and Brittany relented. Ordinarily she loved animals; furthermore, she could usually understand their behavior. "Oh, all right," she grumbled. "I guess my cap blowing in the wind did look irresistible. A brand-new toy to fight and shake. But did you have to gouge out such a big hole?"

As she talked, Brittany's gaze ran professionally over Ivy. Although this particular bitch looked as if she might whelp at any time, Brittany suspected that a German shepherd, still so close to its wolf ancestors both in appearance and behavior, probably had another two or three weeks of pregnancy.

It took nine round trips, but Brittany finally hauled all of her gear and supplies up to the porch of the small stone cottage. At least you're working off those granola bars, she consoled herself. But she also couldn't help feeling annoyed when she glanced up once and saw Paul Johnson standing at the top of the lighthouse, framed in the great expanse of window.

An ironic realization came to Brittany then. For days she had been concerned with trying to learn just who and what Paul Johnson was, and in all that time he hadn't even known she was alive!

Paul had risked a coronary by racing up all the many steps to the lantern room. Here, where the bright lighthouse beacon had once flashed, a large, round glassed-in chamber now existed.

That great light with its valuable Fresnel lens was stored now on the mainland in the museum at the College of the Upper Peninsula. In its place Paul had set up his writing equipment: desk, electric typewriter and file case. Later he had added the narrow bed that had once been Chad's since Paul still couldn't bring himself to sleep in his and Peg's double bed.

Gasping from his own recent lack of exercise and filled with foreboding, Paul yanked open his file case. What had he done with Griff's last letter, the one he'd never quite finished reading?

Midway through the letter Griff had begun to indulge in some fatherly recollections of Peg. Perhaps he had found comfort in relating those childhood incidents to the man who had become Peg's husband, but the attempt to read them had threatened to shred Paul's emotional control. *Later,* he had decided and folded the letter back into its envelope.

Now, cursing fluently, Paul flipped through a stack of correspondence he hadn't answered yet until he found Griff's thick letter. He impatiently scanned first one page, then another. While he was still speed-reading he heard Ivy come panting back up the stairs. There was a plop when she sprawled heavily on the landing.

Ah-hah! Sure enough, Paul found mention of Ms. Hagen on the next-to-last page, although Griff's information was terse and straight to the point. ''An excellent student working toward her master's," Paul read. "Devoted to her study of *Canis lupus*—" which Paul gathered meant gray timber wolf "—and capable of assessing various aspects of wolf-moose dynamics," whatever the hell Griff meant by that.

"I'd appreciate any help you can give her," Griff's letter concluded.

Paul sighed as he replaced the letter in its envelope. Then, in another outburst of unexpected anger, he slammed the file drawer shut with such force that Ivy gave a sharp yelp of protest.

"Sorry, old girl," Paul called out to her, chastened at having frightened a pup-heavy mother-to-be. But, for once, he knew exactly why he was angry as the truth of Ms. Hagen's presence sank in. He was going to have her here on the island, staying at the cottage and getting in his way, for weeks! Now, of all times, when Paul was finally writing well again and about to break through the mental cobwebs that had hung him up on Chapter Thirteen. Was there no justice at all?

Brittany's wolf study elicited no sympathy from him, either. How he hated those miserable, slinking animals! Although he had only glimpsed wolves on three occasions and then only as fast-moving silvery shadows, Paul had never got used to their eerie night howling. With his bias, Paul couldn't imagine why anyone liked wolves or would want to study them, either.

He turned and glanced casually out the closest window just to see what Ms. Hagen was up to at present.

She was dropping an armload of supplies beside a stack already situated on the cottage porch.

I didn't even offer to help her, Paul remembered belatedly. Nor had he extended a genuinely welcoming word. Now he was going to have to unlock that dusty cottage for her and reveal its stacks of dirty dishes and dirty laundry, heaped high and running over.

"Oh—" Paul muttered an unprintable word as he dashed back down the stairs.

But by the time he finally got to the cottage Ms. Hagen had already parted company with her supplies. Indeed, she had pulled out her snowshoes and set off to see the island for herself, her tall straight figure moving along rapidly in the direction of the dark thick forest.

Brittany followed an old Indian trail that led into the snow-covered woods. By the time it petered out a half-mile later she had caught a shimmering blue glimpse of an inland lake and could locate her position on a detailed map of Isle Svenson.

Picking her way around trees and through brush newly freed of snow by the warmth of the sun, Brittany edged down closer to the lake. Then, spotting a large brown shadow through the evergreens, she froze.

According to Dr. Foster the several inland lakes were always favored by the moose population, and Brittany saw immediately that he hadn't been wrong. Standing knee deep in near-freezing water was a healthy and full-grown cow.

With her large, long head, pendulous upper lip and immense ears she was quite an unlovely creature. Also detracting from her appearance were shoulders higher than her rump, a short thick neck and body and a mere stump of a tail. But perhaps the moose's least attractive characteristic was her "bell," that growth of loose skin covered with thick hair that hung from her throat.

"Lady, you are ugly as sin!" Brittany breathed, then gave a low laugh of satisfaction when she saw that this particular moose was also a recent mother.

Twin calves, splashing in shallower water, wobbled over on spindly legs to their mother's teats. Their suckling disturbed the cow not at all. She continued browsing, chewing away placidly on a growth of evergreens that protruded from the bank over the sparkling blue water.

Some distance from Mother Moose and her homely babies, other large brown shapes moved around. They reminded Brittany that adult moose were basically loners—the only exception occurring during mating season. As Brittany moved cautiously away through the underbrush to examine more moose, she spied a large bull whose head was topped with an enormous rack of antlers.

For the better part of the hour Brittany had allotted herself she circled the small lake and studied the various moose, which all looked healthy and fully able to browse. At a first glance the moose population was reproducing satisfactorily and had survived the worst of winter just fine. This was what had been predicted for them by an earlier researcher.

Brittany had already started back toward the cottage when, in a moment of serendipity, she came up on an old cow, thin and visibly arthritic. Ultimately Grandma would probably be prey for this island's as-yet-unseen predator, the wolf. Or would the poor old girl die of disease or starvation? Brittany wondered, seeing the difficulty with which the old cow browsed.

Brittany frankly hoped her fate was the former. Death by wolves was swift in comparison to the other alternatives. But were many—or any—wolves still alive on Isle Svenson? Their numbers when last recorded were perilously low; their continued existence appeared threatened.

It was up to her to determine whether the wolves were becoming extinct, holding their own or staging a comeback. And already Brittany had begun. Automatically her eyes swept the gentle hillside slopes as well as the ground; she looked for likely places for a wolf's den and watched for paw prints or droppings.

That she saw no signs of wolves today didn't necessarily surprise Brittany. They weren't called wily wolves for nothing. And seeing the various moose was enough of a kick for her first day's outing. Now it was time to go back and face the island's thus-far-unfriendly caretaker and find out just what sort of mess he'd left her in the cottage.

Chapter Two

It's all right," Brittany said again to Paul.

She had repeated that phrase over and over until she knew she must sound like a broken record. But she was simply too horrified to think of anything else to say.

She was lying through her teeth, of course. Because, dammit, it really wasn't all right! At least her continued repetition of those three simple words had caused Paul's visibly tense countenance to relax. Now all Brittany had to worry about was how much longer she could control her own facial expressions, even as she wondered what to make of him.

Paul mystified her completely. Either he stared at Brittany intently, as though he found her perfectly fascinating, or he stepped away and glanced off in such a show of colossal indifference that Brittany felt at a loss. He was certainly businesslike to the point of brusqueness.

"Have you ever used this type stove before?" he asked, gesturing as he led Brittany through the rooms of the small, neglected-looking cottage.

She glanced in the direction Paul indicated. "Yes, I have."

"Take a closer look. These stoves are practically antiques—no, make that relics."

As Brittany turned in surprise to stare at Paul, he looked away from her again as though under her scrutiny he grew acutely uncomfortable. Then as if realizing some explanation was called for he continued. "The last graduate student who spent a night here woke me up at 3:00 a.m. Said he was freezing and couldn't start the stove. Frankly it wasn't my favorite time to run to the rescue."

"Look, I promise you I really have used this type of stove before," Brittany protested. And it doesn't work worth a hoot during a blizzard, she felt like adding.

Paul stopped, crossed his arms and leaned back against the wall in a deceptively casual stance. "Where?" he demanded, staring intently once again while that mysterious something flickered in the depths of his eyes.

Brittany threw him a harassed glance. Maybe she should question this man's stability, after all. Maybe she'd been too quick to judge him sane and normal. Because now, in her opinion, he was acting like a borderline paranoid-schizo that she'd be wise to humor.

"This same old type of stove is in my parents' farmhouse in Northern Minnesota," Brittany said, choosing her words carefully. "Of course, their house is practically antique, too."

"Where in Northern Minnesota?" Paul inquired but now he spoke in a casual, offhand way.

"Little Stavanger."

When Brittany named the nearest town Paul gave a short bark of humorless laughter.

"What's so funny?" she asked defensively.

Despite his laugh, the handsome face was cool, his black eyes narrowed reflectively. "'Stavanger' doesn't sound like a town. It sounds more like a disease. A Scandinavian community, huh?"

Brittany absorbed the insult to her hometown in silence and gave a swift nod to his question. "Yes. It's named after Stavanger, Norway. That's a port city on the North Sea, near the fjords.''

"Maybe that's why 'Stavanger' sounded familiar." Paul turned and led the way out of the larger of the cottage's two bedrooms while Brittany tagged behind.

"Did you grow up in Michigan?" she asked Paul politely. A few things about him, including an accent she couldn't quite place, were enough to make her wonder.

"I think I grew up in Vietnam," he replied obliquely. Then he deflected the obvious questions Brittany would have asked by saying, "Please follow me to the kitchen now."

There Brittany's mouth almost dropped open in horror and dismay. Talk about a complete kitchen collapse! Never in her twenty-seven years had she seen such an elaborately teetering mound of unwashed dishes. No, not just dishes, either, she thought, doing a startled double take as she spotted numerous pots and pans as well as piles of silverware.

Paul, ignoring the towering debacle, pointed out the smoke alarm on the wall and water-filtering system attached to the sink faucet. Then he went straight to a cabinet and threw it open to reveal several stacked boxes of plastic sacks.

"Rule No. 1 on this island is do not ever litter or dump," he emphasized, his voice stern.

"I wouldn't think of—" Brittany started to protest only to find herself cut off effectively.

"Here we bundle up all trash in these black plastic sacks. For garbage, use those smaller self-sealing white ones. After you've sealed the garbage sacks, freeze them. Both garbage and trash are always hauled away by the supply boat, in case you didn't notice," he instructed.

"No, I didn't," Brittany admitted.

"That's okay. Anyway, hauling debris is one of my duties. Just handle yours properly and I'll take care of getting them to the supply boat. You see, we try to minimize man's impact on this island in every way possible."

"Woman's, too?" Brittany asked impishly, but her crack elicited only a pained expression from him.

"Please remember to use the plastic," Paul emphasized.

"All right," Brittany said, feeling deflated by him even as she worried about the environmental impact of all those plastic sacks adding up year after year. Better to ask about that some other time, she decided and touched a kitchen counter tentatively. Immediately she regretted her gesture since her fingers came away feeling sticky.

"The machines in the laundry room have directions posted on them." Paul threw open the door to a small utility area that was freezing cold and harbored more appalling stacks and mounds. Unwashed clothes this time.

Brittany was rendered completely speechless by the sight.

"Wash only when it's absolutely necessary," Paul cautioned. "Use the soap that's provided. While it doesn't pollute the environment we still ask that you use as little of it as possible."

Clearly he took his own message straight to heart, Brittany thought. But, of course, she didn't dare say as much.

"Now." Paul leaned back against the washing machine in the small frigid room and crossed his arms again, looking distant and remote. "Do you have any questions?"

Only a thousand, Brittany thought. "No," she said, shivering.

"Once again, I'm sorry I wasn't prepared for you, Ms. Hagen. I'm also sorry that this place is such a mess." Restlessly Paul shifted from one foot to the other as if he were dying to get away from her. Or was she just being too sensitive? Brittany wondered.

"It's all right," she lied again, this time through her chattering teeth.

At last she was all alone, Paul having fled the cottage with visible relief. That wasn't very flattering to her, Brittany thought, although she'd been almost equally relieved to see him go.

Her experience with Howard Pierson had taught her to beware very attractive men, so Brittany had found Paul's striking good looks more than a trifle disconcerting. The mess he'd left behind was more so. What a shame he couldn't carry off all his revolting piles of dirty dishes and laundry.

To give Paul his due, he had already started one wash load churning in the tiny unheated laundry room. And, he had scrubbed up one major pile of dishes and pots before leaving, although "too little, too late" summed up Brittany's frank opinion of these endeavors. She also knew she would simply have to wash those dishes all over again before she dared to use them.

Now that she had the cottage all to herself Brittany inspected it slowly and carefully.

This could be nice, she thought as she savored its warmth, simplicity and rustic charm. The Early American furniture looked old but well cared for and there were built-in bookcases crammed with volumes, a welcome sight to Brittany who was a voracious, if highly critical reader. A fireplace in the living room added to the overall coziness although the hearth was cold at the moment and filled with ashes.

If only this place wasn't so filthy! Brittany silently bewailed as she trailed a disdainful finger through several weeks' accumulation of dust.

She couldn't possibly spend the night here until the cottage had been properly cleaned, the kitchen and bath sanitized and the mattress in the master bedroom aired and sunned. Although Brittany's brothers used to joke that "dust rarely kills and even dirt's only occasionally known to be fatal," she still could not abide either. Fortunately broom, mop, sponges and disinfectants—biodegradable, of course—were all at hand. Apparently Paul's late wife had shared her own passion for cleanliness, Brittany thought with relief. Sighing, she rolled up her sleeves and began.

An hour later she had mopped both the living room and kitchen floors; she had also scoured every kitchen counter and dusted every tabletop along her path. The refrigerator, teeming with pathological-looking leftovers, she had emptied and cleansed. Amazingly the interior of the oven still looked sparkling clean, but as Brittany wiped it out hastily she decided that Paul probably did little if any baking.

Next, she dragged her assortment of rags and bucket of fresh lemon-scented water into the larger bedroom she intended to occupy since it was the only one with furniture. The smaller bedroom was bereft of bed, chair or chest of drawers. Apparently it was used only for storage now although its wallpaper, featuring familiar Disney characters, indicated that it had previously belonged to a child.

It was in the larger bedroom that Brittany spotted the family photograph. It sat on top of the nightstand. Curious, she walked over and picked it up, blowing dust off the glass at the same time.

Three smiling faces looked back at her, and despite Brittany's determination to simply get on with this unwelcome job, her heart gave a lurch. Suddenly a new understanding of Paul Johnson with his mercurial moods and changeable black eyes was born in her and threatened to break through Brittany's own coolly impersonal attitude.

They looked as if they'd been such a happy family. What on earth must life be like for him now?

In the photograph Paul Johnson stood with an arm around his small, red-haired, freckle-faced wife. She was not a raving beauty, Brittany reflected, spotting a definite familial resemblance to Dr. Griff Foster who wasn't one, either. Still, Mrs. Elizabeth Foster Johnson, better known as Peg, had obviously been possessed of both personality and good humor. They gleamed in her pixie face and bright brown eyes.

She was short and delicately built—the petite sort of woman that most men, even six-footers, usually preferred, Brittany thought glumly. A hundred pounds tops was her estimate of Peg's weight, for like most women locked into lifelong combat with calories and bathroom scales Brittany could assess another woman's size quite accurately.

Slowly her gaze returned to Peg's face and all the liveliness etched there. Peg had died young, either in her late twenties or early thirties, in an accident of some kind—Dr.

Foster hadn't elaborated on the details and Brittany hadn't wanted to press him.

Next, Brittany turned her attention to the child. She'd always had a soft spot for kids, and how young this little man was. Chad, she remembered from her earlier conversation with Dr. Foster. At present Chad was six and attending the first grade in Nash, Michigan.

He was cute, dark and thin like his father, but with a spattering of Peg Johnson's freckles across his nose. In the photograph Chad looked very happy, leaning back against his mother's knees. As Brittany studied his small laughing face she felt that pang go through her again.

Why wasn't Paul living on the mainland with his son?

Something about this family didn't quite add up. According to Dr. Foster, in Nash Chad had aunts, uncles, cousins, even another set of grandparents nearby. The devotion of these people kept the boy busy and distracted from his grief.

But from the beginning, when Dr. Foster had offered this explanation, Brittany had sensed another more complex story. Now that feeling grew even stronger, because wouldn't Chad need his father first and foremost?

"Maybe not," Brittany said aloud, remembering again all those divergent opinions of Paul. Just which of them, if any, were correct remained to be seen.

I wonder if I'll ever marry and have a child, she thought as she replaced the photograph on the nightstand.

Oh, what did it matter? Marriage was certainly not her first and foremost goal. Undertaking a valuable biological study here and writing her master's thesis was! Nor did Brittany necessarily feel pressured to marry. If she did remain single, her aunts Greta and Kristen would probably leave her their bakery just so Brittany's safe, solvent old age could be assured.

Of course, it was a little too soon for her to give up on marriage or to entertain thoughts of a late-life change of career, either.

"Howard wasn't the right man for you. But you'll find someone else," Dr. Ingrid Jensen had assured Brittany only yesterday.

In the past year Brittany's mother had frequently said the same thing.

"Look, it's all right," Brittany kept telling people. That she should often reassure them over her own broken engagement was apparently just one more of life's ironic little twists.

At the same time, though, she was no longer sure that marriage was utterly inevitable for her. She certainly wasn't going to count on it any longer. "Do you really want to know how you can help me?" she'd asked her distraught parents just one traumatic year ago. "Stop saving money for my wedding or planning an elaborate one. Help me go back to college instead. I need a master's degree if I'm ever going to advance in my career. And since I've already quit my job and given up my apartment in Duluth there will never be a better time than right now!"

Brittany's father had nodded his agreement. "Just tell me how much you need and I'll go to the bank and get it."

"But..." Brittany's mother had begun, her hand unconsciously caressing the beautiful wedding dress she'd made for her only daughter. Anna Hagen had found it difficult and painful to abandon her own special dreams. But then she, too, had nodded, her lips closed with resolution.

So Brittany had returned to the College of the Upper Peninsula with a new sense of commitment to her career. She'd long been interested in wolves. Now the struggle to save various wolf species in areas of the U.S. where they were endangered, as well as various proposals to reintroduce them into other areas that were once their native habitat, had become a matter of vital concern to her.

But as Brittany finished mopping the bedroom and gathered up her cleaning supplies, her gaze went again to the family in the photograph on the nightstand.

She walked out into the living room—and practically collided with Paul Johnson.

"I thought you'd gone!" Brittany blurted and received a cool stare from Paul in return. Immediately she realized how very unwelcoming she'd sounded. After all, until a couple of hours ago, this cottage had been strictly his.

"You've been cleaning up, I see." Paul moved deliberately away from Brittany to stand in the middle of the living room floor where he slowly looked all around.

"Yes, I have," she said.

"Whatever makes you happy."

Brittany's spine went rigid. She felt sure she heard sarcasm echoing in Paul's voice even though his features remained expressionless. Surely he didn't for one minute believe she actually enjoyed cleaning up after a strange man! Wearily she bent back to her work, determined to ignore him, but when Paul started walking toward the kitchen it was simply too much for Brittany's fastidious nature.

"Look, the floors are still wet," she said. "Either get off of them or else take off your shoes—please."

Paul stopped cold before she'd finished speaking, clearly stunned. That's why Brittany had hastily tacked on that "please" as an afterthought. Nevertheless his thick black eyebrows shot upward at her imperious command.

Oh, Lord, I've done it now, Brittany thought. But when her gaze returned to Paul's feet, shod in heavy thick-soled shoes on which both snow and soil were caked, she couldn't help adding, "Please, Paul! I've really been working very hard."

"Yes, I can tell by the way the place smells."

Was that another crack? At any rate, he had started retracing his steps to the door.

"Thank you," Brittany murmured, determined to prove she could also be gracious.

"I only came over here to switch my clothes. From washer into dryer," Paul said as he stood on the doorstep and tackled his shoelaces.

"I've already done that," Brittany said swiftly. "Then I started a second load of clothes washing for you." As she spoke she hoped that Paul would take her actions in the right spirit.

Another quite different look of surprise flashed on his face. "Hey, thanks!" he said and actually smiled at her for the first time.

No, he certainly didn't mind, Brittany observed. On the other hand, Paul looked so relieved and downright grateful that she knew she'd better make it plain that his laundry was still his responsibility. After all, she hadn't come all this way to be anybody's maid.

"I'm glad you're here now. I'm sure your first load of clothes are dry and ready to be folded," she said pointedly.

"Okay," Paul muttered, his eyes darkening again as he tugged off his heavy shoes.

Maybe he thought she was bossy. Well, she still had too much to do to worry about his reactions. Determined to ignore Paul, she returned to her work.

All the same she remained keenly aware of his presence in the cottage. Over the next ten minutes certain sounds were readily identifiable. The dryer stopped; the washing machine started again. Then some minor disaster must have occurred in the laundry room for she heard a half-muffled curse.

Brittany was briskly shaking dust from her dustpan into a black plastic sack when she heard him return. Paul, still in his stocking feet, carried a laundry basket piled high with clean clothes. Amazingly Brittany felt that strange twinge again that she'd felt on looking at the photograph of his young son. Faced with domestic duties Paul seemed acutely ill at ease, far less able than he'd been when Brittany had first arrived. Or was it simply his being here in the cottage that had turned his expression vulnerable? For now he looked so sad, so lost, so next-to-helpless that he tugged at her heart. Or was it perhaps his overlong dark hair that tumbled across his forehead and seemed to invite a woman's hand to gently push it back. Or maybe it was the way he glanced at his family's photograph on the nightstand, then looked away again almost too quickly.

"Paul Johnson's a flirt...." "—the biggest wolf on the island!"

Those echoes in Brittany's head stiffened her backbone. Hey, you've had enough of fickle men plucking on your heartstrings, remember? she scolded herself silently. Of course, she didn't want to appear hard-hearted, either. Where this man was concerned, could she possibly temper sympathy with wariness?

Meanwhile Paul appeared to be debating something with himself. Well, at some point they were going to have to sit down and have a meaningful talk about Brittany's work, Paul's writing schedule and their mutual coexistence on the island. Had he realized it, too?

With a thump Paul set down the laundry basket and reached for his shoes. "Look—" he began.

For some reason Brittany found herself absolutely hanging on his next words.

"I don't want to be a pain in the neck and pester you," he said, stomping his foot down hard into the first shoe. "On the other hand, it's been a long, hard winter." Paul paused significantly. "I guess you know why."

"Yes," Brittany said quietly. "I was very sorry to hear about your wife." Matter of factly she shook the dustpan again, then glanced back up at Paul. His face looked even more drawn. Was that from the allusion he'd just made to his dead wife or was it just the strong afternoon light?

His eyes had changed once again, moving into a remoteness that Brittany couldn't begin to fathom. Then, suddenly, he stared right at her, his dark gaze almost piercing.

"I'd appreciate it if we could talk for a while, either this evening or tomorrow," Paul went on as he reached for his other shoe. "Feminine companionship would be nice for a change. Hell, *anybody*'s companionship! Not—" he added hastily "—that I meant . . ."

"It's all right," Brittany cut in just as hastily.

Relief crossed his face. Relief that she was a reasonable woman who wasn't going to take offense at his unfortunate slip of the tongue. "Anyway, I have a bottle of good white wine, and I can usually haul a few fish out of the lake, if you're interested, I mean."

Tempted, Brittany hesitated nonetheless. Dinner with a man as attractive as this one and with his particular reputation was quite different from the down-to-earth chat that she'd had in mind.

Still, she had earlier faulted Paul for being too business-like and too unconcerned with her research project. Now that he was reaching out in an obvious attempt to be friendly and reasonable Brittany didn't want to cut him down.

Paul had also been frank, too, she considered—frank to the point of outright tactlessness. He wasn't really interested in her as a woman anymore than she was in him as a man. After all, hadn't he just said anyone would do?

The bottom line was her own curiosity. Brittany was still just plain interested in finding out about Paul Johnson as well as his work. She knew he'd already published two nonfiction books; now he was supposedly writing a novel. Even some of Paul's more severe critics had admitted that this guy had some interesting ideas and entertaining stories.

Paul stood waiting for her answer, but as Brittany continued to hesitate his eyes darted away uneasily.

"To tell you the truth, I've had a long hard winter myself," she said cautiously. "Also, I have to admit your dinner sounds a lot better than any I've been planning. But I'd rather we made it tomorrow evening, okay?"

"Sure." Paul flashed her a spontaneous grin before he bent to tie his shoelaces. Suddenly he became much more than merely attractive to Brittany. Smiling in that swift, devil-may-care way he looked handsome, indeed so much so that her heart slammed against her ribs in a wholly unbidden response. Hey, watch it! she warned herself.

"Tell me, what sort of dinner did you plan?" Paul said curiously.

Brittany gave a rather embarrassed shrug. "A tuna fish sandwich, I guess, with some cold beans on the side."

"I thought so. Later, when you're living in that tent you've brought, you'll have plenty of chances to crack cans," Paul reminded her.

"Oh, a sandwich will suit me tonight," Brittany replied. "I'm tired and intend to turn in early." Now, having successfully quelled her unexpected response to Paul, she tried to pretend that it had never happened. Newfound confidence in her ability to treat him indifferently led her to extend her own offering. "Tomorrow I'll whip us up a fresh green salad to go along with the fish and wine."

As soon as Brittany spoke she knew she was being reckless with her food. Just a few such salads would quickly deplete her supply of green vegetables, and there would certainly be no help from Paul's larder. His consisted almost entirely of snack foods, sandwich mixings and frozen TV dinners, she'd noticed with disapproval.

"A salad sounds good. It's been months since I've had one." Paul bent back down to tie his other shoelace.

"It's a wonder you don't have scurvy!" Brittany exclaimed.

"I take vitamin C, when I remember to, that is. My mother sent me a gallon jug. Look, what time do you want to eat tomorrow?" Paul reached for his laundry basket again, obviously ready to be on his way.

"Seven," Brittany said decisively, having already calculated all that she'd need to do first.

"Anything you want me to do?" Paul asked, then glanced toward the cold hearth. "How about a fire?"

Although Brittany was perfectly capable of building one herself, she knew she'd better utilize Paul's every offer of help. "Yes, that would be nice," she agreed for she was under no illusions about the warmth of these sunshiny days as soon as the sun started its descent.

"Okay, tomorrow I'll run Ivy all over the island first. Then I'll stop back here at five to start the fire."

"Your dog did appear to be sluggish," Brittany noted, bending to wring out her mop.

"I know. Ivy doesn't appreciate exercise right now but it's very good for her." Abruptly Paul's eyes narrowed. "Say, do you really study wolves?"

He spoke as though the notion were entirely incredible to him. "Animal variety only," Brittany quipped. Then, although this was a departmental joke back at the college, she suddenly felt self-conscious about having repeated it to this handsome man. Did Paul know he had a certain wolfish reputation of his own, at least with some people?

Paul's harsh-sounding laugh rumbled again. "Okay, I've got the picture, though I can't imagine why you or anyone else ever bothers with wolves. But I guess I'd better find out what you've got in mind just so I don't do anything to interfere." He hoisted his laundry basket, raising it to a rather broad-looking shoulder.

"That works both ways," Brittany acknowledged. "I'm interested in hearing about your writing, of course."

She could have bitten her tongue off for that revealing "of course." As she saw Paul's drawn face appear to brighten just a little, Brittany hoped she wouldn't have to sit through the recital of some long-winded, multifaceted plot that droned on and on till midnight.

"Okay. See you at five tomorrow, Brittany," Paul said. Then he went out the front door and it swung closed behind him.

It was the first time he had called her by her name.

Chapter Three

Ivy huffed and wheezed in the chilling air. "Come on, Ivy!" Paul urged, setting a brisk pace for the dog as he jogged along their customary three-mile run across the island.

Running was no longer one of Ivy's favorite activities. Now all she really wanted to do was sprawl in a warm corner and wait for this tiring pregnancy to end. Paul could understand that but also knew she *must* exercise, according to the thick book on German shepherds Steve had mailed him months ago.

"C'mon, girl!" he urged his pet again. "You've gotten much too lethargic. Exercise tones your muscles and prepares you for labor. Don't you want an easy whelping?"

Ivy barked a hostile response. Paul could tell she didn't appreciate his attempt at cheerfulness any more than the pace he was setting. Ivy, in fact, just plain didn't give a damn right now.

"It's going to be over with soon," Paul said encouragingly.

Then he raised his head to the cloudless sky. How wonderful the sunshine felt beaming down on his face! In fact, he absolutely felt good all over, Paul realized with something akin to astonishment. The fresh pure air, the forested lake country and the deep blue water—the same shade of sapphire blue as Brittany Hagen's eyes—all combined to fill him with a sudden and spontaneous joy.

Joy was an emotion Paul had never expected to feel again. Now its unexpected appearance, breaking through his wintry thoughts, was like those green shoots he'd first seen yesterday pushing up doggedly through the snow.

Paul still didn't wholly believe in the validity of this joy. He distrusted life's seductive siren song that had suddenly started singing in his veins. Mostly he didn't dare rely on it lest all his zest for life disappear once again.

Still Paul had to admit that he no longer wanted to be lying next to Peg in that gloomy hilltop cemetery, either.

So maybe those know-it-alls had been right. The same know-it-alls headed by Gina and Steve, who had kept assuring Paul relentlessly that life goes on, that time helps heal all wounds and that one day he'd find life rich and sweet again.

Perhaps all the self-appointed sages who had so infuriated him with their clichés knew something Paul just hadn't known until now. Something about the resilience of the human spirit, or mankind's innate response to spring. For just when the sap began to rise in the trees and Paul saw the earth starting to wake once again, he had realized how utterly weary he was of winter and grief.

He, who had dearly loved his wife, was even weary of mourning her. And now this close-to-balmy weather kept luring him out of the old lighthouse to search for other signs of spring. Yet, it wasn't until yesterday, beginning with Ms. Hagen's agile jump off the supply boat and the sight of the bright golden hair streaming out behind her, that Paul had truly awakened.

Not, of course, that *she* had anything to do with these feelings, he hastily assured himself.

Suddenly, fiercely, Paul wanted to see his son. Or, since that was impossible at the moment, between Brittany's arrival and Ivy's approaching labor, Paul decided he must talk with Chad over the radio tonight. Maybe see if his son, too, had noticed any evidence of spring and tell Chad what to watch for if he hadn't.

Chad also needed to hear that both he and Daddy were definitely going to be okay again.

Just thinking of Chad made Paul's chest tighten. He had missed his son unbelievably, missed seeing that mischievous sparkle of laughter in Chad's brown eyes that were so much like Peg's, and missed the boy's chatter.

They had been through their separate crucibles, he and Chad. But now very soon—even sooner than Paul had thought yesterday—it would be time for them to reunite.

Ivy wandered over and shoved her cold nose into Paul's bare palm. As he began automatically to caress her, Paul suddenly wondered if his decision to breed Ivy might have been an unconscious affirmation of life's continuity—or if his stepfather, Steve, had known it.

"No!" Paul scoffed aloud in disbelief. Steve wasn't capable of such subtle understandings. Still and all, Steve had realized that Paul just might not make it through the dark winter days all alone on the island. Thus the gift of Ivy.

She wasn't a present Paul had appreciated immediately. In fact, he had been angrier and more resentful than ever when he had departed for this lonely place with Ivy straining on her leash, whining for Steve.

Furthermore, after they'd arrived, Ivy had steadfastly ignored all of Paul's commands, most of which had been a furious, "Ivy, *no,* dammit!" But gradually they had each earned the other's respect. Within a month, much as Steve had intended, their mutual affection emerged and had deepened steadily.

In caring for his dog, Paul had learned to care for himself. Because Ivy had to eat at least one meal a day, Paul was reminded to eat one, too. Since the dog required exercise, he exercised with her—weather permitting. And because Ivy liked to sprawl near Paul while he banged away on his typewriter, they had spent long hours at his desk in the lantern room.

Now as Paul began running again, Ivy trotting reluctantly at his side, he cast a concerned glance at her. How he hoped Ivy wasn't preparing to spring a not entirely unexpected surprise.

To this day Paul could have sworn that he'd closed the storm door of the lighthouse two months ago, shutting Ivy safely inside. But he'd been in a hurry and apparently careless when his favorite neighbors, Trent and Vanessa Davidson, had arrived to spend the afternoon. As usual, the Davidsons had brought both their child and their dog, the latter a small male terrier named Boots that Trent allowed to run loose while he, Vanessa and Paul enjoyed lunch at the cottage and played with the baby.

Later, after Paul's friends had sped away in their cruiser, Paul had discovered the storm door to the lighthouse ajar. With the weather warming he knew he hadn't bothered to secure the inner door. Could Ivy have found her way out?

Calling her name in alarm Paul had stepped over the several inches of fresh snow that had drifted inside, only to discover that his pet was indeed gone.

With Ivy in season Paul had been completely dismayed. The very thought of her breeding with Trent's terrier left him groaning in despair. Good God, what a horrible mismatch that would be!

Ivy had come bounding home at suppertime, allaying Paul's fears somewhat. But not his stepfather's.

"Surely you don't think Ivy and that little terrier—" Paul had said worriedly to Steve on his last visit to the mainland.

Steve's grim face was less than reassuring. "No, the terrier's not what I'm worried about," he had said tightly. But Steve refused to elaborate further, saying "There's no sense in borrowing trouble."

It was typically infuriating of Steve to simply clam up like that. But, for once, Paul had been too worried about Ivy himself to want to hear Steve articulate the worst—whatever the worst might be.

Now, as they ran, Paul tried to convince himself all over again that in a couple of weeks he would get a nice, predictable litter of pure German shepherd pups. Why, just look how large Ivy was! Surely she wasn't carrying any little half-pint terriers under all that hair.

"C'mon, Ivy," Paul called spurring her on to greater speed.

While they jogged back through the forest of dense trees to the rocky promontory on which the cottage and lighthouse had been built, Paul thought again of Brittany Hagen. He was still puzzled about why he'd impulsively suggested yesterday they share dinner, but he wasn't sorry. Still, it was definitely unusual the way his thoughts kept circling back to her again and again.

Was he just grateful for another warm body nearby? If simple loneliness was the case why didn't he go back to Nash, Michigan, or stay for a while at Trent and Vanessa's guesthouse, as they kept suggesting?

No, in many ways he was a loner who liked his privacy and solitude, Paul thought.

Nor did Brittany seem the most promising of neighbors. So far she'd proved that she was strong-willed, inclined to be bossy and without any redeeming sense of humor—her one frail attempt at a joke notwithstanding.

Furthermore, Brittany seemed to have carried a tendency toward cleanliness to an unhealthy extreme.

Nor was Paul sure of just why he found her so intensely good-looking, either. To a lot of people, he knew—his petite brunette mother, for instance—Brittany would simply be another tall, large-boned blonde in need of a stylish wardrobe and a complete makeover. But something about Brittany's fresh natural looks appealed to Paul, as did those lush, ample curves of hers.

At least a guy wouldn't have to worry about losing someone like Brittany Hagen in bed!

Paul had started to grin at his sudden thought when he grasped its inherent meaning.

My God, what on earth was he thinking about?

Why, he was thinking of sex and all that other man-woman stuff, he realized in surprise so severe that it bordered on shock.

Well, well. Apparently his libido was healing from his tragic loss far faster than the rest of him. Didn't his sneaky subconscious have any decency?

You ought to be ashamed of yourself! Paul lectured himself sternly. Wasn't it for exactly this sort of thing that he'd long condemned his mother and Steve? For falling in love before the bodies of their previous mates were even cold?

Not, of course, that he was in danger of falling in love. Any new love was something far and away down the road, if ever.

Paul's own priorities were perfectly clear. First, he must recover sufficient emotional control of himself to become a proper father to Chad again. Second, he must finish his novel, if only to be done with it so he could get on with the rest of his life. After all, he was approaching his late thirties and had literally nothing to show for it, as his mother had frequently pointed out.

"I have my family," Paul had replied coldly to Gina almost a year ago. "I also have work I enjoy."

"Yes, and I was proud of the reviews you got for both *Lights Across the Sky* and *Wrecks Beneath the Sea*. But, Paul, who read them? For that matter, who bought them? Aren't you ever going to do something to make some money? Why, Ernie Henderson, who was in school with you but not half as smart, owns two hotels now...."

Paul hadn't wanted to hear how well Ernie was doing. Not that he begrudged his old friend his prosperity. But neither had Paul wanted to hear about his own poor performance at an age when most men were hitting the top rungs on the proverbial ladder of success.

So he had stormed out on Gina and headed straight into the backyard where Steve was showing Peg and Chad his latest litter of purebred puppies.

"Let's go," Paul had called and watched as both his wife and son turned to him with a smile.

At least I have my family, he had assured himself once again that day.

Only now he didn't even have them. Was it any wonder he'd virtually cracked up and been monumentally depressed?

But now for the very first time in months, Paul realized he was actually anticipating this evening. For that, he had Brittany Hagen to thank. Because something, though he wasn't sure quite what, had awakened inside him at that first startling sight of her. The image of her rich hair flowing in the breeze and her ripe, shapely body stayed etched on his mind.

Paul and Ivy, both panting now, reached the cottage and clattered up the front steps. There Paul saw that its porch had been swept carefully clean of snow, dirt and leaves. In little more than twenty-four hours this dwelling had become unequivocally "hers."

"Sit," Paul told Ivy, and his tired pet promptly obeyed. Then Paul rapped sharply on the door and waited for Brittany to appear.

Although it was five-fifteen Paul still wasn't there. Maybe he'd forgotten about building the fire or had decided against doing it. For that matter, maybe he'd decided to skip the whole business of their dinner tonight.

I don't care! Brittany thought and tiredly pushed back her long mane of thick hair. A too-short night's sleep in an unfamiliar bed last night and a too-long hike today, burdened with a backpack, had stretched muscles she didn't know she had. She'd seen a lot more moose today and had found both paw prints and droppings from a wolf, possibly two. But she had yet to hear one call, much less have several in full voice sharing their unique "song."

Now Brittany was exhausted and cold and felt in dire need of a shower. She'd also done all the work she intended to do for one day. She just hoped she still had enough energy left to set the table and serve dinner.

If Paul didn't come she'd go to bed early once again.

Outside dusk was fast approaching. Once Daylight Savings Time began in a few weeks the afternoons would be longer and brighter. But now spring's illusion faded rapidly with the setting sun while the gloomy chill in the cottage deepened by the minute. As Brittany waited for Paul, her impatience with him increased steadily.

Beneath her thick clothes she felt itchy and grimy from all her exertions. Yes, she definitely wanted a shower and shampoo and she naturally preferred to take these before the temperature nosedived any further.

Brittany had always been a trifle cold-natured, despite being naturally well-padded and having lived in the Great Lakes region all her life. Not so her dad and her three brothers. They had frequently boasted that they didn't feel the cold, causing both Brittany and her mother to stare at them incredulously.

At least I can start warming up the bathroom, Brittany decided.

The small neat bath adjoined the larger bedroom. There Brittany turned the heat to high and closed the door behind her. She was discovering, alas, that while the fifty-year-old cottage looked snug and cozy, neither its stoves nor insulation were the best.

At least Paul no longer seemed quite the boor she'd thought him for insisting that she display convincing proficiency with these stoves. He had known the truth about life and heat at the cottage.

Rapidly Brittany laid out the clothes she intended to wear tonight if Paul ever showed up. Briefly she pondered her small plastic bag of cosmetics. It probably wouldn't hurt to wear a touch of lipstick tonight, as well as a little eyeliner and mascara, she decided as she set the items out.

Usually Brittany didn't bother with makeup, knowing herself blessed with good skin and natural color. But she'd been neglecting her skin lately, and that lake crossing yesterday in the biting April wind had undoubtedly leeched even more moisture from her skin.

The exceptional use of cosmetics—this uncharacteristic way she studied her face—suddenly Brittany realized that she was preparing as she would for a date.

This was definitely not a date! Tonight was simply a get-acquainted session with the only other resident out here in the big middle of nowhere.

Brittany looked at her wristwatch again and allowed a slow burning anger toward Paul Johnson to build. It was five-twenty. Where in the hell was he?

Rude, inconsiderate people who didn't know the meaning of time had always annoyed Brittany. And Paul was already a likely target for her ire since he hadn't exactly been thrilled by her arrival and she'd spent all yesterday afternoon cleaning up after him.

Now with the afternoon growing steadily darker and the cottage colder, Brittany gave up waiting around for Paul. Angrily she slammed the bedroom door and began tearing off her clothes. Then, carrying her warm white robe over her arm, she stormed into the bathroom only to reel back at the heat that blasted her the moment she opened the door.

At least this room was satisfactorily warm and for that she was grateful, Brittany thought as she set the water in the shower stall to drumming. A minute later she stepped inside and closed the newly laundered shower curtain.

Paul waited for a couple of minutes, then he knocked again on the cottage door—much harder this time.

There was still no answer. After another minute passed, verified by his impatient glance at his watch, he grew annoyed. Where was she? It was now five thirty-five. Or was that tall blonde deliberately ignoring him? Paul's feelings about Brittany were growing less charitable by the second. She was snug and warm inside; he was out here freezing his tail.

Ivy gave a restless whine while Paul began to shiver. His exercise had left a sheen of perspiration on his face and neck, only now that he'd stopped running that same moist sheen was evaporating rapidly in the crisp air.

He was growing colder by the minute and the wind had picked up again, Paul noticed as he fumbled for his key ring. Briefly he debated using the key to let himself inside the cottage. He had retained a set of keys to open all the cottage doors, a fact he hadn't mentioned to Brittany when he'd given her the spare set.

No, I'd better wait a little longer, Paul decided and began to shift from foot to foot, hoping to generate a little more warmth.

Paul barely knew Brittany, of course, but he was still quite sure that the last thing she would appreciate would be his barging inside unannounced.

In the shower, Brittany began to remember her visit the day before yesterday with Dr. Ingrid Jensen.

Dr. Ingrid, who stood close to six-feet and was a woman of Scandinavian descent even taller, bigger and blonder than Brittany, practiced medicine in a small office adjacent to the college's infirmary. She was married to an engineering professor and the mother of two small children.

Now that Brittany was older and wiser she could look back across the years and realize that Dr. Ingrid had been her unconscious choice of a role model. The doctor was proof that a woman really could have it all: interesting career, charming husband and cute kids.

Brittany also wondered if Dr. Ingrid hadn't unconsciously identified with her, too. The lady's recall was amazing considering the number of patients she saw every year.

While Dr. Ingrid popped a thermometer into Brittany's mouth, peered into her ears and pumped up the blood-pressure cuff, the two women communicated with the same ease as if they'd seen each other only yesterday. "So, Brittany, your engagement didn't work out?"

When Brittany shook her head, Dr. Ingrid waxed philosophical. "These things happen. It's better to find out if you're unsuited to a guy before you marry him. Getting out of the situation later is a whole lot messier."

That was Dr. Ingrid, plainspoken yet understanding, too.

Brittany had nodded since she couldn't speak with the thermometer still stuck in her mouth.

"Say, whatever happened to that big towheaded kid who brought you in when you had flu?" Dr. Ingrid, who could do two things at once, wrote "normal" on Brittany's chart.

Brittany took out the thermometer. "Carl Lindstrom? He did quit college. Went back home to become a dairy farmer just like his dad and granddad."

"Some people aren't college material, though it's usually hard to make their parents accept the fact," said Dr. Jensen.

"That wasn't true in Carl's case," Brittany noted. "His folks were delighted that he wanted to take over the dairy."

Dr. Ingrid glanced up, her expression quizzical. "Have you ever been sorry you didn't go back home with Carl as he'd wanted you to do?"

"No!" said Brittany emphatically and Dr. Ingrid laughed.

"That was really all that was wrong with you," she recalled. "Flu was just a symptom. You had a decision to make that looked agonizing at the time."

"You kept me in the infirmary for five days!" Brittany accused.

"You needed time to think. To realize that whatever Carl's own inclinations and limitations, you were smart and ambitious. You'd lived on a dairy farm all your life and, while you didn't knock it, you knew in your heart that it wasn't what you wanted. Oh, I've never forgotten one thing you said, Brittany."

"What was that?"

"You said, 'Frankly, I'm not all that crazy about cows.' Once you'd admitted that, I knew you were all right. But I'm also glad Carl's life turned out okay, too."

"Oh, yes. He married a hometown girl back in Minnesota, and they have four kids now and *lots* of cows." Both Brittany and Dr. Ingrid had laughed at that.

"So what about that quiet, dark-haired guy—Walt or Wade?"

"Warren," Brittany replied decisively. "Warren Petroschi."

"Yes." Dr. Ingrid got out her little rubber hammer and started testing Brittany's knee reflexes. "Warren was so concerned when you broke your wrist ice-skating."

"And you managed to get the cast off in time for him to take me to the Spring Dance," Brittany recalled wistfully. "You know, I was half in love with that guy! Warren was older because he'd been in the service before he came to college. He made the other guys look like boys. He also had more money to spend and more ideas of where to spend it, like nice restaurants and theaters. And Warren bought a great snowmobile—oh, we did have fun!"

"You were impressed but were you really in love?" Dr. Ingrid asked.

"Probably not," Brittany admitted with a shrug. "After Warren graduated he left Michigan for a job with an architectural firm in Chicago. He wrote to me for a while, then his letters gradually stopped. I really thought my heart was broken, at least for a few weeks. I knew he'd met somebody else."

"But you did get over him," Dr. Ingrid said encouragingly. "And you'll get over this latest man, too—say, what was his name again? I never can remember names."

"Howard Pierson." Despite all her resolve Brittany had heard her voice turn shaky. "And this one is a lot harder...."

Suddenly, abruptly, Brittany was jerked back to the present. Back to being alone in a shower stall rather than in an examining room with Dr. Ingrid. Here she was, lathered from head to toe, while somebody kept knocking as if he intended to batter down the cottage door.

"Oh, great. Now he shows up," Brittany murmured in annoyance as she fumbled first for a towel and then for her bathrobe.

Definitely Paul Johnson's sense of timing was not the greatest. He and Howard Pierson were certainly alike in that respect, too, because Howard always used to run late.

Already Paul reminded her quite a lot of Howard.

* * *

Paul was about to storm off, convinced that dinner had been cancelled without his being informed, when Brittany finally flung open the door. And one quick glance at her told Paul that she was in a snit.

Brittany stood wrapped in a heavy white robe, her feet shoved into woolly bedtime booties, her thick blond hair concealed in a towel worn turbanlike on her head. Her strikingly deep blue eyes were glacial. Paul could feel her disapproval radiating toward him in waves.

He stared at her, trying to think of what offense he'd committed. "Come in," Brittany said curtly. "Or do you enjoy standing there watching me freeze?"

Did she think *he* hadn't been freezing, waiting all this time for her to come open the door? Paul wondered as he followed Brittany inside. Still, he was too puzzled by her testy behavior to take immediate offense.

"What's wrong?" he asked warily.

"You're late, that's what's wrong!"

"Late?" Paul blinked, then he recovered quickly. "When I said five o'clock I didn't mean precise, synchronized, Greenwich time," he retorted, hearing his sarcasm but not caring. "Things on this island are a little more laid-back than—"

"I am not laid-back!" Brittany burst out. Then, incredibly, she blushed at her poor choice of words.

"I believe you." Paul sighed as he headed over to the hearth and the full wood box beside it. "Well, do you want a fire or not? It's strictly up to you."

She still looked pink of face and momentarily uncertain, but Paul doubted that this state of affairs would last. "If you hadn't been late then I wouldn't have been in the shower," Brittany said defensively. "I gave up waiting for you. I decided you'd either forgotten or had changed your mind."

"'Oh, ye of little faith,'" Paul quoted. Without waiting for her to make the decision he started selecting wood for a fire.

"How was I to know you take such a lackadaisical attitude toward time?" Brittany asked.

At her caustic question Paul gave a silent groan. Talk about beating a dead horse! He pressed his lips together and worked rapidly and steadily. After all, the sooner he finished building the fire the sooner he could get the hell out of here. Already he had decided to invent a creative excuse to forego dinner. A severe headache? A rare bacterial infection?

Hey, how about a real pain in the butt? he thought.

A sudden scratching noise on the window caused Brittany to jump.

Paul already knew what the sound signified. Ivy, who wasn't long on patience, had grown tired of waiting for him and was letting Paul hear about it.

"What on ear— Oh, it's just your dog," Brittany sighed in relief.

Paul noticed that fear had warmed her chilly voice by at least two degrees.

"Ivy gets restless," he was surprised to hear himself volunteer.

"I didn't know what was happening," Brittany confessed and Paul saw her face gradually clear of fright. Suddenly he could almost read her mind. When Ivy jumped up and scratched the screen Brittany Hagen had been forcibly reminded that she was all alone out here on a small island. Alone except for Paul. Now she moistened her lips to—to do what? he wondered. Was she mature enough to apologize?

"Look, Paul, I'm sorry I was short-tempered."

He was so pleased by his precognition and her maturity that he decided to be forgiving. "That's all right," he said, continuing to work. "I startled you, too, I suppose, banging on the front door."

"Yes. I did truly think you weren't coming."

Paul still wasn't sure whether he wanted to stay around for dinner. He glanced back at Brittany and suddenly every other thought flew straight out of his mind. For when Brittany had jumped just a moment ago in fear and surprise her white robe had parted. Now it exposed one long and shapely leg.

That leg stood just inches away from Paul and it was a work of art, absolutely breathtaking, with creamy-smooth skin tinted faintly rose. Yes, a truly perfect leg and fully revealed, too, from slender ankle all the way up to firm mid-thigh.

Then Paul swallowed hard. He'd never imagined Brittany possessing such an incredible and delectably curved leg. But why was he so surprised? Those ripe nymphs, usually painted by artists such as Titian, Rubens or Raphael, who drifted across a canvas trailing diaphanous streamers and little or nothing else, frequently had legs to kill for.

Come to think of it, dinner with Brittany just might be a worthwhile endeavor, after all.

All at once Brittany grew aware of her robe being agape. She jerked it closed, knotting its belt tightly around her surprisingly slender waist.

Paul sighed in disappointment and Brittany cut her eyes around to him.

"Were you looking at me?" she demanded suspiciously.

So what was he supposed to say? Deny that he'd looked? Start stammering or apologizing like some wimp? Not on your life! What Valkyrie had ever respected a wimp?

Instead Paul rocked back on his heels and stared up at Brittany boldly. "How could I miss? Thanks for the view!"

"Why—" Brittany began, obviously disconcerted.

"That's a fabulous leg, by the way," Paul continued. "Why, I hadn't seen a woman's leg in so long I'd forgotten that yours aren't ugly and hairy, too."

"You . . . you're incorrigible!" she stammered, trying to look properly indignant. But her lips gave an involuntary twitch.

Paul congratulated himself on reading her correctly. Yes, this was a strong woman who would literally mow down a meek, apologetic man. Fortunately for them both, nobody had ever accused Paul of being one.

Reluctantly Brittany smiled and revealed twin dimples at either side of her mouth. There was something young and winsome about that smile. Something electric, too. Even with its wattage turned to dim, Paul still felt almost dazzled. Automatically he grinned back at her. Well, so she did know how to smile—and had he actually uncovered some hint of a sense of humor?

"Incorrigible, you said?"

"Yes, you are!" Brittany continued, swinging around on her heel. "And I certainly hope you don't write such trite clichés about legs in your books or I can't imagine why anybody would bother to buy one."

"So try to tell me you don't appreciate my keen power of discernment," Paul interrupted, frankly teasing her now.

"I don't intend to answer that."

Brittany regally swept from the room. "Dinner has just been bumped up to seven-thirty," she called to Paul over her shoulder. "Don't be late or you'll wait on the porch forever!"

We'll just see about that, Paul thought, fingering his own door key.

Then the bedroom door slammed shut behind her.

Chapter Four

Brittany dropped a black turtleneck sweater over her head, then zipped up her long checkered wool skirt. Thick and warm, the skirt had a red, black and white design. It was the only skirt she'd brought with her to the island, but tonight she rather relished having her legs freed from the confines of slacks.

Also, like it or not, Paul's dark intense gaze had a way of making a woman feel very feminine indeed. Was the long skirt her response? While it didn't positively say "never," it did declare "not now." It also proclaimed its wearer a woman.

Dressed, Brittany fixed her hair hastily, pinning it up into a silken coil atop her head. Then she hurried into the kitchen. It was time to warm up the oven so they could broil or bake their fish. Also, Brittany wanted to stir her scalloped potatoes. Since they had come straight out of a box, she had tried to perk up the packaged sauce mix by adding sharp cheddar cheese, a little extra milk and a tangy dash of dry mustard.

Next, she opened the refrigerator to peek at her salad. Always cut up tomatoes first and put them at the very bottom. That was the secret to making up a salad ahead of time yet having it stay crisp and tasty. This particular salad still looked gratifyingly crisp beneath its glaze of plastic wrap.

The lemon mousse for dessert was another quick mix and an entirely disappointing one, Brittany discovered. It even managed to taste like cardboard, and chilling had improved it only slightly. Annoyed by its failure to improve, Brittany borrowed a dollop of Paul's nondairy dessert topping that she found in the freezer. This she spread atop both portions of mousse, then rapidly grated a little fresh lemon rind on top.

Finished, she washed her implements, dried them and replaced them exactly where she had found them. Only then did Brittany stop to glance at her watch. Seven twenty-five. Why, she was actually ready earlier than she'd thought.

At just that moment she heard a brief rat-a-tat on the back door, then Paul used his key.

He'd already come through the storm door onto the small back porch. Brittany saw a flash of maroon sweater before Paul turned back to retrieve a small bucket of fish. The fish were headless and had been cleaned, although they hadn't as yet been filleted.

"Hi," Paul greeted Brittany as he set the bucket of fish in the sink. "You look nice."

"Thanks, so do you," she murmured and wondered how to politely inform Paul that she didn't want him using a key to barge in here just any old time.

He shrugged out of his heavy gray jacket, hung it on the back of a kitchen chair and reached for a knife in the wooden scabbard mounted on the wall. "I've given our situation some thought," Paul began, speaking before Brittany could. "Why don't we agree that I can come and go out of the back but not the front. That way I won't catch you running around in your flimsies, but I also won't have to freeze waiting for you to answer the door when all I want is to fix a cup of instant coffee."

"Well..." Soberly Brittany considered the idea. Paul was just so—so unmistakably male that the thought of his being close by while she dressed, bathed or slept made her feel a trifle disconcerted. Tonight he looked especially virile and handsome, having obviously trimmed his beard and his overlong hair as well as groomed his moustache.

She caught a scent of woodsy after-shave and wondered if Paul knew that the maroon sweater he wore over black wool slacks made him look devastatingly handsome. Yes, she suspected he would know, and the thought made her more than a little nervous.

"Anyway, that's the single, simplest solution I can think of," he continued. "I guess you'll just have to trust me to be a gentleman."

"Can I?" Brittany inquired pointedly and completely without guile. Since Paul had himself dressed up as if for a date, complete with manly fragrance, Brittany thought she had the right to ask.

Paul set down the knife he was holding and turned around to face her, his black eyes drilling into her own. "Yes," he said emphatically, "you most assuredly can."

Brittany moistened her lips. "Okay. That does sound like a workable solution," she said, determined to demonstrate that she was reasonable, too. "Listen, I've already turned on the oven. I assumed you'd want to broil or bake the fillets."

"Can you tell me how? All I know is boil or fry."

"Oh, sure," she said.

"Good," Paul approved and began to whack away quite competently at the fish.

Brittany turned back to the counter and retrieved her casserole in its ovenproof dish. "It might be a good idea to pop these potatoes back in the oven, too."

"Potatoes?" Paul asked with obvious pleasure.

"Yes, they're scalloped. It's just a mix, I'm afraid," Brittany said apologetically.

Paul flashed her a grin. "There's never been a potato I didn't love!"

"Good," she replied automatically since, for some reason, Brittany found herself feeling quite strange in his presence, almost breathless and light-headed. "Oh, I found a card table and set it up in the living room, in front of the fire. I thought that would be coz—"

Abruptly she stopped, biting down on her tongue in dismay. "Cozy" sounded just one tiny step away from "romantic" or even "seductive."

But to her relief, Paul didn't leer, roll his eyes or make any acknowledgement of her near gaffe. Rather, his reply was strictly matter of fact. "Good. I'd like to eat by the fire. It's getting cold outside and the wind is blowing hard."

Brittany seized the opportunity to snatch up their plates and silverware and flee into the living room where the table and two chairs were already set in place. Why am I suddenly acting like such a ninny? she wondered. Paul couldn't sound more casual, more nonchalant, more clearly uninterested.

And why was she perversely annoyed by *that*?

Yet he had also dressed up for tonight, and his gestures—a smile, a nod, a lift of eyebrows—had started getting to her, making her feel subtly threatened.

Mixed messages. Paul wasn't the first handsome man to train his charms in her direction, but she was far more alert to them now. A man who came on, only to back away, did indeed threaten any woman's emotional equilibrium. Hardwon experience had taught her that.

She looked beautiful but he didn't dare tell her, Paul thought as they sat eating beside the fire. In fact, he doubted if he'd ever seen any woman who was lovelier. Firelight played over Brittany's face and hair, bathing both in a peach-colored glow. And in her skirt and sweater she seemed the essence of pure femininity, a young earth mother with full breasts, small waist, fertile-looking hips and pleasantly trim ankles. Suddenly Paul thought of Sif, the Norsemen's golden-haired fertility goddess.

But Brittany seemed edgy tonight—edgy enough that Paul feared she might misconstrue any admiring expression or comment he'd make.

There was no need to deprive himself of a genuine vision, however, so he glanced back up at her again. Something about a blonde wearing jet black appealed to him and always had. Perhaps it was that contradictory combination of innocence, as personified by the bright fair hair, with the mysterious sophistication and elegance of black. Brittany projected just that innocent sophistication right now.

At least he could praise her food. "Dinner is delicious," Paul said to her sincerely.

"I'm glad you're enjoying it."

He saw the way her hand tightened on the edge of the table when he spoke, even crinkling the snowy-white tablecloth, and he felt all the more puzzled.

What had happened to their earlier easy banter? Tonight something about him really stuck in her teeth and rattled her cage. He couldn't imagine why he suddenly made Brittany nervous. But she was like a high-spirited filly, shifting in her chair and even giving a start when he directed an occasional question to her.

Was it him or would she be like this with any man? Paul wondered.

At least he was attuned enough to feel her vibrations. Having done so, he made his every move slow and easy. In fact, whenever Paul found himself watching Brittany too carefully or for too long he took care to glance away, even though he didn't want to.

Paul did most of the talking through dinner. For that matter, he did most of the eating, too, but everything tasted perfectly delicious. Paul had burned out weeks ago on his own cooking—the little bit he knew, such as boiling fish with potatoes and corn for chowder or boiling fish with canned vegetables for stew. Brittany had actually added even to fish, the grimly familiar staple of his diet, by whipping up a lemon-butter sauce with which to baste the fillets. Then she'd sprinkled them with paprika. Voilà! Paul had faced an entrée that looked and tasted entirely different.

That Brittany might be a bang-up good cook had simply never occurred to Paul, but she brushed away his appreciative comments as though whipping up a balanced meal was nothing. Maybe in her repertoire of skills it wasn't, for Paul remembered that the Valkyrie had supposedly been equally at home in the great banqueting hall, serving food and drink.

Now, as he talked between bites, telling stories from his days on jungle patrol in Vietnam, Paul saw interest flare in Brittany's deep sapphire-blue eyes. Saw her start to relax almost imperceptibly when he began describing that hot steamy green land of turgid yellow rivers. Peg had always sworn that Paul was a born storyteller and now he tested her opinion on Brittany, retelling the stories of the snake, the Vietcong sniper and the tragedy of seeing a good buddy killed by "friendly fire."

"How old were you when you went to Vietnam?" Brittany inquired, her face concerned.

"I enlisted on my eighteenth birthday and went to Vietnam first when I was nineteen. I did two tours of duty there and was almost twenty-two when Saigon fell."

"Two tours! Were you crazy?" she exclaimed bluntly.

Paul's mother had asked the very same thing. "No. I was just young and very angry at my mother and stepfather."

"What's your new book about?" Brittany passed Paul a plate of biscuits.

He took one and reached next for the tub of butter. "That very subject, the fall of Saigon. My book begins with the last group of people waiting on the roof of the American Embassy building for a helicopter to fly them out."

That grabbed her attention, and Paul saw her blue eyes widen.

"I witnessed it all because I was stationed in Saigon during my second tour. I worked mostly as a chauffeur for a colonel in the Information Office and his shady lady. So now I'm trying to write the story of those final frantic days when everyone was trying to get out of Saigon but there weren't nearly enough planes flying in to take them all."

"Oh?" said Brittany encouragingly.

"Fear in Saigon was something you could smell, something you could taste and breathe. We all knew that Vietnam would fall soon—maybe next week, maybe tomorrow—maybe, God help us, even today," Paul continued somberly. "Americans and Vietnamese alike—we were all scared. At least we Americans trusted our government to get us out.

"There were constant rumors and whispers. 'If you fall into the hands of the incoming army you will be punished horribly. Buried alive,' the people of Saigon said. 'Yes, left to bake slowly in the sun and die of thirst. Of course, if the North Vietnamese are in a big hurry to push on, they'll do it fast and cut your throat.'"

For Brittany's sake, as well as his own, Paul censored his memories tonight. Although his book would pull no such punches, some things were definitely not appropriate for table talk.

Also, some stories were so good he reserved them strictly for his novel. Brittany didn't need to hear that the colonel, married and the father of four kids back in the States, had lived in Saigon with Dominique Duvall, an exotic Eurasian. Or that Dominique had abandoned the colonel without even a word of farewell when she'd had the chance to fly off to Paris with a French diplomat. She'd thrown a temper tantrum, cursing Paul in English, French and Vietnamese, when he'd refused to drive her to the airport and she'd had to take a common rickshaw instead.

Dominique's treatment of the colonel had certainly made women like Peg look even more loyal and loving. Then and there Paul had vowed to marry the professor's freckle-faced daughter if he managed to return home safely.

"I was one of several serviceman-volunteers who helped out at a Saigon orphanage," Paul went on, continuing with safer memories. "The Sisters were desperate to get the kids out. Most of the children had been fathered by Americans, you see, and we were afraid they'd be killed by the new regime. So I worked all one morning trying to locate a plane for the orphans, then all afternoon getting them loaded on it. Most of the children only had one toy apiece, and the most unpleasant aspect of my job was to separate them from their precious toy. But the plane was already overloaded, you see. The pilot refused anyone trying to take along their possessions, even the littlest kids. 'You want that, stay with it,' he told anyone who tried to argue."

Brittany looked up from her plate, her eyes troubled. "That sounds so harsh for little kids," she ventured. "Was it really necessary?"

"Yes," Paul said quietly. "It was necessary. Say, could I have another taste of those potatoes? They're great."

"That fish is, too. I love good fresh fish," she replied generously, then motioned to Paul to continue.

"The next day my office got a call from a prominent South Vietnamese family," he resumed. "Since several of the men had been high up in the government they knew they'd be shot—after an appropriate period of torture—as soon as the new regime settled in. Theirs was one of those vast, extended Asian families, and they were all dashing around getting ready to leave Saigon. When they asked me to drive them to the airport I assumed they had already made arrangements and had obtained a sponsor. See, they could only be allowed into the United States with an American to sponsor them. But they waited until we were actually there, within spitting distance of an American plane, to plead with *me* to be their sponsor."

"Did you help them?"

"How could I refuse? I signed up as sponsor for the whole group and off they flew toward Ventura, Michigan, where my mother and stepfather lived at the time. It was quite a long, horrible trip.

"To make matters worse there was no way I could contact my folks and let them know I'd suddenly become sponsor to a huge refugee family. See, all radio communication out of South Vietnam was on a dire-emergency-only basis. So when my stepfather answered the doorbell a couple of mornings later there were thirty-three Vietnamese, shivering on his doorstep."

Brittany burst out laughing at the scene he described. To Paul's surprise he felt a tingle zigzag down his spine. Why, he was actually thrilled at having amused her! He wondered what had provoked this adolescent male reaction. Trying to impress women was usually completely unlike him. Tonight, though, Paul couldn't quite subdue his feeling of pride.

Also, Brittany was leaning across the table toward him now, her eyes shining, her earlier nervousness and self-consciousness forgotten. "What happened next?" she asked.

"My mother has never forgiven me," Paul replied promptly.

"I mean what happened to the Vietnamese—but tell me, too, why your mother hasn't forgiven you. Seems like that was quite an honorable thing for you to do," she rushed on.

"Not to hear my mother tell it," Paul related, chuckling a little. "My mother—Gina Olszewski is her name—is a very small, very determined and excitable woman who is frankly *not* the most altruistic soul in the world."

As Paul described her, he saw Brittany's eyes crinkle. Of course, almost everyone knew somebody like Gina. "You describe your mother vividly," Brittany commented.

"She's a vivid lady," Paul agreed dryly. "All Gina could see was her pleasant life and nice home being turned completely upside down by a 'ragtag bunch of Asians.' That was her description. Even though Steve hustled the refugees into a downtown hotel as quickly as possible that didn't prove to be a well-thought-out move, either. The Vietnamese didn't understand our customs and certainly none of our modern appliances. So the hotel wound up evicting them after they blew out several fuses using hairpins and nails to fiddle with the electrical devices. Of course, all they were trying to do was cook rice.

"So back the Vietnamese came to Gina and Steve's house. Gina collapsed in hysterics, and Steve called every congressman and senator he could think of, as well as trying to track me down—"

"Where were you by then?" Brittany asked.

"Busy researching."

"Researching?"

"Yes. It had occurred to me that I was seeing something that Americans really knew nothing about: losing a war and being conquered, with an invading army on its way. Oh, I know the American South went through much the same thing toward the end of the Civil War. But, after all, that happened more than a hundred years ago.

"So I hung on in Saigon until I was ordered out," Paul went on. "I followed people around, notebook in hand. I watched the brass race to destroy records and ammunition and the South Vietnamese try various ways and means to escape. I saw boats set out to sea, crammed so full of frantic people you knew they couldn't possibly stay afloat. I saw women crying and begging strange American soldiers to take their children. They kept thrusting the kids, even the tiny babies, at any kindly face, although the women knew they would probably never see their children again."

Speechless, Brittany listened to him; Paul couldn't even detect her breathing. "I saw a lot of scenes like that," he added quietly. "Scenes bizarre, desperate and sometimes ennobling. I also saw the nastiness of greed. Thieves stayed busy stealing anything that wasn't nailed down. The death throes of a country aren't especially pretty, but they're definitely worth witnessing and recording for posterity."

"Whatever happened to that poor Vietnamese family?" Brittany asked.

"Oh, their story ends quite happily."

"It *does*?"

Since she acted as though happy endings were something she wasn't especially familiar with, Paul naturally wondered why.

"Yes, they're a very intelligent and resourceful family," he assured her. "By the time I got home a few weeks later, the kids were already speaking English like natives and teaching it to the older people. By then, too, a Michigan church had gotten in on the act and really helped them a great deal."

"Does the family still live here?" Brittany asked, a relieved smile starting to curve her mouth up once again.

"No. A couple of our Great Lakes' winters cured them of wanting to stay. The Nyangs—that's their name—are all living quite happily on the Texas Gulf Coast. They keep writing me to come visit them, and I really must do that one day. Two of the uncles have started an oyster fishing business. Another branch of the family has a truck farm and raises citrus fruit. And three brand new Americans have been born!"

As Brittany's smile brightened Paul added ruefully, "They're doing a lot better than I am. Just ask my mother. She doesn't think anyone wants to read 'another book about that dreary Vietnam.' She says the whole enterprise is doomed, and I'm mired deep out here just spinning my wheels."

Brittany frowned as abruptly as she'd smiled earlier, twin lines marring the flawless skin between her eyebrows. "What do you mean, Paul?" she asked, drawing back into her chair again. "You're already a successful writer. Why, you've been published! Everyone I've talked to is very impressed by your accomplishments."

Brittany stopped talking suddenly. Was it only the firelight or had her cheeks just turned decidedly pinker? Paul wondered. He also wondered who she had been talking to about him—and why. But as he watched Brittany's guard go up again, like a minor Iron Curtain being erected between them, Paul decided not to ask.

Instead he moved to correct her. "My accomplishments, as you're kind enough to call them, have actually earned me very little money. In our present American culture you're not considered a success without plenty of the green folding stuff."

"Oh, what nonsense!"

"Is it?" Paul challenged. "Do you want to tell me that you've never been impressed by someone with money?"

As he spoke, he watched her eyes drop again to her plate and found that answer enough.

In the silence that followed a log crackled and snapped in the fireplace. Then Brittany pushed back her chair from the table. "If you've finished eating I'll take your plate," she offered.

"Thanks. It was a truly wonderful dinner," Paul said again.

"Oh, it's not over yet," she said, flashing another of those quick winsome smiles.

"Coffee?" he guessed, remembering that he'd smelled it a little earlier.

"Dessert, too," Brittany added.

"Dessert!"

Paul knew he probably sounded like a ravenous kid, but he didn't care. A real meal, topped off with dessert and honest-to-God coffee that had been dripped through a filter, was like a veritable feast after his last five months of sandwiches or fish.

"You're easily pleased," Brittany said wryly. She disappeared into the kitchen and returned a minute later carrying two dessert compotes whose contents looked incredibly tempting. "Don't get your hopes up, Paul. This is just another mix," she warned as she went back to bring their coffee.

After she was seated again Paul took a tentative first taste. "It's luscious, Brittany!" he said fervently.

He saw surprise flash in her eyes as he spooned up more delectable bites. Was it because of the way he'd slipped her first name in there? It was a perfectly natural thing for him to do, of course, considering that she had been calling him by his. Yet Paul sensed Brittany's discomfort at anything resembling intimacy.

Rather, it appeared quite all right for her to move at will, to ask him questions and use his first name. But when Paul tried to bridge the distance to her she drew back like a turtle ducking into its shell.

And that was a distance he now thought he might like to span—into friendship, of course. Nothing more!

The setting was perfect, too, if he could just maneuver Brittany away from the table and over to the sofa. The fire's radiant orange-and-black flames were really licking away at the logs now, and Paul thought of how he'd like to just sit quietly, enjoying its warmth and glow. Maybe slip an arm around the pretty woman seated beside him, provided he could ever get her there.

Human warmth. Closeness. Affection. That's all he wanted now, Paul thought. Of course, it probably wouldn't be all he'd be wanting in a month or two, he had to admit candidly. He was a healthy and presently sexually deprived male.

Still Paul subscribed to the belief that two people ought to get to know each other better before moving into a true intimacy that shared bodies as well as minds and hearts. This seemed especially important to him now that he was older and wiser, a widower with a small child.

Yet Brittany's wariness and that distinct chill that had already touched him more than once, like a damp hand dropping on the nape of his neck, also warned Paul that she'd probably misconstrue any such move he made.

So he gave an almost inaudible sigh, wondering how long it would take before she might relax enough to trust him. Or would she ever?

Suddenly out of the dark night rose a distant and eerie wolf's howl. Instantly Paul felt the hairs rise on the back of his neck and arms, felt his heart thud heavily in dread.

Immediately he was aware once again of the crucial differences between himself and Ms. Hagen. For at the mournful wolf cry that reminded Paul of nothing so much as a banshee's haunted wail, her face lit up like a child's.

You would think she'd just heard merry-go-round music or sleigh bells.

Chapter Five

Paul didn't merely dislike wolves, as Brittany had suspected earlier. That he absolutely detested them was a fact made immediately obvious, especially when the initial wolf's cry sparked a veritable wolf chorus, full-throated and mournful. Paul's face changed at the sound, growing grim and taut. A slight shudder even ran through his body.

But at that first moment Brittany was simply too exhilarated and too intent on listening to the wolves' song to concern herself with Paul's reactions. So they are still here, alive and well on Isle Svenson, she thought excitedly.

When dealing with endangered species a biologist never knew what might happen from one year to the next. Even though the wolves on this island were protected, they still numbered less than twenty, according to the last estimate. It wouldn't take much to wipe them out.

Sometimes entire herds of animals starved during a particularly cruel winter or when a disease spread rapidly through their ranks. The wolves might even have climbed atop an ice floe and drifted far away, since that was undoubtedly the way they'd originally arrived here. But none of those dread things had happened, and Brittany's relief was close to overwhelming.

With a murmured excuse, Paul pushed back his chair and walked over to the fireplace. He stood there, both hands gripping the mantel, while he stared down broodingly into the brightly glowing flames.

"Why, you really despise them, don't you?" Brittany heard herself say.

"*That*," he said emphatically over the wolf echoes and yelps. "*That's* what I can't stand about wolves! That demonic howling. The worst of it is when they get Ivy started, too."

Brittany could barely resist a smile and Paul noticed it. "That's not funny," he said stubbornly.

"Don't you know what those wolves are doing?" she asked Paul quietly.

"No, and I don't care!"

"I thought writers were usually interested in communication. That's basically what wolves are doing on a night hunt, just communicating with each other."

Paul raised his head and stared at her. "Seriously?"

"Sure. According to ethologists who study animal behavior they're just talking back and forth. Locating one another's positions. The first howl was probably the wolf pack's head honcho—the 'dominant male,' we biologists call him. 'Hey, where are all you guys?' he asked. So the others all checked in. You just heard from George and Martha, Charles and Evelyn."

"Are you putting me on?" Paul asked skeptically.

"Not a bit," Brittany protested. "Wolves also howl to warn away potential trespassers. Or they may howl begging you not to attack them because they've learned, as a species, to fear men. You see, wolves are exceptionally sensitive and intelligent as well as having extraordinarily keen senses of sight, hearing and smell. They're loyal animals, too, committed to their pack and they mate for life. When they have pups they make wonderful parents who are affectionate and playful. Because they're real softies for their pups a wolf baby can get away with murder!''

And I certainly hope I get to see two or three of them doing just that, Brittany thought fervently.

Paul appeared to be listening to her, but as the wolves started their keening howl again his face twisted anew. ''Personally I'd like to see them all murdered!''

''You can't mean that,'' Brittany protested as sharply as she'd ever spoken to anyone. But that sinking feeling in her stomach combined disappointment and dismay that an intelligent man she had just started to like quite a lot and to whom she had felt sympathetically drawn during dinner was capable of such a cruel and unreasonable attitude.

''Yes, I do mean it,'' Paul contradicted, his voice tight. ''You just don't know how damned many nights your precious wolves have kept me awake, or given me nightmares. I think there's something inherently evil about wolves and something in the human psyche that knows so.''

Brittany's lips clamped tight with disapproval, then opened again almost immediately. ''What an ignorant, benighted attitude!'' she blurted. ''With people like you running around no wonder the poor wolves have been pushed to the very brink of extinction!''

She knew, of course, that wolves inspired a similar revulsion in much of mankind. That's why people fought them so brutally, using horrible weapons such as poison or setting fire to their dens to torture and kill.

She must try to educate Paul. It wouldn't do at all for him to harbor, much less possibly display in print, such gross ignorance and superstition.

Counselling herself to patience, Brittany tried again, attempting a cordial tone. ''You remind me of my mother and my best friend. They both thought they hated wolves, too, because of their howling, but they simply didn't understand them.''

''Oh, I think I understand them well enough, like I understand pit vipers and black widows.''

''There's no comparison whatever,'' she scoffed, thinking that it was exactly this sort of attitude that had already seen most of America's native wolf population annihilated. Don't lose your temper, she warned herself. "Why, just tell me, what are your first associations when I say 'wolf'?" she asked Paul.

He shrugged his shoulders. Actually, what flashed immediately into Paul's mind was a story his father had read to him when he was a child about the monstrous wolf cub Fenrir. But he didn't cite that, thinking an old Norse legend too obscure.

"Little Red Riding Hood, I suppose," he said tightly. "Isn't that the first story about wolves that any kid hears?"

"Yes, unless it's the one about the boy who cried 'wolf.' Of course, in real life wolves don't attack or eat human beings."

Paul looked unconvinced. "No? A couple of times when Ivy and I were out running I'd see silver shadows back in the trees. They seemed to be tracking us."

"Believe me, you were just being observed, not anticipated," Brittany assured Paul. "Maybe you were close to a den and the wolves were afraid for their young."

"Yeah, sure," Paul said, clearly unconvinced. "So what about all those jolly legends and stories from Russia, Poland or Hungary? Why, their literature is chock-full of stories about savage wolves that tear out the poor peasants' throats."

"Pure fiction," Brittany said decisively, her gaze searching Paul's tense face once again. He has the very blackest eyes I've ever seen, she observed irrelevantly.

"I feel sure a few wolf attacks on Russian peasants have probably been documented. Or are you saying those reports were all lies?"

Brittany decided she'd better leave herself a little leeway. When she was dusting yesterday she'd noticed quite a number of reference books crowding the shelves here in the cottage. She didn't want Paul waving some bizarre incident in her face and crowing with triumph.

"Oh, I suppose if a Russian winter lasts long enough and if wolves are at the very brink of extinction, their survival mechanism might override their normal instincts. Under those circumstances they might find themselves tempted by a juicy tender human morsel,'' she conceded. ''But I still doubt they'd ever attack a full-grown adult.''

''But you admit the possibility exists?'' Paul challenged.

Before Brittany quite knew how she'd gotten there she found herself standing in front of the fire, directly across from Paul. ''Oh, there are occasional renegade animals, just as there are renegade humans. For instance, bears and alligators don't usually attack humans, either. But an occasional one will. That's why, once animals get the taste of human flesh, they have to be destroyed immediately.''

''And the sooner the better,'' Paul muttered.

Brittany began to doubt that Paul actually knew so little about the wolf species. ''Are you really as ignorant about wolves as you seem?'' she asked, her voice reflecting her sudden suspicion.

''What do you mean?''

''Wasn't your wife a biologist?''

He gave a visible start, then recovered slowly. ''Not really. Oh, Peg had acquired two degrees, elementary education and biology. But the latter was strictly to please Griff. After we moved here Peg did keep some records for him on herring nests or some damned thing. But biology never turned her on the way teaching kids did. Both of us usually found Griff's projects about as interesting as watching wet paint dry.''

Paul spoke rapidly—a little grudgingly, too, Brittany thought—as if he were annoyed that she had dared drag Peg into this discussion. His rapid changes of mood were beginning to disturb her. Was she supposed to ignore the fact that Paul had been married for years to Dr. Foster's daughter?

She was also galled by Paul's slurring reference to her profession, and she could tell by the obstinate look on his face that she was still a long way from convincing him of the worth of wolves. And that made her angry, deeply and coldly angry, because too many big-mouthed yahoos like Paul Johnson were running around these days maligning wolves.

"I won't bore you further," Brittany retorted, her voice icy and her back ramrod straight. "Anyway, I've always found it impossible to talk to someone with a closed mind."

"My mind isn't closed. I just fail to be impressed by slinking, sneaky, howling wolves, as well as by studies that have absolutely no practical application," Paul shot back.

"Why, you don't even know what I've come here to do!" Brittany charged. "So how in the world can you presume to know whether or not my work has any practical application? Actually it does! Incidentally wolves are not slinking and sneaky. Rather, they are a valuable and attractive species who help keep nature in proper balance. But why should I waste my breath talking to you?"

"Search me," Paul agreed with a negligent shrug.

Brittany tried to quell the rage that had erupted inside her, but it refused to be stifled. And even though she knew it was pointless to keep on talking to Paul, she heard herself lashing out once again.

"My God, how did an unappreciative person like you ever become caretaker of a natural island laboratory?" she charged.

"I don't pretend to be a rabid nature freak," Paul said flatly. "I'm only here because I find this a cheap and mostly pleasant place to live. I enjoy the solitude that most people—however much they profess to adore nature—really can't endure." Pointedly he added, "Also, living way out here, I don't often get pestered by outsiders—"

Brittany saw her chance to interrupt him and she took it. "Meaning me?"

Paul shrugged again. "You said it, I didn't."

"You don't have to say it! For the past two days you've demonstrated it quite eloquently." Brittany's bosom rose and fell with her wrath, but she was too angry to care that the motion had caused Paul to stare blatantly at her chest. She was also too angry to feel chagrined or embarrassed, either, by the obvious feminine endowments that had attracted his bold stare. Brittany had quite a temper of her own, and by now it was all fired up and had collected quite a head of steam. "In fact, you made it crystal clear that you didn't even bother to note that I was coming here," she accused. "God knows, you certainly didn't knock yourself out cleaning up for me! And although I was assured before I ever left the mainland that you would prove helpful, you left me to struggle all alone, starting with how I had to haul all my gear from the dock—"

"If you hadn't been in such a damned big hurry I would have helped you!" Paul shot right back. "I carried it in off the porch, didn't I? And while I'll admit the cottage wasn't in the very best shape—"

"A pigsty would look clean by comparison," Brittany charged and watched his face whiten with anger.

"My God, talk about a woman stretching the truth—"

"Not by much!"

"So there was a little dust—"

"There was filth and grime everywhere! There was spilled food in the cupboard and mold in the bathroom!" Warming to her topic and growing more indignant by the minute, Brittany now exaggerated shamelessly.

Abruptly Paul dropped his head, his chin jutting out stubbornly, until it was within a scant inch of hers. "Speaking of things you dislike, being constantly interrupted is one of mine," he said tightly. "Don't do it again or I'll—"

"What?" she taunted.

Even as she interrupted Paul, Brittany knew she was living dangerously. Although she didn't really think he would strike a woman, she still didn't know him well enough to be sure.

Nor was she exactly sure just how they had gotten into this ridiculous shouting match when earlier tonight they had each been quite pleasant and polite. Then Paul had been complimentary of their food, and Brittany had found his war stories both poignant and entertaining.

Was it solely because of the wolves' howling? Or was it when I mentioned Peg? Brittany wondered.

She didn't know. She didn't care! Brittany herself had just recovered from long, long months when she'd felt hurt, rejected, abandoned, publicly humiliated and depressed. God, yes, most of all she had been so very *depressed*!

But she wasn't depressed now. It felt good to speak her mind bluntly and truthfully for a change. It felt even better to yell. This time she wasn't letting some handsome, smug, know-it-all male get the better of her. This time she'd met his every volley with fire of her own, standing eyeball to eyeball with him.

Except that this situation was rapidly getting out of hand. Brittany allowed herself to wonder if Paul had deserved all of it. He probably did, she thought scathingly.

Still, he'd been hurt by life, too, she remembered. It was time to bring charges and countercharges to a screeching halt.

Leaning back against the mantel Brittany crossed her arms over her chest. Paul had fallen silent, too, but now she saw an annoying and supercilious amusement glinting in his pitch-black eyes.

"Look, we seem to be miles apart on this," Brittany began again when she thought she could control her voice. "Since it's unlikely that either of us will change the other one's mind, I think we'd better call it a night. I need to be at work early tomorrow morning."

Paul's voice, when he replied, was just as controlled as Brittany's. "Yes, I think we can finally agree on that. Good night."

He turned abruptly and stalked off toward the kitchen where he'd left his heavy jacket, his scarf and gloves. Suddenly a thought occurred to Brittany.

"Wait, Paul," she said, stopping him and streaking off in the opposite direction.

"What?" he demanded so impatiently that she felt irked as she entered the larger bedroom.

"I found some personal things in here that I'd like you to take," she called back to him.

She had left the cardboard box packed and waiting by the bed. Brittany scooped it up and returned to the living room where Paul waited.

She walked over and extended the small box to him. "Here," she said. "Take this away."

If Paul had ever wanted to throttle a woman this was definitely the moment and she was certainly the woman.

In fact, as he looked down and saw the contents of the box that Brittany had as good as labeled "garbage," Paul felt something threaten to snap deep inside of him.

The photograph of his family, with all three of them smiling so brightly, lay on top. Below that was a small blue-and-white sneaker that Chad had misplaced a year ago. "How can you lose a sneak?" Paul had teased his son, but no matter how carefully they had looked they still hadn't been able to find it.

Below the sneaker lay the coil of an inexpensive white necklace, and Paul's stomach tightened painfully at the sight. He'd bought that for Peg to complement a red-and-white summer dress. "It's nothing, Freckle Face," he'd said of his purchase, made at a small inexpensive shop on Catt Island. Even then he'd yearned to buy her real pearls instead of cheap beads. But Peg had continued to exclaim in pleasure. "It's so pretty, honey," she had said ecstatically and then hugged him.

Below the necklace lay a shaggy, now shapeless object. Paul's second glance confirmed that it was the brown stuffed poodle that had originally belonged to Chad until Ivy had confiscated it. Now it had been gnawed and drooled on to such an extent that Chad would never recognize it. In recent weeks Ivy had hidden her favorite toy and apparently couldn't remember where. Each time Paul had allowed her into the cottage Ivy had raced from room to room, searching in vain.

What was the last item, lying beneath the toy? Paul tilted the box, then felt a lump rise in his throat. It was a small lacy bra. On what night had he swept that scrap of lace off Peg and tossed it away in hot-blooded abandon, only to later have it recovered and hidden by Ivy?

Every important aspect of Paul's adult life lay represented by the items jumbled in that box, an unacceptable pile of discards to this tall blond woman. "Take this away," Brittany had directed Paul briskly.

Wrath swelled inside of him. Earlier it was Brittany who had been the angrier one, Paul merely irritated and annoyed. But now he was gripped by a near-frenzied rage. "Why, you bitch!" he said, speaking each word slowly and softly although they rumbled in his chest like a violent eruption ready to spew forth fire. Then Paul did explode, glowering at her. "You petty, mean-minded iceberg!"

Momentarily Paul had the satisfaction of seeing Brittany's smooth face pale. Of hearing her shocked gasp and watching her step back from him as if he had suddenly frightened her. He just wished he could think of more and worse insults to heap on her shining blond head. But Paul's mind had temporarily gone blank. He felt himself shaking and sweating, gripped once more by that deeply violent fury that he kept trying and failing to curb.

That she had erred grievously dawned belatedly on Brittany. "Look, Paul, I didn't mean—" she stammered.

He simply stared at her as if she were the lowest specimen of human life in existence. Meanwhile he clutched the box as he would have clutched the people its contents represented, if only he could. Oh God, if only he could!

Paul lowered his face to Brittany's once again. "No one, absolutely no one, puts down my wife and kid. No one gathers up their things—theirs—and acts like it's so much trash!"

Brittany was aghast, dismayed and frightened by his fury, but Paul no longer cared. Impressing her favorably, winning her friendship and trust had ceased to matter to him. Let her flee in horror. Let her send a frantic S.O.S. to Griff: "Your son-in-law is a madman!" He didn't even care if the college sent someone after him with a straitjacket and a butterfly net. Whenever he got this angry Paul just didn't give a damn.

"Look—" Brittany tried again. "I know it's personal stuff, that's why I gave it to you in the first place. I wouldn't want my personal mementoes lying around for some stranger to paw over—"

"That's not why you gave them to me," Paul interrupted her coldly. "You wanted to get rid of them."

"Is that so unreasonable? You act as if I've committed a crime. But I'm living here now—"

"Yes, I think your absolute and complete insensitivity is a crime!" he shouted. "It's not your place to discard my possessions or those of the two people I loved!"

Paul heard his voice rise to a roar. He knew he was probably the unreasonable one now, but that didn't matter to him, either.

Nothing mattered anymore, when you really got right down to it.

"Look, I'm sorry. Hey, simmer down, won't you? I didn't mean—"

Paul never heard the rest of Brittany's protests. Maybe her arguments made sense; maybe they didn't, for suddenly he grasped the why of his near-killing rage. By boxing up the various possessions that were Peg's and Chad's, things that dated from those happy days when the three of them had lived together here on the island, Brittany had unwittingly underlined and emphasized the full extent of Paul's loss. The two most important people in his world weren't here anymore—indeed one of them was gone forever. Death, as sinister and unpredictable as always, had snatched her away.

That box with its emotionally charged contents underscored the appalling fact that Paul's life would never, ever be the same again. And it felt as if some deeply hidden part of him was just beginning to acknowledge it. Peg, my poor, dear, lost little Freckle Face!

Had he unconsciously been living with the childlike wish to wake up and find it had all just been a dream? A dream? Oh no, this was his life's worst nightmare come true.

Damn it all, he was tired of feeling victimized. Tired of his life not ever working out and of things always going wrong. Even now, in spite of everything that had happened, Paul knew his life should still be better than this.

By God, it would be, too! Silently he swore it, both to himself and to the haunting memory of Peg. Somehow he was going to find the way back to a better life for Chad and himself. *"We're going to be together again, son, just the minute you're out of school!"* He'd told Chad that earlier this evening when they were talking on the radio. But that was just for starters. Because if he'd gotten this angry and still hadn't killed Brittany he was in better control of himself than he'd thought.

Meanwhile Brittany kept on protesting in her own defense. My God, whatever happened to the silent, stoic Scandinavian? Paul wondered. Had they gone the way of the dinosaur? Earlier, this one had exhibited plenty of Nordic reserve; he would definitely prefer that wintry aloofness now.

Or maybe she wasn't really chill and wintry, after all.

"Paul, are you even listening to me?"

"No, I'm not listening to you," Paul snapped, because he considered her apology insincere. "I think you've definitely got a mean streak, and I don't like it. In fact, I'd toss you the hell out of here right now, if I could, because this cottage where I lived with my family is still important to me!"

A little color was creeping back into Brittany's face, Paul noticed. She lifted her chin defiantly. "How dare you accuse me of being mean?" she shouted.

Brittany's hand swung back and Paul realized she intended to slap him. Furthermore, if she put her full weight behind it, she might land a substantial blow.

With the realization of what was coming, Paul reacted automatically. First, he dropped the box. Second, he sidestepped swiftly so he no longer stood in the spot where he'd been just a minute ago. Third, as Brittany's hand whistled past him, Paul reached out and seized it. Then, before she could recover her balance, he had captured and imprisoned her other hand as well.

For a couple of seconds they swayed, struggling together. What a shame I can't really kill her, Paul thought regretfully.

But unfortunately quite a number of state and national laws took exception to murder. So, since Paul felt abso-

lutely impelled to take some kind of action, he seized the
only one left to him and jerked Brittany hard against him.

His impulsive action succeeded because she was already
off balance, and for all his present thinness, Paul had quite
a lot of wiry strength. The move also worked because it had
the element of complete surprise. Even Paul didn't know
exactly what he intended to do until he kissed her, pressing
Brittany's petal-soft mouth beneath his own.

He'd kissed too many women in his life not to know just
exactly how to do it.

Only then, as his senses started swimming in sheer delight, did Paul understand that this was exactly what he'd
wanted to do from the first moment he'd seen her.

Chapter Six

For a stark moment Brittany's surprise changed to terror. She half expected to feel Paul's hands close around her throat. Then, when his almost equally shocking action achieved its aim, she zigzagged back into total and complete surprise. Paul's mouth now covered hers so completely, so deftly and, yes, so—so warmly that her terror gradually died away. Then all thoughts of protests ended as she slowly stopped struggling.

He might have been born knowing just exactly the right way to kiss her.

In the shadow of his moustache and beard, Paul's lips earlier had appeared virtually nondescript. But they weren't—oh no, not at all, Brittany discovered when she felt their fullness and firmness, their incredible warmth and the way they made her heart lurch and splutter into vibrant life. Momentarily she forgot everything else, turning like a sunflower seeking the sun, to accept the mounting pressure of Paul's lips on hers. Indeed, incredibly, she welcomed them.

The arms that had seized her and caused her to panic just a moment ago were already loosening. Then Brittany felt Paul drop one of her hands to wind his fingers into her hair. Holding her head securely he continued to kiss her with increasing fervor.

Brittany didn't realize that she held him, too, not until she felt the ripple of his back muscles beneath her fingers. She didn't realize she was sagging and melting against him, until she felt her breasts crushed against the wall of Paul's firm chest.

She could never have responded, of course, had she been even a fraction less surprised, or if he had hurt her in any way. But since she was, and he hadn't, her lips parted instinctively, inviting his deeper insertion. She felt his tongue gliding past, then moving inside to delicately stroke the soft vulnerable contours of her mouth. Before Brittany could recover from this ecstatic sensation he'd suddenly returned to take tiny nipping kisses at the corner of her lips.

"My God, you taste so sweet!"

It was his voice that snapped Brittany's spell, ending the moment's enthrallment and her utter abandonment to it. Those words returned her to a semblance of sanity.

Reacting belatedly, Brittany shoved at Paul's chest with her fists.

Dear God, what had she gone and done? She stumbled backward—indeed she fairly staggered. That Paul should have that impact on her was maddening. As was his standing there looking so—so totally unconcerned, maybe even smug.

She dragged her hand across her still pleasantly tingling mouth as if to wipe away his kiss and looked at Paul through eyes narrowing to furious slits. But Brittany also felt her face starting to smart as she reddened with steadily deepening embarrassment.

"How dare you!" she said.

"You want an apology?" Paul taunted. "You should be congratulated instead."

"Congratulated?" she gasped, her voice sounding strangled and her outrage complete.

"Yes, you got lucky, Brittany. After all, I didn't slap you silly even though I sure wanted to."

"You barbarian!" she shot back and dragged her other hand over her mouth, trying to emphasize once again how utterly distasteful she'd found Paul's kiss. Angrily she added, "If you ever touch me again I'll cut off both your hands!"

"Oh? Then why were you hugging me and kissing me back?" Although Paul's voice began as a jeer it softened perceptibly toward the end.

But Brittany didn't permit herself to hear that. "Get out!" she screamed.

"Don't worry, I'm gone."

With that, Paul bent down and snatched up the small box whose contents had ignited this imbroglio. That was the right word, wasn't it? As he charged off to the kitchen where he'd left his jacket and gloves, his bemused mind found refuge in the writer's trick of picking over words, then debating their meanings. Imbroglio meant a confused and intricate situation. It could also mean a damned embarrassing one.

Yes, definitely the right word, Paul thought, before he flung open the door. Immediately an arctic blast rushed to meet him as he plunged out into the night.

The wolves were singing again, their sharp calls echoing in the dark cold night. Music to Brittany's ears, but now she lay in bed and shivered. Clearly she was faced with an absolute worst-case scenario: stranded on this island and at the mercy of a lunatic!

Dramatically she told herself that Paul Johnson wasn't what anyone had said. Oh no, he was worse, dangerously much worse. He ought to be committed. Incarcerated in a well-padded cell. Probably confined there, too, for the rest of his natural life.

A yawn stopped Brittany's own satisfying scene of Paul in a medieval dungeon, chained to the wall, and her weary eyes grew heavy.

Gradually a sleepy honesty compelled her to admit that she really didn't believe her diagnosis of Paul as mentally disturbed. The interplay of emotions across his handsome face had been far too revealing.

I should never have flung that box at him without some kind of warning, she thought, cringing to recall his desperate, unguarded look when he'd stared down into it. Paul Johnson had looked like that not because he was angry, vicious or crazy. But simply because the sight of its contents had plunged him into so much pain.

No, that was definitely not a kindly move on my part, Brittany admitted to herself in the darkness. In fact, it was bloody well mean, just as Paul had said.

But her original motive in carefully gathering up each of the items she'd found hidden beneath a sofa cushion had also not been as base as Paul had thought. Brittany had told the truth when she'd said she wouldn't want strangers pawing over her personal things. But, of course, not everyone was as concerned with his privacy as Brittany.

Now, all alone in the cold darkness of her room, she winced from regret. She also wished she hadn't tangled with Paul. Of course, he certainly shouldn't have retaliated as he had, either. What sort of man kissed his adversary?

Well, she could never be interested in a man who hated wolves and didn't even try to understand them.

Nope. Never. Absolutely never. No matter how well he kissed, even such melt-you-down-to-the-ground kisses.... Obviously he was overly experienced and naturally gifted in that department. But she'd soon forget all about the way he'd kissed her or how she'd felt when he did—all hot and cold at the same time and so—so...

Sleep swallowed her up.

Good God, what was wrong with him? Paul wondered almost desperately as he followed the familiar and well-worn path back to the lighthouse. But then, instead of heading up into the tower's warmth and safety, he turned and hurried along the stone walk that led down to the dock and the ice-filled water.

The wind hitting his flushed face as it blew off Lake Superior felt as if it could freeze flesh but, for the moment, Paul barely noticed. His hotly churning senses probably needed a dash of ice and freezing spray to chill him back to normal.

What on earth had come over him? he wondered, embarrassed to recall how he'd snatched Brittany close and kissed her. No wonder the woman had looked so stunned!

Yesterday Paul had been fairly sure he was well along the comeback trail. Tonight he gave himself mixed reviews. Yes, he had a better grip on his emotions, but after grabbing and kissing Brittany he might also be fired as the Isle Svenson caretaker.

Paul's behavior was all the more puzzling since he had never been a violent man. He'd hated war with its random killing and pointless waste. Hadn't he written almost an entire novel that was, in Peg's telling phrase, "an anthem to peace"?

Certainly Paul had never abused women nor had he ever wanted to. In fact he had always agreed with feminists about the cultural immaturity of males who did.

Feeling as strongly as that, why on earth had he grabbed Brittany? Frightened her? Kissed her?

Paul allowed himself to admit that for some reason he had wanted to kiss Brittany. Even though he hadn't known it, at least not consciously. Not until he was actually swooping down to claim possession of her incredibly soft and tender mouth.

At least the reality of her in his arms and that touch of soft womanly flesh beneath his hands had destroyed any incipient tendency toward violence—if, indeed, that's what it had been. And what else could it have been? Paul thought, stalking the length of the walk like a panther on a leash.

When, a second or less into that kiss, Brittany's lips had eased open beneath his, Paul's sense of triumph had been complete. Not only was her mouth warm and sweet, like nectar to his suddenly flaming senses, but her full young breasts crushed against the wall of his chest had tantalized him with the brush of their nipples. Especially when he felt those oh-so-soft nipples start to harden.

That involuntary feminine response had immediately unleashed an erotic tornado inside Paul. Suddenly every male hormone in his body had kicked in—aroused, excited and rejoicing.

Paul knew exactly what he'd wanted to do. First he would bury his face in Brittany's clean fragrant hair, then kiss her throat and shoulders and the tender nape of her neck, working his way around gradually yet inexorably to that delectable mouth of hers. Then, an inch at a time, he would tug her black sweater slowly up over her shoulders.

Her skin below would be like palest satin. The flash of her leg that he'd caught earlier today had told him that. How would it feel when his rough hands, victims of a long winter, glided over that satin skin?

Stop it! Paul commanded himself, outraged by the very same imagination that had created his books and earned him his livelihood.

To know he had been thinking about making love to Brittany Hagen absolutely appalled him.

Not the fact of raw base desire. That Paul could understand, even sympathize with. He'd been forced by circumstances into monklike behavior that certainly didn't come naturally to him. Nor was this what years of a happy marriage had accustomed him to, either. He'd been used to indulging his senses, not keeping them tightly reined in.

So it was natural now, after months of stark and unnatural deprivation, that the male beast might stir.

At some point he might be driven to seek a basic and uncomplicated satisfaction of that desire, he allowed himself to admit. But he'd want a partner who was faceless in the dark—nameless, too. A deliberately meaningless physical encounter to be swallowed up by merciful night and dismissed as inconsequential long before morning.

No strings, of course. Absolutely, positively no strings!

Only that wasn't the way Brittany Hagen had made him feel, Paul knew. Not once her soft mouth parted beneath his in honest, receptive female response. Suddenly Paul hadn't thought nearly as much about the raw act of lovemaking as he had about simply loving her. About holding her close and leisurely exploring every soft lavish inch, first with his hands and then his lips and tongue. He'd even thought about sleeping with her, too, maybe curling up spoon-fashion to share their bed.

Paul faced deliberately into the gale and refused to let himself think of anything more. Because he was nowhere near ready to fall in love!

Peg had not been gone nearly long enough for him to start thinking about anyone else in the way he'd once thought of her.

But tonight his mind didn't picture Peg. Rather he saw shimmering hair like waves of gold, drawn gently back and pinned high on the crown. Saw a tall strong body and pure clean-cut profile.

"No!" Paul wasn't aware he was speaking aloud until he heard his own anguished cry.

How had that...that woman so totally invaded his thoughts and claimed possession of his mind? Something about all of this—something about her—seemed almost supernatural, now that Paul thought about it.

Immediately, as if to validate his bizarre notion, he heard fresh howls. Rising and falling, goose-bump-inciting, hair-raising howls, the local wolf pack made its presence known. As the cries rose even higher, Paul turned and ran all the way back to the lighthouse.

Brittany didn't stir all night long, except perhaps to roll over once or twice. But next morning she came awake instantly, feeling rested and remarkably clearheaded. This wasn't her usual state of lethargy and muddled thinking, of endless yawns and a deep, abiding reluctance to heave-ho and face a new day.

No, today Brittany woke up thinking about...about the wolves and moose, of course. Not the other resident on the island. Why, the only reason she felt so excited, so eager, so ready to get cracking today was that the wolves she'd heard last night had to live somewhere and she was determined to find their den.

Paul Johnson didn't figure into any of her calculations, whether he came or went, lived or died. All that mattered today was that the sun was shining brightly, in another hour the temperature would be tolerable and she had been entrusted with performing an important mission.

How wonderful it was to wake up not feeling depressed!

Brittany even startled herself by humming as she washed her face and pulled on her warmest clothes. Then she hurried into the kitchen, the only room she had to share with Paul.

He'd better not show up to ruin my breakfast, either, she thought vengefully, fairly skipping through the door despite her heavy boots. Still, if he did she was ready for him. Today she felt as if she could lick a cage of tigers with one hand tied behind her back!

She'd fix pancakes, she decided. And she wouldn't offer to share with that . . . that lecher, either, not even if he does look thin and hungry. Regardless of how many wistful looks he trained on her mom's cherry preserves, he'd be strictly out of luck. Paul Johnson needed to learn that there were penalties for boorish behavior and that she, for one, wouldn't tolerate—

Brittany's thoughts broke off abruptly as she spotted the unwashed coffee mug sitting by the side of the sink. She picked it up to discover that it was still faintly warm. And there were blackened toast crumbs, too, messing up the sink that she'd left in such immaculate condition last night.

So Paul had already come and gone, she realized, not understanding her suddenly deflated feeling. Of course, the only reason she might have wanted to see him was just to treat him as icily as he deserved. Then if he should persist in either his comments or his unwelcome attentions she was primed to tell him off. Even to warn him that if he didn't cease and desist immediately she would notify college officials of his unprofessional behavior, starting, of course, with Dr. Griff Foster.

"Boor!" Brittany muttered and set the teakettle on to boil.

She settled for a cup of tea and a bowl of instant oatmeal, having lost her taste for a more elaborate breakfast. After all, busy women like herself really didn't have time to cook. At least the oatmeal would warm her up and stick to her ribs till noon.

Brittany ate as she suspected Paul probably had, standing up by the sink. Unlike Paul, however, she intended to wash her dishes. She fixed a baleful eye on his coffee mug and the mess of blackened toast crumbs.

So the biggest crumb around here had burned his breakfast. Good! It served him right. Her lips tightening with disapproval, Brittany swept away all of Paul's offending signs. She decided that it annoyed her less to clean up after him than to continue looking at what he'd left behind.

Finished with her tidying up, Brittany tucked a cheese sandwich and an orange into her pockets. That ought to suffice for her lunch on the go.

She went back into the living room and drew on her parka, scarf and gloves. She tucked a ski mask into the pack she would carry, just in case the wind got too brisk to endure. Then she collected snowshoes, map, notebook and pens, camera and binoculars.

Outside the sun sparkled, casting golden crescents on the old and slushy-looking snow. Brittany locked the front door carefully behind her, then stood for a minute on the porch savoring her surroundings before resolutely starting down the steps.

For the past two days she had gone east; today she decided to begin hiking across the western edge of the island and enter the forest there.

She had to pass the lighthouse, of course. There was no way to avoid it. But Brittany barely allowed her gaze to move, casting only a furtive glance up, way up, to the top of the tower.

She didn't see its inhabitant. But, of course, she'd looked so quickly that Paul might have stood there but been obscured by a shadow on the wide glass window.

Not that she was really eager to see him again. Oh, maybe she did owe him an apology for apparently being so insensitive about that box last night. But since he hadn't listened to any of the earlier ones she'd attempted, Brittany decided she probably ought to save her breath.

After all, Paul certainly owed her an apology, too! Remembering, she gave another resentful swipe across her lips with a gloved fist.

There were only two things Brittany found herself still genuinely curious about.

Last night Paul had discussed the fall of Saigon from his own unique vantage point, telling her various stories and anecdotes of things he'd witnessed. Yet hadn't he also said he was writing a *novel*? Was he going to take all those facts and render a fictionalized account of them?

And what had happened to his poor Peg that she had died such an untimely death?

Brittany really wished she could ask Paul about those matters.

So the she-wolf was off again to do whatever she did. She'd cast one swift, disdainful glance at Paul's ivory tower, then turned her head in the other direction.

What was she doing on this island, anyway? Paul wondered irritably. Merely writing another dull paper on wolves' family structure and the reasons behind their behavior patterns? Or was she a numbers freak, gathering more predator-prey statistics?

If Brittany expected to observe wolves in daylight she was strictly mistaken. About the only time to spot those shadowy, slinking critters was on a night of the full moon. Maybe she'd even go out to howl with the wolves, too.

It was more than a facetious thought. A previous graduate student in residence here had done that very thing, howled for all the world as if he had wolfsbane in his blood. He'd given both Paul and Peg the creeps, and they'd cracked jokes about the werewolf in their midst.

Was this ice-blooded blonde as weird as that?

Of course, Brittany had said her own particular project did have a practical application.

Now he walked over to the broad window and stood framed there blatantly while he glowered down at the back of Brittany's departing figure. Paul had slept poorly last night and had awakened early and in a foul mood this morning. Today it seemed as if everything that had gone wrong lately was her fault.

Seen from this altitude, Brittany Hagen looked very tall and long-legged. Quite athletic, too, as she strode along with her blond hair in a single thick braid swinging over her shoulder and snowshoes sticking out of the pack on her back.

Once again, something about the sight of her tantalized Paul's mind, filling it with thoughts of ancient cultures and old Norse legends.

Enough! Paul thought, tearing his gaze away from her. She was about to plunge into dark thick woods, anyway, and vanish from view. Maybe she'd get lost in there and never crawl out, Paul thought savagely, starting toward his typewriter. He knew he ought to get fired up and finish his book but he turned away. He just simply wasn't in the mood to write.

If Brittany got lost he certainly wouldn't play Saint Bernard and go looking for her, either!

He whistled to Ivy who was snoozing again, nose-down on her bed. "C'mon, girl, it's time for fresh air and exercise," he announced, then started descending the lighthouse stairs rapidly. Reluctantly Ivy rose and came shuffling after him.

First, though, Paul intended to check on the condition of the cottage. As caretaker he usually gave it a cursory going-over when students stayed longer than overnight. Couldn't have them chopping up the floorboards for firewood or doing coke and crack. Not that Paul suspected Brittany of anything like that. Still, he would be negligent not to take an occasional look.

After all, who really knew what a she-wolf did all alone in her lair?

As he left the lighthouse, Paul's boots crunched down on old snow that was firm and packed full of ice crystals. Each step he took was preserved in snow, he noticed, glancing behind him.

Since Ivy's paw prints were also a visible trail, there was no way Brittany could miss the fact that Paul had visited the cottage in her absence.

That suited him just fine. It was time she understood that he was in charge. He'd be damned if he'd keep going through the back door only, Paul determined. By God, he'd go straight through the front door whenever he liked.

On the porch he gave his boots one knock apiece to rid them of excess snow, then opened the door with his key. He didn't care if he tracked up her floors. Matter of fact, Paul half hoped he did, although he wasn't petty enough to do so deliberately.

To find the cottage in absolutely flawless condition only irked him more. "My God, the woman simply isn't human!" Paul exploded, having taken a close look around. Since the cottage didn't look as if anyone even lived there, Paul wondered for a wild moment if he had imagined Brittany Hagen. If, indeed, she had escaped from Valhalla and materialized on earth to haunt him.

That bed, so crisply made, had surely not been slept in. And where were her nightclothes or slippers? Since Paul could detect no signs of pajamas, nightgown or robe he thought maybe she'd left them hanging on the hook behind the bathroom door. That's where he and Peg had always hung theirs, when they'd worn anything, that is.

No nightclothes hung on the hook, and the bathroom's condition was immaculate, toilet lid down, wash basin and tub freshly scrubbed. No damp washcloth or towel hung here, either. The only ones draped over the rod hadn't even been unfolded. Didn't the woman bathe? Or had she lied about being in the shower yesterday?

The small mystery intrigued him. While Ivy whined outside—finally letting loose with impatient barks and scratching against the window to express her further displeasure—Paul tried to detect any evidence that Brittany slept, ate or washed like normal mortal beings.

Ah-hah! In the top dresser drawer Paul saw a stack of nightgowns, and the one lying on top didn't look quite as stiffly untouched as the others. A granny gown, too, Paul thought with disgust. Those things were about as sexy as feed sacks.

But what did he expect a woman to wear to bed all alone? The practical voice in his mind told Paul that Brittany was taking eminently sensible precautions against freezing to death in the drafty old cottage.

He also found her woolly white bedroom slippers in the closet, lined up with near-military precision along with her other shoes and boots.

Okay, so she actually had slept here last night, he concluded. She hadn't really drifted off to Viking heaven, only to return today to plague him.

Satisfied, Paul left the bedroom and headed into the laundry room next. As he passed the kitchen stove he automatically flipped on the burner beneath his teakettle. He'd left plenty of water in the kettle earlier just so he could make himself another quick cup of coffee.

In the laundry room Paul was gratified to discover a damp washcloth and towel. So she did wash. But, my God, did she intend to go through a clean towel and washcloth every single day?

Since he now had to do laundry himself, Paul never discarded a towel or washcloth until it was in imminent danger of souring. Of course, he had to admit that Peg had been plenty picky, too. Maybe it was a universal feminine trait.

Closing the door on the small chilly laundry room Paul returned to the kitchen. He hefted the teakettle only to drop it instantly, cursing in rage and fury. It was blazing hot, entirely empty and he'd just burned its bottom black. Since he always left the teakettle half-full of water he damned well knew who had emptied it. Just what did Her Majesty think she was doing, tampering with the way he had always done things?

Grudgingly Paul cleaned off the bottom of the kettle with a scouring pad, then added fresh water to it only to look around in bewilderment for his favorite coffee mug. He always left it sitting by the side of the sink, but now it was gone.

He finally found his mug washed, dried and put up in the cabinet. At least Paul thought this one was his. Since there were five others exactly like it in the cabinet, it irked him not to be able to make a positive identification of his now that its characteristic coffee stains and odor had been eradicated.

Paul fixed his instant coffee, drank most of it, then returned the coffee mug to its customary place by the sink and stalked back out of the cottage.

"C'mon, Ivy!" he called to his dog.

Ivy looked confused by their schedule change. Usually Paul worked all morning and took her out running in the afternoons.

Of course, Ivy didn't appreciate writer's block, either. It wasn't an affliction from which Paul had often suffered while he was on the island but tired and cranky as he felt today he doubted if he would get any real work done. Undoubtedly that was all her fault, too!

Chapter Seven

This was war!

It began with a lull—the calm before the storm, as Brittany was later to recall.

Three days passed before Brittany and Paul confronted each other again. They had spent that time reassessing their respective positions, sharpening their weapons of tongue and pen and going to elaborate, even ridiculous means, to avoid bumping into each other. But, after that, they were each too curious about the other to resist, as well as being primed and ready for Round Two.

Brittany knew their war had returned to an active phase when, on Friday afternoon, she returned to the cottage feeling tired and discouraged. Her work was not going well, at least not in her own estimation. Oh, she had already located a couple of winter casualties, so Dr. Foster would be pleased. Predictably, too, the moose carcasses she'd found in the snow had been of old and infirm animals, as she confidently expected her bone samples to prove. But she was still no nearer to finding a wolves' den or anything that re- motely resembled one.

So Brittany was not kindly disposed to discover *his* dog, Ivy, parked and waiting on the front porch—not the back, as he'd promised.

Immediately she began to feel a whole lot better. Newly energized and with the lust for battle like a tangible taste in her mouth she stormed inside and started shedding her backpack, coat, scarf and gloves. Nor was she going to worry one bit about Paul Johnson's recently widowed state. He had proved that he didn't deserve her kindness and con- sideration, so from now on her heart was hardened against him.

She had started toward their mutual arena, the kitchen, when its door swung back and Paul stood framed there. He was munching on a sandwich and, naturally, with a slob like him, crumbs were flying everywhere. Didn't it ever occur to him to sit down to eat?

Despite her rising ire at his lack of table manners, at the sight of him Brittany's stomach gave an excited flutter and her heart banged hard against her backbone.

Paul wore a brown sweater over matching brown slacks, and the overall effect heightened his dark and clever looks. He might have been a research scientist working on a new rocket fuel, Brittany thought irrelevantly, or perhaps a psy- chiatrist about to describe a breakthrough technique for curbing aggression.

Suddenly, too, those steamy kisses they'd exchanged came flashing back into Brittany's mind, especially when Paul raised one black eyebrow in her direction.

At that look of his Brittany began to feel overly warm, as though she were wearing too many clothes.

"Hello there," Paul said, his greeting deceptively casual.

"Hi." Brittany's reply was brusque. She sank down onto a footstool beside a comfortable old living room chair and began working the knots out of the laces on her boots. Al- though her feet were killing her, that was the only source of discomfort she'd experienced until just now. But suddenly her mouth had gone dry and her mind was a blank. Belatedly a thought occurred to her.

"You've chosen a novel way to commit suicide," she remarked as Paul stepped into the room.

"What are you talking about?"

"Eating the sandwich meat on your side of the refrigerator," she declared. "Most of it has turned ripe and green. Both the cheese and turkey slices probably harbor food-poisoning organisms by now. Which, by the way, are you eating?"

It was a good thing she'd run out of conversation, Brittany thought privately, because she'd also run out of air. She didn't know why he made her feel so strangely breathless and light-headed, but it was infuriating.

"I rarely try to identify my food." Paul raised one slice of his sandwich and peered down. "Looks like cheese."

"Good. At least I'll know what to tell the paramedics." With that, Brittany tugged off the boot on her right foot and let it drop with a thump.

"Very funny," said Paul without the trace of a smile.

"Actually very true," she retorted, starting on the laces of her other boot. "Anybody who eats food as old and moldy as you do obviously has a death wish."

"You wish!" Paul shot back.

"You said it, I didn't." Brittany wondered why she was all thumbs today. Normally she had no trouble unlacing her boots and shedding them. Today it took five tries per foot instead of the usual deft one. "By the way, your bread has gone bad, too."

"Now that I did notice. Which is why I'm eating yours. I didn't figure you'd mind loaning me a few slices. I mean, it's not like you need extra nourishment or anything."

For a moment, sheer outrage kept Brittany speechless. Why, he had just as good as called her fat! "Matter of fact, I do mind," she said, rearing up off the stool as angrily as a rattlesnake that had just been jabbed with a stick. "That food's got to last me until the supply boat comes next. And while I'm telling you about various things I mind, having you come in and out of the front door is one of them. Another is having you open my dresser drawers and paw over my personal things."

"I see no reason to bother using the back door when I know good and damned well that you're out," Paul snapped right back. "And what makes you think I've been 'pawing over' your things?"

"I've noticed a few signs. Enough to make me wonder if maybe you have a problem in that area," Brittany replied, sitting back down on the stool.

Silently she congratulated herself on having landed a clever strike, especially since now she could watch the satisfying sight of Paul's handsome face turning purple with rage. "Yes, I opened a few drawers. I am, after all, the caretaker here. That literally means I look after things, particularly when the person in residence is a woman as unusual—dare I say peculiar?—as you."

He walked over closer to where she sat, his sandwich forgotten. "Incidentally I don't have problems in the area you implied. If I was ever going to get turned on by women's underwear it would take more than basic white cotton panties and jogging bras for the fuller figure to light my fuse."

Those cracks about her utilitarian undergarments made Brittany so angry she had to bite her tongue and count to ten before she dared try to respond. By then, too, a comeback had occurred to her. "Oh, I don't know," she drawled, deliberately looking Paul up and down. "If, say, you were into wearing it rather than just pawing it, I'd guess my stuff would fit you pretty well."

"I'm not interested either in handling or wearing women's lingerie!" Paul roared now, waving his sandwich for emphasis.

"Good. It might make for difficulties if we were sharing the same wardrobe," Brittany said briskly, then stood up in her stocking feet.

"You're really a very odd person, did you know that?" Paul said coldly. "Your mind is definitely warped."

Brittany felt amused that he was reduced to aiming silly cracks at her. It showed a person caught off guard. "You're the first to complain," she said and went into her bedroom where she closed and locked her door to finish undressing.

After Paul had left, banging the front door shut behind him, Brittany allowed herself a cool smile. Had they been keeping score on their skirmishes she could have recorded this one: BRITTANY 1, PAUL 0.

But, wouldn't you know it, he evened things up the very next day.

Of course Paul caught her off guard by coming in the back door while Brittany was in the laundry room disposing of the towel and washcloth she'd finished using. As she walked back into the kitchen, absorbed in her own thoughts, Brittany suddenly grew aware of Paul's lean figure standing by the sink she'd filled with soap bubbles.

Previously he had always come and gone before Brittany even arose, but today, for some reason, Paul was apparently running late. Or was he merely lying in wait?

He wore the maroon sweater that emphasized his olive complexion, but the expression in his eyes as he turned to look at her could have cut glass.

"Oh!" Brittany cried, taken aback by the surprise of his presence. Then before she could accuse him of scaring her by coming inside so quietly, Paul launched his first strike.

"You are the most compulsive neurotic for cleaning and washing I've ever seen," he said, looking critically from the sink to the laundry basket in Brittany's hands.

"It's not neurotic to like things to be clean," Brittany protested. As she spoke she wished her heart would stop its jumping-bean act each and every time she happened to see this unpleasant man.

"It's neurotic the way you do it," Paul said, setting down his coffee cup carelessly. As Brittany watched, brown droplets sloshed over the sides of the cup as well as the sink. "This place used to be a home," Paul said, gesturing sweepingly around the room. "Now just look at it!"

"What's wrong with it?" Brittany demanded in surprise. "It looks fine to me." Although fresh belligerence echoed in her voice, Paul was way ahead of her this morning.

"For starters, I've seen cheap motel rooms that have more warmth and charm," he charged. "As for its smell—"

"What's wrong with the smell?" Brittany interrupted just a trifle defensively. She knew, of course, that he was deliberately trying to get her goat. Still, if there was one thing she couldn't abide it was unpleasant smells.

"Use your nose," he directed.

Brittany succumbed to a sniff, even though she hated herself for letting this man make her self-conscious. Were the onions she'd cut up for soup last night still lingering? Or was it the butcher's paper in which the ground meat had been frozen?

"Every time I walk in here it reeks of antiseptic, that's what's wrong," Paul said accusingly. "I keep thinking I'm back in the men's room at the Detroit bus station!"

"I don't like germs. Furthermore, I have to clean up after you," Brittany huffed in her own defense. Defiantly she pushed past Paul to return to her breakfast dishes left soaking in the sink. But even that swift brush against his lean, hard body reminded her stingingly of things she didn't want to remember, like the warmth of his lips and hands.

"Believe me, no mere germ could survive the Brittany Hagen attack. But, frankly, honey, it's strictly overkill," Paul said patronizingly.

"Don't you dare call me 'honey'!" Brittany snapped, lifting her dishes from the suds to rinse them off. "Anyway, for all I know you may be bringing in anything since you never wash your dishes or clothes. Or, if it isn't you, it's probably fleas and lice off your mangy dog!"

"I do, too, wash my clothes—" Paul began heatedly.

"Not very often," Brittany chimed in.

"And Ivy is not mangy!" he continued indignantly. Then Paul reached down for his coffee mug only to grope all around; the mug was no longer by the side of the sink. Even Brittany didn't realize the truth immediately and wondered where it had gone.

"What have you done with my coffee mug?" Paul roared. "Oh God, as if I didn't know. You've grabbed it and washed it!"

Although Brittany started to deny that she'd done any such thing, she was so taken aback by his angry vehemence that she reached down automatically into the suds. Sure enough, she immediately retrieved the mug since it was the only item still left in the sink.

As Brittany silently rinsed it, then handed it back to Paul, she could feel her face reddening. It was rather hard to deny that you weren't a compulsive neatnik after a revealing little slip like that.

But she wasn't allowed the opportunity to simply feel embarrassed. Already Paul was carrying on as if she'd committed a crime.

"Why did you wash it?" he demanded. "Why are you always washing it?"

"Because you never do!" she shot back. "And what's wrong with—"

He loomed over her, his face changing to that dangerous-looking purplish shade. "Listen, Ms. Clean, I hadn't finished drinking my coffee yet, that's what's wrong! Furthermore, I have kept a mug sitting here by this sink every day for the past seven years until you—you of all people—came here. Now I'm never able to find my own coffee mug! The damn thing's always gone. Well, let me tell you something, lady. If you ever dare to move it again, even one inch, even once more, I will take considerable pleasure in kicking down your bedroom door, emptying out your dresser drawers and setting every damned sterilized, cast-iron, military-issue garment you own on fire! Do I make myself clear?"

Brittany's heart began pounding erratically as she tried to hide a sudden rush of fear as well as an even more disconcerting feeling of arousal. Something to do with Paul's threat to kick down her bedroom door had spawned this disgustingly primitive reaction, she supposed.

"Sure. You're about as clear as any other raving maniac," Brittany replied coldly, then managed an offhand shrug. But she still felt intimidated. Taken aback. Thrown for a loop and unable to think of the right sort of comeback in just the properly ironic words that she sought.

So, tilting her nose into the air, she marched past Paul Johnson, making certain to shrink back from any contact with his tense body this time.

Reaching the bedroom, Brittany slammed and locked her door, then leaned back against it, shaking both from rage and a sudden eager apprehension that she didn't understand and completely deplored.

Without question Paul had won today.

She was really starting to get on his nerves now, Paul conceded, pacing his big lantern room at the top of the lighthouse while Ivy lay sprawled beside the desk that held Paul's neglected typewriter.

Three more days had passed. Three days since he'd threatened to batter down Brittany's bedroom door and seen a momentary spark of fear touch her hostile face and chill blue eyes.

Paul still wasn't sure why he'd said "bedroom" except that it had come most handily to mind. Why not bathroom? Why not the laundry room, for that matter?

Always analytical, about himself as well as other people, he suspected that his crack about Brittany's bedroom door might be some sort of Freudian slip.

Still, he'd kept her bluffed for two days, or so he'd thought until this morning when she'd retaliated so simply, yet so effectively, too.

Paul had still been sipping his first cup of coffee when Brittany had appeared, and she'd looked really nice, too, at least for her. That long shining golden hair had been braided, then the braid coiled around her head. With her blue Scandinavian eyes and that flawless complexion she looked like a fresh, innocent schoolgirl.

Paul also noticed that Brittany's figure appeared trimmer. Since the weather had warmed up she probably wasn't wearing two layers of clothes over thermal underwear any longer.

"Good morning, Paul," she sang out with a sudden disarming sweetness. The winsome and completely unexpected smile she'd flashed his way had looked deceptively sweet, too.

But Gina Olszewski hadn't raised any fools, Paul thought cynically. So he'd set down his mug of coffee in its usual place by the sink and regarded her cautiously. "Hello, Brittany," he had replied.

"You don't need to move," she'd cooed. Then she had slipped beside him to take a cereal bowl down from the cabinet. For a moment her scent surrounded Paul, enveloping him in the natural essence of total cleanliness—skin, hair and clothes—as well as a touch of perfumed fragrance. Her toilet soap, he surmised.

Paul inhaled deeply just as Brittany turned back. Then, abruptly, her elbow accidentally-on-purpose brushed his coffee mug, and before either of them could react it went crashing down to the floor. There it shattered, leaving only a hundred tiny pieces of broken crockery and one very large brown stain.

"Oops," Brittany had said.

Paul knew full well that this contrary woman was anything but cowed, anything but subdued.

Oh, she'd kept playing the innocent all the way. "So-o-o sorry," she'd apologized even while her blue eyes almost sparkled out of her head. "Just let me clean it up— Oh, but you don't like me to clean things up, do you?"

Paul went crashing back outside a scant minute before he might have killed her. Even though as he left he knew—yes, he absolutely knew—that she was standing in the middle of the kitchen, holding her sides and reeling with fiendish laughter.

Brittany Hagen was undoubtedly the most maddening and infuriating woman he'd ever met, Paul had thought, clenching his teeth as he stomped back to the lighthouse. Too bad the army didn't know about her. She could become a new secret weapon in their arsenal of dirty tricks. Someone to sic on any unsuspecting male they wanted to drive completely crazy. Valkyrie Power! Why, ultimately it might even replace espionage.

Now, alone with Ivy in the lighthouse, Paul paced some more. Then he tried to sit down and write once again. But soon he'd x'd out the only paragraph he could manage.

This sort of writer's block had certainly never happened to him before. Not the kind where a completely unimportant person absolutely consumed him. In fact, until it had happened to him, Paul had always thought most writer's blocks were just a lazy person's excuse not to do any meaningful work.

Now he thought differently because, for some strange reason, he just couldn't stop thinking about and constantly watching for that tall blonde. Paul was still seething as he remembered how Brittany had broken his favorite coffee mug. Deliberately, too! Never mind that five others just like it were still sitting in the kitchen cabinet.

The Middle Ages had dealt with such evil-eyed women by burning them at the stake, while the city fathers of Salem, Massachusetts, had hung them as witches.

Always, in the past, Paul had sympathized with the witches, knowing that they were merely women who had been misunderstood. But now he was gaining a whole new understanding of the Salem city fathers!

Abruptly Paul felt hunger stir, making his stomach rumble. With surprise he glanced over at the clock on the lighthouse wall. It was a quarter past noon. Although he used to regularly forget to eat lunch he never forgot lately.

At least he'd find the kitchen empty. Brittany had been gone from the cottage for hours, which made it all the more ridiculous for Paul to be pacing around thinking about her.

What in the hell did she do for such long hours all alone in those dark woods? Look for moose and the more elusive wolves and translate all such sightings into dreary statistics? Or did the forest suddenly become enchanted while she changed into a goddess? Did she go riding away on spectral horseback, her golden hair streaming out behind her, to her magical palace just over the rainbow? Although Paul grinned at his own images his smile faded away just as swiftly.

Not knowing what she was up to kept bugging him, which was ridiculous. But at least it told Paul that he needed to reduce even further his amount of contact with the wretched woman.

For the next several days they avoided each other completely, writing notes back and forth when they needed to communicate.

P.J.
This telegram rec'd Catt Island today. Delivered by yr. neighbor, Dr. Trent Davidson, who followed ice-breaker in Lake Super. Couldn't find you at light-house. Guess you/Ivy running. Found me. Dr. D opened telegram. Yr. NY editor wants to see rest of yr. book. Write her.

B.H.

P.S. Dr. D said you've been writing that book for three yrs. Do you ever plan to finish or are you making it yr. life's work?

B.H.
Wrote editor. No, novel is not my life's work. Will finish soon. However, a literary endeavor like creating original fiction is not quite as easily accomplished as counting moose hides.

P.

P:
Stay out of my food! I know you ate soup.

B.

B:
Why be stingy? You've still got plenty of soup bones in freezer.

P.

P:
Those bones are from very old and/or diseased moose
who died during the winter. I don't advise anyone—
even you—eating them. Or does this warning come too
late?

                                             B.

B:
Diseased moose? Great God! And you worry about
mere household germs! Get those diseased moose
bones out of this cottage *immediately*!

                                 Isle Svenson Caretaker

P.S. I call supply boat headquarters tomorrow. Leave
your grocery list.

Caretaker:
Relax. Bones double-sealed in heavy plastic. Anyway,
freezing prevents multiplication of most bacteria. Bone
samples will be sent to Dr. Foster on next supply boat.
Grocery list follows:
Bread
Eggs
Butter...

                                             B.

Hunger seized Paul's attention even more keenly than
before, and when he wasn't preoccupied with Brittany he
was thinking about food. He didn't know why he felt ravenous almost all the time when he'd had such scant appetite before. Of course, he was still almost twenty pounds
under his normal weight, and that was why his clothes hung
on him so loosely and why his face looked so thin.

Shock and grief had caused Paul's unintended weight
loss, he knew. Added to that was the prosaic fact that he'd
simply burned out on his own wretched cooking. But lately,
even the stuff he'd slopped together in sometimes weird and
inappropriate combinations was tasting good to him.

Nothing, though, tasted quite as good as the few bites he filched from Brittany's side of the refrigerator. Now that she was aware of his pirating, Paul had limited those to very few. But, Lord, how could he resist when she fixed what were, for him, rare and wonderful things: hot homemade soup or chili, fresh slaw or salads, breads and desserts. Sometimes Paul thought she baked those appetizing pans of Scandinavian rolls and pastries solely to torment him, especially since he had run completely out of anything even resembling bread and was presently reduced to eating stale crackers.

Brittany had also brought various delicacies that Paul never thought to request, like smoked oysters, Danish ham and a whole assortment of unusual cheeses. Today just thinking about the infinite variety of food crowding Brittany's side of the refrigerator made Paul's mouth water.

Five minutes later when he actually stood looking at the food he felt so famished he was driven to raid without compunction. Rapidly he combined Danish ham with cheese, constructing a huge Dagwood sandwich on twin slabs of newly baked whole-wheat bread while succulent vegetable soup simmered, reheating in one of his scarred pots.

Then Paul sat down at the table and began enjoying Brittany's food. He began with a big bowl of soup, which he ate between bites of his sandwich. Halfway through the soup, which was superb—at least the contrary woman could cook, he'd grant her that—Paul paused just long enough to build a second sandwich.

Finished at last, he dropped his dirty dishes and the soup pot into the sink, just as he always did. Usually Paul had smiled quite maliciously, since he knew by now that dirty dishes drove Brittany absolutely crazy.

But today, this seemed like one too many dirty tricks. To devour her food and then leave her such a mess to clean up was simply too much. Reluctantly, and annoyed by his better nature, Paul turned back to wash and dry his dishes.

The small gesture made him feel so much better that a new inspiration struck. Why didn't he leave Brittany a tasty peace offering in the form of some freshly caught fish? After all, hadn't she said on that night they'd shared dinner—that night that now seemed so long ago since it had happened back while they were still speaking to each other—that she dearly loved good fresh fish?

Almost before Paul knew it, he was down on the dock, whistling and enjoying the sunshine as he set out his fish lines. After all his years on Isle Svenson he knew the local fish pretty well, knew just which bait they found irresistible and which they ignored. In record time he caught two beauties: large white fish that he left in the water swimming in his trap.

He returned to the cottage to write Brittany a note, and for the first time in days Paul was able to express himself eloquently. Why couldn't he do as well on the all-important project that was his novel-in-progress?

There—that should suffice. Straightening up, Paul slapped the note on the table, then reached for his jacket.

On the porch he nudged his reluctant dog up with an insistent foot. "C'mon, Ivy, it's time to run."

Ivy grew larger with every day but since she hadn't had much appetite of her own lately, Paul now cast a worried look at her.

Ivy's lack of hunger was definitely suspicious since this was one of the signs of approaching labor cited in the dog book. But when would it begin and what should he expect? Paul wished he could ask Brittany about Ivy. Not only had she grown up on a dairy with lots of animals, but since she was a biologist she was bound to know more about dogs than Paul did. For that matter, almost anybody knew more!

All at once Paul felt quite lonely and more than a little afraid for Ivy.

His feud with Brittany had enlivened the otherwise dreary and monotonous days. But lately there were moments when Paul wished, more than ever, that the two of them could stop their stupid bickering and just simply be friends.

On Paul's return from their run he turned his attention to the trash and garbage sacks. Since the supply boat would be back tomorrow he must have all of his and Brittany's debris organized and waiting down on the dock. First, he needed to find out exactly what she had.

A couple of small garbage sacks had been frozen by her, as he'd requested. Brittany had used only one trash sack, but it was close to full, Paul noted. He decided to go ahead and tie it up securely for its boat ride. As he bent to do that Paul ran an experienced eye over its contents.

A flash of navy blue on top caught his attention. Was that . . . yes, it was! Tugging out the woollen scrap Paul saw that it was the once smart-looking cap Brittany had worn two weeks ago on her arrival to the island. The very same cap Ivy had also riddled.

I should have offered to replace it, at least, Paul thought belatedly.

Or could it possibly be mended? Although Paul had no way of knowing, his mother was a great one for sewing and knitting. Why didn't he send this cap to Gina and see what she could do with it, if anything.

Paul had started to close up the trash sack once again when he noticed a stiff-looking invitation now on top where the navy cap had been. He sent a curious hand delving back down, then he was surprised, even stunned, by what he drew out.

An engraved wedding invitation had been torn quite neatly in two. Reading it Paul felt an intense jolt deep inside.

Mr. and Mrs. Rolf Siegfried Hagen
request the honor of your presence
at the marriage of their daughter
Anna Brittany
to
Mr. Howard Eric Pierson
on Saturday, April 30,
at Grace Lutheran Church
Little Stavanger, Minnesota

After he stuffed the torn invitation back into the sack again Paul glanced at the kitchen calendar to confirm what he already suspected. Yes, that invitation, which evoked more questions than it answered, was exactly one year old today.

Had the wedding actually taken place? Paul wondered with concern. Was that the mystery behind Brittany's sometimes caustic tongue and aloof behavior? Was she one of the casualties of yet another modern marriage that had ended almost before it began?

Or had her planned wedding been called off?

Surely the latter. If Brittany had been a recent divorcée, Griff would surely have mentioned it to Paul. Also, Brittany seemed to exhibit the habits of a single person. She even knew how to cook just for one.

Suddenly Ivy lunged against a window to express her impatience and Paul yelled, "Oh, all right. I'm coming!"

His mood thoughtful, Paul left the cottage only to discover Ivy standing alertly on the edge of the porch. "You ready to go home for a nap?" Paul asked.

Ivy whined softly in response, but she didn't bound over to Paul's side as she usually did. "What is it, girl?" he asked, aware that his dog found something disturbing.

When Ivy's response was simply to whine again, Paul moved swiftly to her side to see what was bothering his dog.

Brittany. She sat on the dock down at the water's edge. That was where the fish he'd caught earlier were still swimming in his trap. Her back was to Paul and Ivy, and she must have unbraided her long golden hair for it streamed over her shoulders like a glorious burst of sunshine. But her head was ducked, her shoulders hunched and her arms were wrapped around her knees, hugging them.

Something plaintive in her bent posture—something desolate and even close to despair—communicated itself silently to Paul. Was she hurt? he wondered. Or ill? She certainly looked entirely miserable.

Or was this just another of her tricks? One more attempt to make a sucker of Paul Johnson?

Maybe there was a way to find out, Paul decided. Even though Brittany obviously had no use for him she did apparently like animals.

"Go see her, Ivy," Paul said quietly. Then when his German shepherd raised her alert, intelligent face to him questioningly, Paul repeated his command more specifically, "Go to Brittany."

Ivy understood. She gave an almost springy bound for such a pregnant dog as she jumped off the porch, then started trotting down the long stone walk.

Brittany didn't appear to see Ivy until the dog was almost upon her. Only then, when Ivy sniffed at her figure affectionately, did Brittany turn around. As Paul watched from the porch, Brittany's arms, which had earlier been wrapped around her long legs, now encircled Ivy's neck instead.

Then when Brittany dropped her face down into the animal's thick pelt, Paul stepped instinctively off the porch and started walking toward Brittany as well. For now he was more than half convinced that this was no act; rather, that something was really and truly wrong.

Chapter Eight

When she felt this sad and blue, comfort of any sort was welcome, Brittany thought, even when it took the form of a dog's cold wet nose.

Everything had finally caught up with her today. First, Brittany felt lousy from a miserable, streaming cold. Second, today marked a very melancholy anniversary. Last, as if that weren't enough, when Brittany was burrowing through her suitcases earlier today hoping to find a cold capsule, what she had found instead—pressed between a pocket and the lining of her suitcase—was one of the wedding invitations for a ceremony that had never occurred.

And that, of course, was precisely the melancholy anniversary she was trying so hard *not* to think about!

Today, though, Brittany couldn't help thinking about it, probably because she felt more isolated than she ever had in her entire life.

Part of it was simply her present geographical isolation. Here she was, all alone on a small island, in the middle of a vast and stormy inland sea and the only other resident wasn't speaking to her. In fact, ever since she'd knocked over his coffee mug—and very childish of her it had been—Brittany admitted, they had communicated in writing and only then when it was absolutely necessary.

Brittany had not even felt this inhumanly alone in the midst of Howard's defection. Despite her shock and pain over their abruptly cancelled wedding she had still had her mother close at hand and Amber, standing by loyally.

But on Isle Svenson she had nothing and no one. Nor was Brittany's work going well. Not being able to find a wolf's den and observe the predators in their natural state remained a major disappointment. She was beginning to be sorry she'd even come here to try. She should have known it was too long a shot. But if she gave up now what on earth could she write her master's thesis on?

Brittany was also sorry by now that she'd been such a witch to Paul, not that he didn't royally deserve it. But winning a couple of rounds in their ongoing battle had not really made her feel good once the moment's brief triumph had passed.

Also, Paul might have proved a help to her in finding a wolf's den had she only thought to ask him sooner where he'd seen those silvery shadows. Now that she'd completely alienated him he would probably be delighted to refuse her, Brittany's practical nature reminded her each day.

So when she had returned from work early this afternoon with a splitting headache and a stuffed-up nose following another long, lonely, futile tramp through the forest she simply didn't feel up to renewed hostilities. With Ivy crouched on her porch and Paul clearly inside the cottage, undoubtedly doing something to annoy or infuriate her, Brittany chose to pass up their otherwise inevitable argument. Instead, she had walked down to the water's edge and sat on the dock, determined to wait Paul out. She just prayed he'd leave soon.

But now here was Ivy, licking her hot face, and only then did Brittany realize that at the welcome contact her eyes brimmed with tears. Numbly she hugged Ivy closer and buried her face in warm, clean-smelling doggie fur.

What a relief just to give up and yield to that empty, aching chasm yawning within her—until she heard *his* footsteps, that is.

Paul. Since she definitely wasn't up to facing him, Brittany wished she could disappear and let Paul think what he might. Because absolutely nothing in her whole life was working out right.

"Is...something wrong, Brittany?"

She listened for an insult, then evaluated his tone of voice. But, for once, Brittany found no reason to take offense. Paul had actually sounded...well, almost concerned. "I'm all right," she muttered, dashing the tears from her eyes. Belatedly she added, "Thanks."

Paul didn't reply for fully a minute. Apparently Brittany's feeble expression of gratitude left him equally stunned. "You ah, looked lonely," he said at last. "That's why I sent Ivy down here to see you. She's very sensitive to people's feelings. At least I think she is, though I guess some people would say I was crazy."

"I don't think that's crazy," Brittany answered, glad to be diverted from her own dreary train of thought. "Animals are a lot smarter than most people give them credit for being. We humans are just beginning to learn some of the ways they can communicate with each other, as well as with us, if we just take the time to learn their language. And I was feeling very lonely." To Brittany's amazement, making the admission didn't kill her, and Paul didn't laugh out loud, either.

"So was I, today." Without asking if he might join her Paul simply dropped down beside Brittany on the dock. But now she didn't feel like objecting to his company any more than she had to Ivy's. The waves were growing choppier as the afternoon waned and the wind picked up. Far off in the distance a loon—probably newly arrived on the island after spending winter in the South—let loose his own lost and forlorn cry.

After a minute Brittany raised her head and began to gently stroke Ivy's neck. "You've got a nice companion here, Paul."

"Yes, I do," he agreed. "Actually, Ivy was my stepfather's idea. One of the few good ones he's ever had."

"You really don't like him, do you?"

"Actually, I may have to revise my opinion upward. Steve's not quite the blockheaded Swede I used to think he was."

"He's Swedish?" Brittany said, rubbing at her stinging eyes.

"No offense if you are," Paul added hastily. "Steve's Swede as well as Czech. Matter of fact, I'm half-Swedish myself."

"That I would never have guessed," Brittany said and found herself smiling faintly.

"I know. You look at me, all you see is Italian. I resemble my mother's side of the family." While Paul talked he leaned back on the dock, bracing himself on his elbows, and stretched out his legs.

Brittany stole a quick glance at him. My, this guy really was good-looking! He might even prove as handsome as Howard, if it weren't for all that hair hiding his face. For the first time she found herself hoping to someday see Paul minus his moustache and beard.

"I would never have guessed you were Italian, either," she said truthfully. "So how does a Swedish-Italian wind up with a generic name like Paul Zachary Johnson?"

"My parents' idea. My father had these two Old World names—Pohlson and Johanssen—hung on him and he hated to do the same to me. Also, since my mother's maiden name sounded something like 'zucchini' they decided to spare me all the teasing they'd gone through. So they Anglicized everything and here I am, one more child of the great American Melting Pot."

Brittany laughed, unable to help herself. Then she admitted, "I'm half-Swedish, too."

Paul tossed her a wry look. "Guess we should have known?"

"Two blockheads, you mean?" Brittany asked, staring down at the toes of her boots that lay only inches from his.

"You said it, I didn't!"

She remembered other times when they'd used that particular phrase on each other, then she decided not to resurrect them.

"You were thinking it, though," she chided.

"No, I wasn't. Actually I was wondering how you got named for a province in France. Or else, do I dare really say it, for a Brittany spaniel?"

Brittany swung around with a mock-fierce stare and gave Paul a light, reproving slap on the arm. "Spaniel, indeed!" she said with such haughtiness he started to chuckle. "Paul Johnson, are you calling me a dog?"

With that, Paul burst into full-scale laughter. "No, I'd never dare! And you're certainly not!"

"Anyway, Brittany spaniels did come from that particular province in France, that's how they got the name," she informed him.

"I didn't know that. Probably I should have guessed. So you're not really French?"

"No. Well, not that I know of, anyway." Brittany qualified her answer. "I mean, who knows what those marauding Vikings were up to—or with whom. Oh Lord, now, you're probably going to make some quite dreadful pun!"

"No. But since those lusty Vikings weren't exactly known for leaving women untouched I'll bet they sailed back to Norseland with any number of French beauties aboard. Maybe that's why we're both so good-looking! Maybe that's even why you were named Brittany."

It was her turn to laugh. "No, I don't think so. My first name is a good plain Scandinavian Anna. Mother just tacked on Brittany because she liked it."

"I like it, too," Paul agreed. "It suits you."

"How do you mean?" Brittany asked with a return to skepticism.

"It sounds kind of regal."

Regal? To Brittany the pleasant word conveyed presence and poise. Did he really think of her like that?

Then Paul sighed regretfully.

"What?" she asked, still stroking Ivy.

"Okay, I'll tell you," Paul began slowly. "It's been nice to sit here and talk to you. I've really enjoyed it. So I dread what I have to say next because you're going to get good and mad."

"I am?" Brittany asked warily and tried to think of all the various things that could provoke her. She had to admit the list was extensive.

"Yes. You'll probably storm and yell, too. You see, I effected a trade of sorts—at least, I had planned to. You came back before I had quite finished my end of things."

"What sort of trade?"

Paul looked like this offense stopped barely short of murder. "I ate some of your soup. I've really been hungry lately."

Brittany felt frankly relieved. And with Ivy still snuggling up so warmly against her knees, she decided to grant him amnesty, at least for today. "That's all right," she said.

He stared at her so incredulously that she added, "It's a big pot of soup and, frankly, I'm sick of it by now. Take more. You're welcome."

Paul still hadn't completely relaxed. "That isn't all," he warned.

Now Brittany was the one who sighed, even as she studied the relative size of their hands. Since it was much warmer today neither of them wore gloves, and their hands rested side-by-side on the dock. Two quite different looking hands. Paul's were large with long tapering fingers. Competent, capable hands, Brittany decided, their backs liberally dusted with jet-black hairs. Her own smooth hand looked downright girlish in comparison. "What else?" she inquired of Paul.

"I ate some of your ham and cheese. A lot, actually, and four slices of bread."

A hanging crime? She shrugged. "It's okay. I brought a lot more food than I've needed."

Now Paul did look frankly relieved. "I was going to trade you for a couple of fresh fish I have in a trap right here at the end of the dock. I left you a note. It's in the kitchen."

"I'll take the fish," Brittany said promptly. For some reason fish appealed to her today, although her cold had robbed her of much of her appetite. "Consider us even."

"Gladly," Paul said fervently. Then he peered at Brittany more closely. "Say, are you sick or something?"

Now Brittany did bristle, as if she didn't know just how terrible she looked! "What makes you ask?" she demanded.

"Your nose and eyes both look like they hurt. They're kinda re—pink, I mean. Just a little pink."

"They're both red and I know it," she admitted ruefully. "I've caught a cold."

"Oh. I'm sorry. Do you have some vitamin C?" Paul asked with such concern that Brittany knew she might have to revise her opinion of him upward, too. Well, a mite, anyway.

"No, I don't have any vitamins. But that's all right. I'm going to call it quits for today. Just go inside and go to bed," she concluded, aware now of her aching arms and legs.

"I'll bring over some vitamin C," Paul said decisively. "I have some other stuff, too, that may help."

He got up off the dock and went striding up the long stone walk. Ivy arose, too, and went lumbering after Paul.

Brittany was frankly sorry to see them leave even though she knew she did need to turn in. Wearily she pushed herself up off the dock and realized for the first time how sleepy she was. Well, wasn't rest the best thing for a bad cold?

"Paul, just leave those things in the kitchen," she called after him, and he gave her a thumbs-up signal to show he'd heard her.

Brittany was halfway to the cottage when she grew aware of the fact that her stark, acute loneliness had just miraculously eased.

She drank a glass of water in the clean kitchen—and thank God it was for once. She'd been braced for Paul's usual mess.

Next, she read his note about the fish, then turned toward her bedroom, yawning.

Shedding her clothes, she reached gratefully for one of her long, warm flannel nightgowns, then crawled into bed, pulled the covers up to her chin and fell asleep before her head hit the pillow.

She took quite a long nap. Two hours had passed before Brittany awoke in a cottage warm, dark and still. At least everything appeared quite dark until she opened her bedroom door. Then she discovered that Paul had left a lamp burning in the living room. Its rosy glow was cheery.

He had left a number of things for her in the kitchen. There, at the table, was a clean place setting for one, complete with paper napkin. Three medicine bottles also stood by the plate in prominent display: vitamin C, aspirin and cold capsules.

Over on the kitchen counter was a larger bottle of another sort, one containing brandy, and Brittany smiled wanly. She didn't want any brandy now, but maybe later she'd take a nightcap to help her sleep.

A new note from Paul rested in the center of her plate. "Baked fish and potato in oven," he wrote. "Maybe they're edible. Also try peaches in fridge. If you need help stick a light in the window."

Had he really tried to cook some food? she wondered, turning in the direction of the oven. Brittany's stuffed-up nose did not allow any aromas through to give her a clue.

Yes! A large baked fish lay just inside, along with a medium-sized potato, and all the food was still warm. Tentatively she pinched off a small piece of fish and popped it into her mouth. Not bad. Its firm yet tender texture tasted appetizing, and suddenly Brittany felt almost weak with hunger.

The potato she found a trifle raw in the center, but its warm skin was quite tasty when slathered with butter.

She ate most of the fish and potato, then almost bypassed the peaches. Cold and canned in a thick sugary syrup they couldn't possibly be good for one, she thought disapprovingly. But since Paul had already opened the can, Brittany dutifully forked up a single slice. A minute later she was eating them all ravenously, one slice after another.

Of course, her appetite was often a little quirky when she was ill. But Brittany wondered how Paul knew that peaches would just hit the spot. Maybe her body needed the sugar for energy.

Finished, Brittany cleaned up the kitchen and by then she was feeling pretty tired and achy again. Although she left the brandy untouched, she did open the three medicine bottles in turn and dutifully swallowed a pill from each.

When she crawled back into bed and extinguished her bedside light Brittany was ready to grant Paul one more concession.

He really wasn't like Howard, despite certain similarities of behavior. But Brittany couldn't conceive of Howard ever tending a sick person. Of course, as she had been discovering for the past year, Howard had been style with little substance.

Now, lying awake in the dark bedroom of the cottage, Brittany at last allowed her memories of Howard to return. She hadn't dared to really look at them before, but if Howard hadn't scuttled their plans and if their marriage had taken place on schedule this would have been Brittany's first wedding anniversary.

Instead the date was now a morbid reminder of one man's deceit and her own self-deception, both experiences so painful that Brittany knew why she hadn't dared to remember.

He looked like a golden prince and the answer to a maiden's prayers. That was Brittany's first impression of Howard and, oddly, it would remain her last.

The prince. Only very young and romantic girls still believed in one, of course, and Brittany had not even had the excuse of extreme youth. She was twenty-five when she met Howard so she should have known better. Yes, she should definitely have known that a prince did not really exist, except perhaps in her imagination.

But there he was, a man so dazzling that women other than Brittany couldn't look away, either. Hadn't Amber noticed Howard first, as she and Brittany sat at breakfast their first morning at the ski lodge in Canada?

"Good Lord, take a look," Amber breathed. "That guy is Prince Charming come to life!"

Oh yes, Howard dovetailed nicely with other women's fantasies, too. Tall, trim, silvery-haired gods with chiseled features, cleft chins and eyes of pale green were meant to inspire feminine rhapsodies.

Brittany turned to look where Amber indicated and—wouldn't you know it?—Howard immediately intercepted Brittany's stare.

Over his grapefruit half he smiled at her. It was a blasé smile, delivered with a shrug of his shoulders. The sort of shrug that said, "This happens to me all the time."

Except that Brittany flushed in embarrassment and Howard looked amused. Then he scrutinized her, too.

Later, on the ski slopes, Brittany tried to ignore him. But with his royal-blue ski togs and his ash-blond hair, that was hard to do. Also, his skiing was flawless—another attention-getter.

Brittany made herself look away. She hadn't come to Canada to watch some handsome, conceited show-off. Rather, she and Amber were at the ski lodge to enjoy the first real vacation either had allowed herself in years.

Brittany, who was a teacher of grade-school biology in Duluth, was also readying herself for an ordeal to come. As soon as her ski vacation ended, she was signed up for night classes so she could work toward her master's while continuing to teach by day. It would be a real grind, of course, and she wasn't exactly anticipating the next couple of years.

Then Howard walked across the ski lodge that night to introduce himself to Brittany and the next thing she knew her future plans were in shambles.

Brittany could still visualize Howard just as he'd looked that night when he smiled down on her: his styled hair attractively tousled, his cheeks ruddy from a day spent on skis. He wore an obviously expensive Norwegian sweater, and the reindeer dancing across his chest later seemed symbolic to

Brittany of the elegant and carefree life-style Howard represented.

"Saw you on the slopes earlier," he began and soon offered to buy her a drink. He really wanted to get to know her better.

But, as things developed, Howard talked mostly about himself. Brittany learned that his parents were prominent in Detroit society and hobnobbed with the Fords, as well as the other automotive first families. The elder Piersons also summered at their house on Mackinaw Island and visited Europe at least every other year. Howard, the product of an Eastern prep school and a graduate of Harvard, practiced corporate law in an old established Detroit firm.

Why was he talking to her? Brittany wondered after those facts fell out. Guys like Howard spent their time with debutantes, heiresses or the boss's daughter. They weren't attracted to big, tall, well-scrubbed Scandinavian blondes from hard-working dairy families.

But Howard appeared so eager, so earnest, so obviously sincere in his admiration of Brittany that the next step was to convince herself that a miracle had conveniently occurred. Why else would this absolutely fantastic man be so interested in her?

Before the evening ended—an evening Brittany spent dancing in Howard's arms and savoring the first of their ardent kisses—she managed to convince herself that she was the one with a problem.

Yes, she was acting like a snob in reverse. Class distinctions didn't matter in America. Why should she and Howard concern themselves with the creaky, outdated customs of an obsolete society?

She felt like Cinderella, especially after she discovered that Howard had to leave early the next morning. But before Brittany could curse cruel fate he promised to come see her in Duluth very soon.

Only Howard waited almost six weeks before he finally phoned her. By then Brittany had given up hope of ever seeing him again.

"I waited to see if I'd forget you," Howard explained candidly, and she felt jarred by his self-absorption.

In fact, Brittany might have spared herself quite a lot if she'd just had the strength to say then and there, "No, Howard, don't come." But how could Cinderella say that to The Prince? Especially since she'd been thinking of him, dreaming of him and praying that he'd call ever since they'd said goodbye.

So Howard visited Duluth and he was just as handsome as Brittany remembered, just as attentive and loving as any woman could have wished.

He also opened a new world to her, the world of the monied, privileged few. His financial status shouldn't have mattered, of course, but Brittany couldn't resist taking pleasure in Howard's sleek black Jaguar or in the glib sophistication he displayed at the best restaurants and clubs. Such attributes did not really represent a gulf between them, she assured herself. Rather, they were pleasant assets that smoothed life and made its passage easier.

Knowing a prince could soften even a sensible woman's brain. And, eventually, as their romance escalated, Howard could almost make Brittany believe he spent those many weekends when they weren't together all alone and missing her.

Nor was Brittany worried about introducing Howard to her family. Of course not! The Hagens were decent, honest people of whom she would never, ever be ashamed. But she had such a knot in her stomach before the planned meeting that she couldn't eat for a week.

Amazingly Howard fit right into life on a dairy farm. Chameleonlike, he always appeared utterly at ease anywhere and seemingly with anyone. Howard charmed the Hagens—most of them, anyway.

"My, Howard has the nicest manners," Brittany's mother exclaimed.

"He's really interested in the way we operate the dairy," Brittany's father chimed in.

"And he's *so-o-o* good-looking!" giggled one of Brittany's sisters-in-law.

Her parents, of course, thought any man would find their daughter desirable. But Brittany's three older brothers knew better. They had considerably less to say about Howard, and Brittany saw the furtive glances they exchanged. These she tried to write off as evidence of overprotectiveness on their part. Or maybe her brothers were simply jealous, envying Howard his glibness and charm, his designer clothes and globe-circling travels.

All year Brittany gave herself pep talks as her involvement with Howard deepened. Still, she could never quite drown out that persistent inner voice that reminded her over and over that this was all simply too good to be true.

Did a man who got his hair styled once a week really enjoy going on field trips with Brittany? Howard might be a good sport, but could he actually have fun lugging her packs and gear through mosquito-infested wilderness to sleep out in a tent? He swore he did, but only an absolute fool could have believed him.

And Brittany was not really such a fool, despite being in the throes of extreme infatuation. Several times during that year with Howard she woke up briefly to reality.

"Of course, I don't believe you, Howard!" she snapped once when he offered the feeblest of excuses for not having phoned her in three whole weeks. How dare he try to convince Brittany that he'd been out of the country on a case. What country had courtrooms but no telephones?

Although she slammed down the phone in Howard's ear Brittany fell across her bed sobbing. It was all over. She knew it was. First, Howard had ignored her, then he lied to her so clumsily.

She cried half the night, trying not to notice that along with all her grief and anger came a certain measure of relief. But at dawn Howard woke her up hammering on her door. He loved her, that's why he'd jumped on a plane and come immediately to tell her so. He didn't know what had gotten into him or why he'd acted as he did. Nerves? Cold feet? But when he thought about actually losing her...why, she was the only real person he'd ever known in his life! Tears gathered in Howard's beautiful green eyes.

By then Brittany was in his arms.

Because she didn't really want to listen to her intuition or the logic rattling around in her own capable mind. She didn't want to be right. She wanted Howard's version to be the right one, wanted him to be telling her the truth, wanted the romance and excitement of loving so fervently and intensely.

That persistent dream of Cinderella and The Prince was so very slow to die.

Of course, Howard also had a couple of other hooks into Brittany. She'd dropped her night classes and put all her future plans on hold because there just wasn't enough time to go to school nights, teach days, grade homework, keep up an apartment and a car, her clothes and her appearance—and still be available to see Howard, too.

What woman wanted to admit that maybe she'd sacrificed her valuable time for an impeccably tailored suit and a flashy smile?

Also, Brittany and Howard were lovers by then.

He was the first man she had ever slept with, and she simply couldn't treat a close and intimate relationship casually. Oh sure, sometimes after Howard had fallen asleep Brittany did lie awake beside him and think in disappointment, "Is that all?"

Then she'd argue with herself that it must be, of course, for didn't you always get the best of everything with a rich, handsome, silvery-haired Prince?

Definitely! If Brittany ever dared to suspect differently she set her doubts aside once she wore the most beautiful engagement ring in the world. This proved The Prince's love and, not so incidentally, his classic good taste.

Brittany had quite a lot of heart-stopping moments before that ring glided onto her finger. Nights when Howard didn't phone. Days when he disappeared for a whole week or longer before returning to her with various excuses. Because they lived in separate cities, it was impossible for her to keep track of him completely.

So along the way there had been more than a few fears and tears—more than a few fights, too. But for a year they were caught in a mutual addiction when neither could quite let go of the other.

Once their engagement was official Howard's parents were clearly disappointed although, to Brittany, they were also quite polite. But she simply didn't fit their image of what a suitable daughter-in-law should be. Since they'd wanted someone who would assist in maintaining their social position, their ideal wife for Howard could organize a charity ball and then shine as its star.

Brittany ignored the well-bred disquiet of Howard's family and began preparing for her spring wedding. Soon she and her mother were busy poring over brides' magazines and making endless lists.

But all the time Brittany's inner voice of reality kept reminding her that this was magic, a dream, a cinders-to-princess fable that would not, could not, last.

Only one person ever voiced any reservations over the forthcoming wedding. That was Amber, speaking as Brittany's trusted and long-time friend, and even she chose her words cautiously.

"You know, opposites always attract," she said to Brittany one day when she happened to be visiting in Duluth. "You're a deep and serious-minded person, but Howard isn't. In fact, he's always ready for a party and . . ."

"*What?*" Brittany's voice was dangerously sharp, although her insides were churning and rocking. As staunchly as she defended Howard to herself day after day, she was honor-bound to defend him even more vehemently to anyone else.

Amber, who anticipated being Brittany's maid of honor, caught the warning and backpedalled deftly. But her dark eyes were clearly troubled. "Oh, Howard's so lighthearted and outgoing I can understand why you would each find the other refreshing."

"Yes, we do," Brittany replied, her hands gripped so tightly in her lap that the diamonds and emeralds of her custom-made ring dug into her skin. She wondered if Amber had started to tell her that Howard was shallow. Or that, like a flighty butterfly, he might alight briefly here or there but would soon be off again to sniff the fragrance of many flowers.

Most of all, as Brittany looked across the table at her willowy, dark-haired friend, she suspected suddenly that Howard had made romantic overtures to Amber.

If she asked, she knew Amber would tell her the truth. And Brittany knew she ought to ask.

Of course, she had too much pride. She also feared an answer that, as yet, she simply couldn't face.

Now, a year away from that conversation, Brittany silently marked this melancholy anniversary: one year since she'd at last stopped being a self-deluded fool.

Perhaps the hardest thing was admitting she'd been dumb enough to believe in a dream, an image, a storybook version of The Prince. Not to mention a rags-to-riches illusion that tracked the American image of success and the mirage of happily ever after until she'd tumbled straight off the edge of a cliff.

She could blame Howard for a lot but not for that. In her heart, Brittany knew she had only herself to blame.

Perhaps the greatest irony of all was that it still hurt. Brittany had only to close her eyes and she could remember Howard just the way she'd seen him first, and last—the perfect golden boy with the Greek-god physique—and her heart throbbed anew.

Why should it hurt so much to give up someone who was really all wrong for you? she wondered, fumbling in the dark for another tissue with which to blow her nose.

Of course, Amber, a reformed chain-smoker, claimed she still missed cigarettes, too.

Paul was talking by shortwave radio to Chad when he saw the lights go out in the cottage. So Brittany was abed for the night. He hoped she woke up tomorrow feeling better.

Then he picked up the conversation with his son. "So you want to go see that rabbit movie again the next time I come?"

"Yes, Daddy. Will you take both me and Dickie?"

"I sure will," Paul agreed. "But what about your cousin, Danny?"

"Dickie and I don't like Danny. He's always telling us what to do," Chad explained earnestly.

"I expect that's because Danny's older, Chad. He may feel responsible for you younger guys. Tell you what, maybe if you invite Danny to go with us he'll be nicer to you and Dickie."

Chad considered the suggestion. "That might work, Daddy," he conceded.

"Try it. And remember, Chad, I'll see you soon—just as soon as Ivy's had these puppies of hers. Right now I can't go off and leave her alone."

"That's okay, since I'm gonna get one of her puppies. I still am, aren't I, Daddy? I want a big boy dog!"

"Still don't have any use for girls, huh? That will change one day, my man," Paul promised. "And, yes, you can get first pick of any puppy in the litter."

"And I'm gonna spend the whole summer with you on the island?" Chad pressed his father.

"You bet you are, Chad," Paul vowed and heard his voice growing husky. "Now I guess I'd better talk to Aunt Vicky."

"Aunt Vicky!" Paul heard Chad shout. "Daddy wants to talk to you." After a minute, Chad came back. "Daddy? She's coming."

"Hey, my man, are you doing okay—honest?" Paul asked anxiously.

"Yes, Daddy. But I miss you."

"I miss you, too!"

"I still miss Mommy."

"I know you do, son. I do, too."

"I just wish we could all be together like we used to be!"

"So do I, Chad. Oh God, so do I!"

Then Paul sneezed.

Chapter Nine

Brittany awoke next morning feeling quite a bit better, although when she washed her face it looked less than reassuring. Her lips were chapped, her nose still red and swollen. Her skin had an unnaturally dry, taut look to it and her eyes—still pink as a bunny's—were deeply, darkly circled.

"You look like hell," Brittany muttered to herself and decided to stay in all day. That would give her recovery a better chance to take hold.

Accordingly she took a quick warm shower. Although she dispensed with her usual shampoo she brushed her hair well and braided it. Then she drew on a clean flannel nightgown and wrapped herself back into her thick robe and woolly slippers, filling both robe pockets with tissues. Only then did she head toward the kitchen.

Paul had not been over yet, she noticed in surprise. The coffee mug he was using these days was still cold, so Brittany started a pot of ground coffee dripping. Undoubtedly Paul would show up soon and she felt generously inclined to repay him for fixing her dinner last night.

Eggs scrambled with ham, biscuits and Mama's cherry jelly, Brittany decided as she reached in the cupboard for her biscuit mix. She stirred the biscuits up quickly and popped them into her warm oven. They were browning nicely when the back door rattled. As Brittany heard Paul come in she felt a rush of pleasurable excitement. He'd been so very nice yesterday that she hoped he was still in a pleasant frame of mind.

Ordinarily Paul entered the cottage very quietly. But Brittany would never have missed his arrival today—no, not even if she'd been in bed fast asleep.

First, Paul sneezed. Next, he went into a veritable spasm of coughing. When he finally could speak at last, he chose to swear in colorful and profane language. Then the door slammed shut behind him.

Uh-oh. He must have caught it, too, Brittany thought, her heart rhythm accelerating by several beats although she wasn't sure whether it was from eagerness or apprehension. She could already tell Paul felt rotten as she tilted the skillet she held, the better to melt butter into which she intended to pour her freshly beaten eggs and finely chopped ham.

Paul stumbled into the kitchen, wearing a black glare and holding a handkerchief to his chin. Immediately Brittany revised her opinion of her own appearance. She merely looked bad. Paul looked like walking hell. His face was chalk-colored; his eyes and nose clearly poised to stream.

"Good morning," Brittany sang out. "Are you sick, too?"

"I've caught your—cold!" Paul replied, his voice accusing. He sneezed again, which sent him into another series of racking coughs.

"Thanks for making me the scapegoat," Brittany snapped back, feeling offended as well as deeply disappointed. "I didn't even have the damned cold until yesterday!"

"You still had it first," Paul snapped back. Then he sank down into a chair at the kitchen table.

He was the moodiest, angriest man she'd ever met. As he glowered at her the cheerful speech Brittany had planned to deliver, the one that graciously thanked Paul for dinner last night and aimed their relationship toward a higher level of consciousness, flew straight out of her head. When she felt Paul's bloodshot gaze sweep both her and the kitchen, Brittany was simply sorry that she'd taken the time to prepare a special breakfast for such an oaf.

Paul noticed her preparations, too, including the tub of butter and the cherry jelly she'd placed on the table. "Who are you cooking for, the army?" he inquired critically.

Brittany managed a shrug. Although her feelings were hurt, she wasn't about to reveal it. "Actually, I'd planned to invite you to share breakfast," she said, carefully setting down the bowl of raw eggs. "Since you're obviously not interested and only want to insult me I think I'll go back to bed."

With that she swung around and headed straight back to the bedroom, slamming its door behind her. She knew she was still weak from illness when her eyes immediately brimmed with tears. Oh, damn that unpleasant man, anyway.

She heard Paul march over to her closed door. "Oh, all right," he grumbled. "I'll eat breakfast with you. Come back out."

That did it, cracking her resolve to be much more adult than he. "Don't do me any favors!" Brittany screamed through the door.

A brief pause followed. When Paul spoke next, his voice held a note of controlled panic. "Brittany, things out here are starting to burn. The grease in the pan on the burner and the rolls or whatever they are—"

"Let 'em all burn!" Brittany yelled again.

"But that's going to set off the—" Suddenly it was already too late as the smoke alarm in the kitchen began shrilling insanely. "Oh, for—!" Paul shouted a few more words that were usually spoken in maximum-security cell blocks and not among gentler folk.

"Oh, for—" Brittany muttered a couple of similar ones to herself as she came crashing out of the bedroom.

Paul stood in the middle of the kitchen, looking around wildly as if wondering what to tend to first. Deftly Brittany scooped the skillet containing the melted butter off the burner, threw open the door to the oven with one hand and flicked the oven switch to OFF with the other. Then she snatched up a dish towel, which she fanned rapidly in front of the screeching smoke alarm.

Paul watched her, open-mouthed. When the alarm's ear-splitting cry abruptly died away, a trace of sardonic amusement showed in his red-rimmed eyes.

"You're very good in a kitchen," he commended, but Brittany had already turned back to the oven to rescue her biscuits.

"Those look nice and very brown," he added hopefully.

"Help yourself," she replied, her voice glacial. "Since I don't plan to eat any you can have them all."

"Hey." Paul walked over and dropped a hand on top of hers. Despite her intention to storm right back out, Brittany went very still instead. Indeed, she didn't even feel as if she could move. That was ridiculous, of course. Why should mere skin-to-skin contact affect her like this? But she could instantly feel the entire imprint of Paul's long warm hand, as if her eyes had actually seen it and her mind had memorized it, although she had yet to even look down. That's how natural his touch felt to her. "Look, I'm a bastard and I'm sorry, Brittany."

"Sorry you're a bastard or just generally sorry?" she inquired in a brittle voice. But she still didn't pull away from Paul. At the same time she wondered why he should feel so known and familiar to her.

"Either. Both," Paul went on wryly. "I know it's not your fault I've caught a cold. Certainly it's not your fault I'm in a lousy mood. That's because I talked to my kid last night, and he needs me, but I'm stuck out here since I'm a hothead who can't control his temper and also because I'm playing midwife to a dog!" Paul stopped to draw another breath. "It was very kind of you to cook breakfast for me this morning and I do appreciate it."

"Sure, sure," she said cynically. But now his black eyes met hers, and the sincere regret she saw in their depths undid her completely. Brittany's eyes stung and her lips quivered. Promptly and without warning her nose also started to run. She barely got a tissue from the pocket of her robe and up to her face in time.

"Oh hell, now I've made you cry," Paul sighed. "I sometimes forget how sensitive women are."

Then, to Brittany's amazement, he simply wrapped his arms around her and drew her close, very close. She was aware of his thin hard body and its radiant heat, feeling it even through their clothes.

"It's not that," Brittany choked. "I'm only crying because . . . oh hell—" She stopped because she didn't know exactly why she was crying.

"You're sick. I snarled for the same reason."

Now Paul was rubbing his chin against the crown of her head, back and forth, to and fro. It was a gentle, undemanding caress, although his arms continued to hold her quite tightly. How strong they felt, Brittany marvelled as she blew her nose, then groped for another tissue to dry her eyes. In fact, she thought that no other arms that had ever held her had felt quite this treacherously good.

Anger into sweetness, dark into light, turnoff into come-on—memory crashed down reminding her that she'd been through similar scenes with Howard.

Oh God, was she starting to make the same mistake again? Yet here she stood, welcoming Paul's apology and his tenderness with the same vast, sweeping relief she'd always felt with Howard's.

She supposed he would be the yardstick against which she measured men forever. While Howard and Paul actually had little in common overall, both had a decided and distressing tendency to blow first hot, then cold. It wasn't a characteristic Brittany liked, nor did she intend to topple into that same trap again. Swallowing hard, she drew back from Paul and he released her immediately.

"Hey, how about some cold breakfast?" he suggested, then turned his head rapidly to deflect a sneeze away from her.

"Okay," Brittany agreed, and gave Paul a pat on the back as he began coughing again. She could certainly sympathize with how miserable he must feel.

By the time they sat down to eat the biscuits were cold, the coffee lukewarm and only the eggs, which Brittany scrambled in a clean skillet, were served hot. Nothing she ate this morning tasted quite right to her but, of course, that was undoubtedly the cold playing havoc with her sense of taste.

Paul's seemed unaffected so far. "Everything's good," he said to Brittany as he reached for another biscuit. "Tell your mother her jelly is super."

"Okay," Brittany said and dabbed a little more on her own biscuit. With Paul's mood apparently mellowed again she dared a personal question. "You said you were upset about Chad. Is anything wrong?"

"Probably not," Paul conceded. "Chad says he's okay though he did admit to being lonely."

"Is that why you don't quite believe him?" Brittany inquired.

"I don't know—that's the real total hell of it!" Paul said explosively. "You see, Chad has his mother's sweet disposition. He's not a crank like me. If my kid has any kind of motto it's probably, 'That's all right.' Sometimes I wish he was like those kids who are real pains in the butt, always griping and whining. At least I'd know when things were wrong. But Chad's the cooperative sort."

"Must make him easy to raise."

"Yes, but he's a sensitive one, too. It doesn't always show when he's anxious inside, or hurting." Paul set down his fork and looked across the table at Brittany, his expression clearly troubled. "I guess I'd feel better if Chad did more romping and stomping. If he'd scream and kick and curse the way I do when things go wrong. Why, even the child psychologist who's seen him a few times says Chad's just a little too pleasant."

The child's small freckled face flashed before Brittany's eyes again. Chad sounded like a naturally sweet little boy who would be very dear. "I'd like to meet him sometime," Brittany remarked to Paul.

He looked across at her in surprise. "You like kids?"

"Very much." Then honesty got the better of Brittany. "Rather, I like the kind of kid you've described. I sometimes have trouble liking the cranky, whining ones who are, as you say, a pain in the butt."

"Were you a nice cooperative little kid?" Paul asked her, flashing her a sudden grin that made his black eyes twinkle.

"God forbid!" Brittany said wryly with a further burst of truth. "My parents have often said that even three rowdy boys still didn't prepare them for me. I guess I was a natural kid crank. I didn't like a lot of foods and I wouldn't wear certain colors. Or shoes—I couldn't stand tight shoes. I still can't. But at least Mom and Dad think I've turned out pretty well."

"That puts you ahead of me," Paul said, his manner turning glum again. "According to Gina Olszewski I've never done anything right, and am probably not ever liable to."

"Don't listen to her," Brittany advised.

"I haven't so far. But she's like that famous Chinese water torture."

"That what?" Brittany interjected.

"You know, the kind that drips and drips continuously until, finally, it even erodes stone."

"She's another crank," Brittany surmised, pushing back her plate.

"For sure," Paul agreed.

That treacherous closeness was creeping back between them again, Brittany noticed. Why did talking to him come so easily? Looking across the table into Paul's handsome bearded face she wondered if he was aware of it, too. At least, while it lasted, this closeness made her bold enough to make a request of him as well as a personal admission.

"Paul, I've looked all around for your books, but I haven't found them. Where are they?"

"Books? Which books?" he asked, taking a second helping of eggs.

"Those two books you've had published," Brittany said patiently. "I went through all the shelves here in the cottage, but I couldn't find either one."

"You were looking for my books?" he repeated. Then Paul suddenly gave her a smile so warm, friendly and, yes, so downright surprised that Brittany didn't mind what her admission of interest had cost her.

"Yes," she went on a little more diffidently. "My friend Amber Villet read them and said they were both quite good."

"You know Amber?" Paul demanded, his breakfast forgotten.

"Yes. She's my best friend. She wasn't sure, though, if you'd remember her," Brittany explained.

"Not remember!" Paul exploded. "How could any red-blooded man not remember Amber?"

Amber, who was as attractive as she was intelligent, wasn't usually a person Brittany envied. Now, though, for the second time in a year, Brittany found herself feeling jealous of a woman she usually thought of as a sister. Such an unseemly feeling was very puzzling to Brittany.

"Amber said one of your books was about shipwrecks here in the Great Lakes," Brittany continued.

"That's *Wrecks Beneath the Sea*," Paul cut in eagerly. "The other one on the lighthouses of the region I called *Lights Across the Sky*. I never could come up with a better title. They all sounded pretentious. Anyway, mariners didn't refer to 'lighthouses' per se. To them it was always 'the Isle Svenson light' or 'the Split Rock light.'"

"Oh," said Brittany, who hadn't been aware of this.

"In both books I retell the old stories and oral histories of this region," Paul informed her. "I had to go poking around in plenty of archives and library stacks to verify my facts. For the shipwreck book I learned to scuba dive, too, and checked several out for myself. And writing about the various lighthouses involved climbing fully ten thousand steps up and down. Anyway, I'll bring you a copy of both books."

"I'd enjoy that," Brittany responded, thinking how animated Paul became when he discussed his work.

He returned to his eggs, finishing them in a few quick bites. Then Paul dropped his paper napkin onto his plate and pushed back his chair.

When he stood up he began coughing again—hacking, actually, one deep rattling cough leading to another. "Why don't you stay in today, too," she suggested.

"Can't," Paul wheezed, barely managing to quit coughing for even a minute. "The supply boat's coming, remember? I've got to get our trash, garbage and those precious moose bones of yours down to the dock."

"I'll help you," Brittany offered.

"You'll do no such thing! It's my job," Paul said sharply. Then he leaned over the table and touched Brittany's hair lightly, taking the sting from his words. Briefly his hands framed her face. "You stay in. You're still looking a little peaked."

"That's putting it mildly," she conceded, trying not to let his gentle touch matter quite so much.

His long warm hands dropped away from her. "Another reason I've got to keep going is that Ivy's acting awfully antsy," Paul said. "I built her a whelping box a month ago and introduced her to it last week. Now she doesn't want to get out of it. She doesn't want me to leave her side, either. She whined when I started down the steps this morning, and before I got through the door she'd really started howling. I felt like a criminal."

"Uh-oh," said Brittany, raising her eyebrows knowingly. "Is Ivy still eating?"

"Not much. I could still tempt her yesterday with a few goodies. I haven't tried today. Guess I'd better go do that, huh?"

"When animals refuse to eat, labor is usually not far behind," Brittany observed. "How about Ivy's temperature?

It should elevate if she's within twenty-four hours of delivery."

"I know," Paul said glumly. "That's in my German shepherd book, too. But have you ever tried taking a very pregnant dog's temperature?"

"No, I have to admit I haven't," Brittany said, trying to smother a smile.

"Believe me, they resist the procedure. Oh well, I guess all she can do is bite me."

"Keep me informed," Brittany said and thought of how fond she'd grown of Ivy in a short period of time.

"I'll do better than that," Paul said forlornly as Brittany pushed back her chair. "I'll let you bandage my dog bite."

After that, they worked silently yet companionably at their separate chores. While Brittany washed the dishes, Paul hauled out the various trash and garbage sacks. He had also produced a box labeled Isle Svenson Scientific Specimens—Handle with Care, and into this he packed Brittany's icy and double-sealed moose bones.

After Paul had left the cottage Brittany took a peek at him through the living room window. Today was gray and overcast, unlike the sunny pleasant days they'd enjoyed recently, and from the way Paul walked hunched against the wind Brittany knew it must be quite cold again. At least he was all bundled up, wearing the cap, scarf and gloves he'd shed a few days ago.

Brittany turned back to her bed, grateful to simply stay inside. Gradually the heat of the cottage combined with the gray, dusklike gloom set her nodding, and she drifted off to sleep once again.

She didn't wake until after one o'clock. Then, although Brittany felt lethargic and groggy from so much sleep, her facial color had definitely improved, and she was also ravenously hungry, always a reliable sign of health's return.

Paul had been in and out several times while she'd slept, Brittany saw at once. Brown sacks of groceries were stacked in the kitchen, although he had removed all perishable items to either refrigerator or freezer.

Also, set in prominent display on the kitchen table were the two books he'd written. Wonderingly Brittany hefted one. She studied the dust jacket and traced Paul's name there with her finger, then turned the book over to see his picture and the brief biographical sketch.

Why, I know a real, live author! she thought. The books made Paul's accomplishments more real to her, and Brittany felt duly impressed. She also felt a renewed curiosity about his present project, that novel set during the fall of Vietnam, and wished he'd tell her more about it.

For lunch Brittany fixed herself a sandwich and a bowl of canned clam chowder, then put up the remaining groceries, Paul's as well as hers. She also spared him a moment's concern because he obviously hadn't bothered to fix himself any lunch. Had his cold worsened? Or was Ivy keeping him busy delivering her puppies? Or both?

Maybe I ought to go check on him, Brittany thought, and realized then that she was still extremely curious about the interior of the lighthouse. Now she especially longed to see Paul's sanctuary since this was where he wrote all his books. Although she'd been here for two weeks, she still hadn't set foot inside the lighthouse. How glad she was that she and Paul were on friendly terms again.

A glance outside, through the kitchen window this time, was enough to deter Brittany's interest since fresh snow drifted down heavily. "Oh, no!" she wailed at the sight.

Obviously she and Paul would have to forget any fond hopes they harbored for an early spring.

Brittany retired to her bedroom again to begin reading Paul's book. But first, in a gesture celebrating her new feeling of well-being, she shed her nightgown and robe and dressed in slacks that she topped with a couple of warm sweaters. Then, buoyed by the psychological lift of being in her regular clothes, she settled down to read.

Where was he?

By ten o'clock that evening Brittany had grown almost as apprehensive as she was hungry. She hadn't seen or heard

from Paul since breakfast and now she felt the unusual stir-
rings of panic.

He had missed two meals, of course, and Brittany didn't
admit to herself that one reason for her annoyance was that
she'd cooked up a huge pot of hot potato soup—from
scratch, mind you. Not only did it taste superb, it was the
sort of hearty, healthy stick-to-the-ribs fare that should help
a sick man throw off a cold. Only Paul hadn't been
thoughtful enough to turn up and eat a bowl.

Of course, the way he'd been hacking earlier today he
might be ill. Or he could be up to his ears in a veterinary
emergency. But if either of those had occurred why didn't
he signal to her from the lighthouse?

Also, it was snowing like crazy.

Twice Brittany had thrown on her parka and tied a scarf
over her head, then gone out onto the front porch for better lighthouse visibility. Even there she could barely see the
lantern room through the swirling, fast-falling snow, so the
second time Brittany had trained her binoculars on the great
glass window. Nothing. It looked entirely normal for this
time of night, lit up, of course, but only with ordinary in-
candescence. There were no red flares, no rhythmic SOS
signals and no glimpse of Paul standing in the window,
desperately clutching his head, heart or stomach.

Still, it was getting so late, and he hadn't eaten for hours.
I guess I've just got to risk a relapse and trudge over there
to see about him, Brittany thought grimly, taking out her
gloves again and going for her snowshoes.

After all, she couldn't let a man as talented as Paul
Zachary Johnson succumb for lack of care. And he really
was talented. As annoyed as Brittany was at present by the
man's behavior she had to allow for his exceptional gifts,
although it didn't really seem fair that someone who could
write as well as Paul should be so good-looking, too!

She truly hadn't expected to be grabbed around the throat
by a book on shipwrecks. It had sounded entirely too
scholarly to qualify as escapist thrill-and-chill reading. But
Paul had seized her attention very effectively on the first
page when he wrote about imperiled people on a vessel

caught in a famous Great Lakes' storm, their ship freezing up rapidly in dangerous packs of ice.

Part of her annoyance at the moment undoubtedly stemmed from the fact that Brittany was eager to keep reading. Instead she had to go plunging out into a freezing storm herself. But now, with each minute that ticked by, Brittany seemed to feel something driving her; various worries that grew at a pace all their own pushed at her, prodded her, nagged her. Premonitions of trouble were not the sort of thing she had experienced often, but this one gradually grew too vivid and insistent for her to ignore.

"Moral: Don't read any more books about disasters," she muttered to herself as she patted the zipped pocket of her parka to be sure her house key was still there. Not that Brittany had any intention of locking either door. She scarcely expected company—welcome or otherwise—on a freezing snowy night like this. However, bizarre things were occasionally known to happen, and Brittany intended to take no chances on finding herself locked outside in the cold dark night.

"So here goes nothing," she said to herself, then plunged through the door.

Her timing was right on target. Another hour and she would have found Paul dead from exposure. Even another half to quarter-hour might have been too late.

But when Brittany stumbled on his dark figure crumpled on the path between the lighthouse and cottage Paul was only lightly dusted by snow so she knew he hadn't been lying there unconscious for very long.

Paul kept waking up by slow degrees, reluctantly and painfully. There were a lot of reasons why he didn't want to rouse and resume living, but there were also a couple of compelling reasons why he did. Uncomfortably he seesawed back and forth in an emotional tug of war.

He lay in his old bed for he was back again in his former bedroom, that room he'd shared for years with Peg. It was haunted by memories of her. That was one reason why he kept his eyes so tightly closed.

He didn't want any more encounters with her ghost.

While Paul had been at his sickest he'd seen Peg and had talked to her, or had it been a dream or hallucination? Merry and mischievous, her brown eyes twinkling and her red hair aglow, she reminded him of a few things that Paul had elected to forget. Oh, not that Peg had reproached him. Even in death she was always so pleasant, just like Chad.

No, it was his own mind that still reproached him, Paul realized. Now guilt kept his eyes closed, indeed made him squeeze them shut even more tightly.

But then he started thinking about how sick he'd been and that was no fun topic, either. When the nausea and fever had first struck Paul, soon after the supply boat had arrived, he'd feared leaving Ivy alone in the lighthouse since by then her sides were rippling rhythmically.

"I've got stomach flu," Paul had thought with a sigh, then lost his breakfast before going back to stroke Ivy's head and murmur soothingly to her.

By the time the first puppy was born a short time later Paul had thrown up so many times he feared for his stomach lining. Dazed and dehydrated he'd collapsed on his narrow bed and tried to oversee Ivy from there.

She did just fine, too. Born to be a mother, Paul had thought, taking pride in his pet as she lovingly lapped her long rough tongue over her new offspring.

Six puppies had been born, all alive and active. Cute, too, though all their coats looked gray rather than having Ivy's desirable gold-and-black coloring. But despite the color of the puppies' coats or the way Paul felt he was pleased by the day's events. He closed his eyes and drifted off into uneasy slumber.

It was night when he awoke, pitch-black outside the windows, although lights blazed all around him in the lantern room. Ivy needed to be fed, and she was also whining to be let out so Paul stumbled up.

Oh God, I'm really sick! he thought as misery made its way into his consciousness. He felt on fire and soaked by perspiration. His head throbbed unbelievably; his nose, throat and stomach were aflame; his arms and legs all ached as if they might drop off at any minute. His back felt as if it had been cracked open on some torturer's rack.

Never in his entire life had Paul gotten so sick quite so fast. But he no longer had his body's normal strength and resilience, either, he realized with a sense of near panic.

I've got to get to the cottage, some part of his brain prodded him, although he couldn't remember just who was at the cottage to help him. Peg? No, Peg is dead. It's someone else . . .

Slowly and painfully Paul made his way down the seemingly endless stairs, Ivy already well ahead of him. He opened the heavy door just a crack and she whizzed out while Paul was still struggling to get his arms into his jacket.

By the time he started to leave the lighthouse Ivy was already back and eager to return to her puppies. Paul let her fly past him, then he stepped out to a Christmas card scene—the falling snow, the cozy cottage whose every room blazed with lights. As he stumbled further down the walk he could even see a figure pacing inside the cottage. Tall and golden-haired. Oh yes, the beautiful, magical, fierce and uncompromising Valkyrie.

And that was the last thing Paul remembered clearly until the same blond woman was cruelly rubbing his face in snow and screeching at him to wake up. After that, he remembered leaning heavily on her, his feet stumbling and shuffling quite strangely, as they made their way toward the cottage. Then she was pouring pure liquid fire down his throat, making him cough uncontrollably and his eyes water. Not that she cared since she still insisted remorselessly, "Drink the brandy, Paul!"

After that, nightmares and reality got all mixed up for him.

Chapter Ten

"Hey, sleepyhead, aren't you ever going to wake up?" a voice taunted Paul.

Brittany. More than once in the past however-long-it-had-been her voice had reached down to him just like this. That clear voice, though rarely tinged with today's humor, had resounded through his dreams, just as the sight and touch of her were like a lifeline thrown down into a cold, black, bottomless pit. Even though Paul lay far away, broken and hurting all over in that pit, her voice kept calling him to climb back up to warmth and light, to her.

So now he tried to open his eyes again and discovered that the process wasn't as painful as he had feared. In fact, from the moment she had called out to him, Paul ceased dreading the moment of awakening and actually began to anticipate it.

His eyelids still felt weighted down. They rolled up very, very slowly, but then he was looking up into her lovely smooth face. Although Brittany wasn't smiling, as Paul wished she'd do, she still regarded him pleasantly and her deep blue eyes held concern.

"How are you feeling, Paul?" she asked.

Paul swallowed, his mouth almost too dry to speak, so he ran his tongue over equally parched lips. "Not too bad," he said, but the froglike croak of his voice startled him. His throat still felt swollen and raw and numerous aches continued to afflict him, but, at least, he could identify them all now. His body was no longer one gigantic, throbbing mass of pain.

"Good. Your fever's down, too," Brittany said with a trace of satisfaction. "Do you think you could eat something?"

Paul considered her request since that was actually what it was. Although he appreciated Brittany's eagerness to feed him, even the thought of food was abhorrent. He shook his head. "Maybe later," he temporized.

"How about some grape juice?" she tempted.

He reconsidered. He would have rejected orange juice as too sharp for his sore throat, but grape juice sounded almost good. "Okay."

"Be right back. Don't go anywhere without me," she teased, then rose from a chair set beside his bed.

Paul watched her movements, finding them graceful and womanly. She was really quite a startlingly attractive woman, he thought once more. Even with her hair hanging in a neat simple braid down her back, her face devoid of makeup and her attire a simple white sweater worn over dark slacks she was still pretty.

She'd been an excellent nurse, he remembered, gentle and soothing. Those were two characteristics he hadn't associated with Brittany Hagen before, but they'd been apparent as she'd deftly coaxed him into drinking the fluids his burning body required as well as swallowing aspirin, cold capsules and vitamin C. She'd even had a remedy when those deep coughs shook his whole frame, measuring out spoonfuls of a lemon and honey mixture that temporarily lulled his cough mechanism and allowed him to sleep again.

Paul also remembered several hot toddies made from his brandy, fragrant and strong.

Brittany had fed him regularly, spooning in potato soup and chicken broth or baked potatoes. Fruits, too, he remembered, thinking of mashed bananas and scraped apples. Paul could still easily remember her coaxing voice ringing in his ears. "Take this, Paul...swallow that...here, let me hold your head. Won't you eat just a little bit?"

Most of all, Brittany's voice kept banishing the ghost of Peg, and even though that sprightly ethereal spirit might come bouncing back an hour or two later—or was it a day or two later—Paul had only to cringe or cry out and he'd feel Brittany by his side, hear her voice assuring him that everything was all right and ringing out for truth and reality.

The reason Paul kept resisting the merry ghost of his late wife was that Peg was dead. Yes, he knew that now. Even in the throes of sickness, with all its fever-induced dreams, Peg remained irrevocably dead and buried. That was why her presence, even here in her own bedroom, startled him so. Peg just wasn't real anymore. But Brittany was.

He remembered the warmth of Brittany's body and its clean scent as she'd bend down to lift his head. Now, as Paul struggled unaided to push himself up on his pillows, he remembered the smooth gliding touch of her hands. Remembered his own arm thrashing out at some point and encountering one of her soft, rounded, ample breasts.

"Hey, watch it, fella." She'd chuckled in good-natured protest, and Paul had felt a moment's chagrin, knowing he'd done something wrong. But because he couldn't honestly regret finding and touching that sweetly curved breast, he hadn't croaked out an apology, either. Not when it would have been so fake and insincere.

Now as Brittany came back into the room, bearing a small glass of purple liquid and looking so clean, neat and pretty, one of Paul's hands crept up his cheek to discover that both his beard and moustache were shaggy and overgrown. "I must look like a wild man," he muttered ruefully as Brittany again took the chair drawn up to his bed.

"You've been better-looking on other occasions," she admitted, winding a paper napkin around the base of his glass. "But at least you're getting well now." Again that trace of satisfaction crept into her voice, a satisfaction that her next words explained. "If you hadn't been dramatically improved by today I was going to have to leave you and go for help. Frankly, that had been worrying me a lot. You and I stayed so busy fighting each other that a couple of the dire need-to-knows fell through the cracks."

"Like what?" Paul coughed, trying to concentrate on Brittany's words, which seemed to be overlaid with irony. His brain wasn't functioning as quickly as it should, he realized.

"For instance, I didn't know how to operate your short-wave radio, and I still don't," she admitted. "I couldn't find the manual. Anyway, even if I'd found it I'm just not good at mechanical things. Of course, I don't know how to start your boat, either, but I expect I could figure that one out. At least I've operated a few other boats. But there's still so much ice in Lake Superior I was scared to try to take it to Catt Island." Brittany sighed. "In short, I didn't know what the hell to do in an emergency like this, and I definitely should have known."

"It's my fault for not teaching you," Paul said contritely.

"Actually, I don't believe I ever bothered to ask. I was deriving too much pleasure out of just being mad at you to learn a few little things like how to call med evac."

Now Paul knew he heard irony in her voice. "We've really been fools, haven't we?" he said wearily, for the effort of talking had already started to tax him.

"Fools playing with fire," Brittany agreed. "Hey, drink your juice. Then maybe I can ply you with other goodies."

The grape juice tasted sweet and fresh; finished, Paul felt strengthened enough to ask Brittany a question. "How long have I been lying here?"

"Four days."

"Four days!" he echoed incredulously.

"Yes. You can see why I was getting so worried," Brittany admitted, low-voiced.

Paul handed the juice glass back to her. Just as Brittany took it he seized advantage of their proximity to let his hand curve over hers. "Brittany, I'm so sorry," he apologized thinking of all the trouble he'd caused her.

She looked astonished. Indeed, if Paul wasn't mistaken, her eyes leaped first to his hand covering hers, as if she found his touch more significant than his words. "Goodness, what for?" she blurted.

Paul wondered if it was just his imagination or if Brittany's eyes had turned a deeper blue. Imagination, he concluded as she carefully disengaged her hand from his. Again, though, he received a message at variance with her action. Something in Brittany's expression hinted that she wasn't pulling away because she found him repugnant. Rather, it was as if each brush of his skin felt equally tantalizing to her.

Breathlessly Brittany added, "After all, you couldn't help being sick." Then she looked carefully away from Paul.

No, he decided he'd definitely been imagining things. Since he could sense how truly awful his appearance must be it was little wonder Brittany wouldn't look at him. Maybe, when he felt a little stronger, he could drag himself into the bathroom to bathe and shave. He probably smelled like a goat. If only he didn't feel so damned weak and helpless! As Brittany rose and left the room again, Paul was ready to sink back against the pillows and close his eyes. Various tremors running through his weakened hands and body were telling him his energy store had just been depleted.

Suddenly, wafting into Paul's nostrils, came the most delightful smells in the world, cinnamon and chocolate. Incredibly hunger stirred inside him.

He heard Brittany return a few minutes later. With his eyes still closed Paul sniffed, then smiled. "You're bringing something that smells great," he whispered.

"Just cinnamon toast and cocoa," she replied, her voice matter of fact.

"I didn't think I was hungry," Paul marvelled, then looked up through half-closed eyes to view Brittany's clean-cut profile and shimmering hair. "How do you always know just exactly what to fix?"

"Sick people always revert to childhood," she explained.

Since Paul's hands were still trembling, Brittany had to help him eat. But when he managed to swallow every bite he could tell she was secretly pleased.

"Ivy?" Paul inquired, using the last dregs of his stamina. The only reason he hadn't inquired immediately about his pet were various memories he'd had of Brittany reassuring him regularly about Ivy.

"Ivy's just fine," Brittany confirmed now. "So are her puppies. Just wait till you see them! They're fat and cute, changing and growing bigger every day. Still blind, of course, but their eyes should open in another week."

Since Brittany had apparently answered his question fully Paul wondered why he detected a certain reticence. Was she holding back some information? If so, why?

"Brittany, what aren't you telling me?" Paul asked her bluntly.

He heard surprise in her near-gasp. "Okay, there is a small thing wrong with the puppies that won't please you," she began.

"Oh God!" Was she about to tell him that Trent's little white terrier was their sire? "Not the terrier, please!"

"Terrier? What terrier?" Brittany asked, surprised. Then, lowering her deep blue eyes until they were level with Paul's anxious gaze, she added, "No, these pups are much too large to be terriers—"

"What then?" Paul interrupted and felt cold sweat breaking out on his body. He couldn't bear to think of disappointing Chad, who was counting so on a puppy. For that matter, Paul had counted on earning a modest sum from the sale of the remaining puppies, provided they were pure-bred.

"Paul, calm down, please!" Brittany urged. "What's wrong is...I think...in fact, I'm close to certain...that their daddy is a wolf."

* * *

Half-wolves or not, all the pups were cute as the dickens, Brittany thought an hour later, kneeling beside the large box over which Ivy presided with new dignity. Gone were Ivy's own puppyish antics. Motherhood had transformed her to full maturity. Even as the puppies crowded around her side, whimpering in their desire for a warm milk-filled teat, Ivy lovingly lapped her tongue across their small gray heads.

Uh-oh, the little runt of the litter was getting short-changed again, Brittany noticed. Carefully she disengaged a pup almost twice the size of the grayish runt. "That's enough for you, Big Boy. You're round as a butterball," she scolded as the displaced puppy began to whine. In his place she deposited the runt who immediately began suckling greedily.

"You may be tiny but you've got all the right instincts, haven't you, Little One?" Brittany crooned to the runt.

Instincts. They were quite amazing, she reflected, watching Ivy's tongue caress the runt now. Instincts told Ivy just what to do with her offspring and the same sort of inherent instincts had guided Brittany while she'd tended Paul through these last harrowing, horrible days.

She'd had quite a time at first, fearing that he might have food poisoning in addition to quite a bad cold. It was scarcely a farfetched theory considering the deteriorating condition of much of the food he'd consumed. But instincts plus a thick first-aid manual she'd found on the shelves had helped Brittany to decide that while Paul might deserve food poisoning for all the chances he took, he had still escaped.

That meant he had plain old winter flu, which could still be plenty serious given its tendency to escalate into pneumonia or severe ear and throat infections.

So Brittany had followed all of the instructions in the manual, trusted her instincts as well as what she'd learned nursing animals at the Hagens' dairy. And she'd also been very lucky because Paul was now on the mend.

She wondered if he would ask her any questions, such as what he'd said while he was unconscious or in the grip of severe nightmares. Occasionally Paul had imagined he was with Peg and they were talking. A couple of times he'd even apologized to her in tormented, poignant words. "I'm sorry, Peg—oh God, I'm so sorry. I know you deserved the best. I always meant to be a better husband, too, and make things up to you. I thought I'd have years to take care of that. I didn't dream you'd ever die!"

When Paul began to call out to Peg and thrash around in torment, Brittany always moved immediately to his side. She'd take his fever-hot hand and speak his name quietly. "Paul, it's all right."

"Oh!" On a couple of occasions his eyes flew open and he had looked up at her in recognition. "Brittany."

Even if he didn't become completely lucid her voice still seemed to lull him down into gentler, deeper sleep where he was clearly less agitated.

"Paul, what do you think you did to Peg?" Brittany asked him once, her old perpetual vice—curiosity—overcoming her.

The sins he'd muttered, about not thanking Peg when she'd tiptoed all the way up the lighthouse stairs to set a sandwich by his elbow or for washing his dirty clothes were, to Brittany, mere oversights. But in Paul's weakened condition they had assumed, to him, the proportion of major flaws.

Of course there might be something bigger that he wasn't talking about, Brittany had reflected cynically, her mind filled with images of extramarital lovers. But now, remembering Paul's broken words and the tears that had streaked down his thin cheeks, she really doubted he'd been capable of holding back much.

Would he remember those scenes? Brittany wondered, automatically soothing the dispossessed and whining puppy she'd gathered up into her lap. Or, if he should ask, ought she to tell Paul how he'd imagined Peg's presence?

He might be embarrassed if she did. So Brittany decided to heed this instinct, too.

Suddenly, at a warm wet touch and a small sucking sound, she laughed aloud. The still-blind puppy she held had discovered Brittany's little finger and had decided this was exactly what he sought. How alive he was, rooting around in her lap and groping with his small wet mouth! How alive all of the puppies were, Brittany marvelled, watching and rejoicing in their wriggling, babyish antics.

Somewhere out there, across a bleak landscape of still-blowing snow, were newly born wolf pups behaving much like these? Not that she was apparently ever destined to find out, Brittany thought with a trace of sadness for her side-lined project. Between the weather, her own bad cold, seven animals and a seriously ill man, Brittany's work was now far behind schedule.

She was upset about it, too. The real wonder was that she wasn't more upset, given her methodical nature and innate fondness for things clicking along nicely on schedule. She should have been pacing the floor, tearing her hair and cursing Paul because he was keeping her from completing her assignments. Instead those menial duties she'd performed on his behalf had somehow become the most important things in the world—and that kind of lapse naturally left Brittany deeply suspicious of her own motives.

Abruptly Ivy stood up, shaking off her pups. She climbed out of the big box and went to investigate her bowl of dog food. Brittany had filled it faithfully, since she knew a nursing mother required more nourishment than usual. For several long minutes Ivy ate hungrily. Finished, she lapped noisily at her water dish, then started down the circular iron stairs, clearly intent on air, exercise and a bathroom break.

More instincts, Brittany thought, hastily returning the puppy she held in her lap to the box with his siblings. Ivy needed Brittany to go downstairs and open the heavy door at the bottom of the tower to let her out.

As she followed Ivy down, Brittany kept glancing all around. She still wasn't quite used to the lighthouse, but she found it interesting and cheerful and could certainly understand why Paul enjoyed working here.

For one thing, it was considerably warmer than the cottage, since its original bricks had been reinforced later with several inches of solid concrete, and the lighthouse was also a lot brighter with its great expanse of glass at the top and whitewashed walls below.

Most of all, the view from the lantern room was just as spectacular and inspiring as Brittany had imagined. Daily she savored the landscapes that lay before her in all four directions: rock-strewn shorelines, canopied forests of evergreens and icy clear water with fish galore.

Now, as Brittany wound around to the lower levels of the lighthouse she passed two much smaller areas that had been partitioned off to serve as additional rooms. First came a miniature bathroom with a skinny-looking shower stall but no tub.

Below that was the storeroom, lined with a number of inexpensive metal shelves on which quite an array of items lay jumbled. Most of it was emergency equipment designed to cover everything from lost at sea to storm-stranded. There were lifejackets in all sizes, battery-operated lanterns and an emergency generator. Although firearms were banned for students staying on the island, Paul was allowed to have both a rifle and revolver. But a couple of sniffs at gun barrels told Brittany that neither had been fired in ages. There was also a two-burner hot plate and a generous supply of canned goods and bottled water designed to see the caretaker and kin through whatever the elements might fling their way.

Parked in the corner of the room was a snowmobile, obviously broken since its interior parts lay in a box. There was also a child's sled and a small red wagon.

I'll have to move Ivy and the puppies down here soon, Brittany thought now, passing the storeroom. It wouldn't be long until the pups were clambering out of their box and venturing off to explore the world. She certainly didn't want them toppling down the stairs. But, for as long as possible, they needed the light and warmth of the lantern room.

Brittany trailed Ivy outside into a cool spring day where snow was melting once again. Shading her eyes against the glare Brittany watched as Ivy scampered around and around the lighthouse, getting her daily exercise by running in circles. While she waited, Brittany's mind drifted back to

Paul's second book, which she'd finished reading late last night.

Lights Across the Sky had been just as fascinating as his first book. How could he make a series of lighthouse stories exciting? she had wondered on opening the volume.

While she'd sat beside Paul's bed—*her* bed, actually— and watched him sleep Brittany had soon found out. Paul just naturally had a knack for bringing things alive, whether it was shipwrecks or all the small homey details of light- keepers and their families. By writing about the people who had lived here at Isle Svenson, as well as at other Great Lakes' stations not so long ago, Paul had illustrated how life had been made less dangerous for the vessels traversing such treacherous waters.

Brittany had been equally unable to put down *Lights Across the Sky* and had held the book with one hand while dispensing aspirin, water or cough syrup with the other. Long after she should have been asleep on the lumpy cush- ions of the too-short sofa in the living room she had been propped up on an elbow, reading far into the night.

Of course, she had always been a sucker for people who did a job really well, whatever it happened to be. This and, of course, this alone accounted for her new appreciation of Paul, or so Brittany tried to tell herself now as she watched Ivy come loping back.

Ivy stopped before Brittany and whined, a request that Brittany open the door and let her back into the tower. Ivy also performed her new job well, Brittany thought approv- ingly as she moved to oblige. In fact, as canine mothers went, Ivy was a prize. While her puppies were so little and helpless she never wanted to stay away from them for more than a few necessary minutes. Yes, Mother Nature had surely sent each creature into the world encoded with a whole set of natural instincts to guide its behavior and re- production.

"Good girl," Brittany said with an approving pat on Ivy's backside as the dog scooted past her and climbed back up the spiral stairs. Then, with Ivy tended to temporarily,

Brittany headed back to the cottage, since that was exactly where she wanted to be again.

More instincts to contend with? Brittany wondered. Unlike dogs, humans sometimes had to be quite wary of theirs, and right now Brittany certainly was. Oh, she wasn't going to pretend that she'd been exactly unmoved as she'd helped Paul through the previous days. Cradling his dark head and discovering anew the soft texture of his hair, wiping perspiration off his brow or spooning something into his mouth, she'd gotten far more involved with the man than she should have. After all, women had been given crucial feelings, too—feelings for the opposite sex as well as maternal feelings to help insure the survival of the species.

Paul's helplessness had activated Brittany's feelings, bringing out all her strength and protectiveness. Paradoxically, perhaps, she'd felt especially protective of Paul since she knew now the extent of his talent and perception. Since Brittany had new respect for his abilities, she was determined to see him through this period of illness and to make certain that he was kept safe during his temporarily unguarded state.

But, right now, Brittany wasn't quite sure, either, where simple humanist feelings left off and those other, far more perilous female emotions began.

Her relationship with Paul had changed so clearly and so suddenly that she could actually mark the place. It had happened on that afternoon when she'd felt so sad and blue, the day when he hadn't left a mess in the kitchen for once and when he had sent Ivy to comfort her.

Brittany had certainly been agreeable to giving up their previously hostile relationship. Indeed, she'd felt downright good about the change. But then their relationship just kept on developing until, ironically, she had found herself becoming progressively more enmeshed—possibly entranced with—an only half-conscious man.

No wonder she felt so wary and so threatened. Obviously Paul's feelings would not have changed along with hers. While he might be grateful to her, Paul hadn't spent most of a week learning all about her as Brittany had now learned about him, both from personally tending him as well as from all that his books had revealed.

As she stepped up onto the porch of the cottage, Brittany stopped to inhale deeply of the pure, fir-scented air and also to quell that sense of elation that started welling up spontaneously. Instead she forced herself to remember the flip side of such emotions. To recall exactly what it had been like to depend on someone else for her happiness and feelings of worth.

Being forewarned as she was now was like the way she'd been in childhood, wading out into untried waters and knowing that the lake floor beneath her feet would disappear suddenly. Even when you expected it you could still be left floundering, gasping in water over your head.

But it was much, much worse if you weren't prepared.

Whatever might conceivably happen between herself and Paul, Brittany still remembered Howard yanking the rug out from under her feet at the moment when she was least prepared.

She knew then, as she knew now, that she mustn't ever let that happen to her again.

An hour ago she'd left Paul asleep, which was probably the best thing for him considering his obvious dismay over Ivy's mixed-breed puppies.

"What am I going to tell Chad? Or Steve? He was going to sell the puppies for me. Well, by God, I know one thing. As soon as I get out of this bed I'm going to find a wolf and shoot it!" he'd threatened.

"Good luck," Brittany had replied drily.

Paul still slept but lightly now. In fact, by the way he was stirring and frowning, Brittany expected him to awaken at any time. After peeking in on him she went back to the kitchen to wash all the dishes she'd left stacked in the sink.

Until this past week, Brittany had never abandoned dirty dishes, but between the dual demands of Paul and Ivy she'd simply had to sometimes. Of course, if Paul had been right about such compulsions it wouldn't hurt her to loosen up a bit. It also wouldn't hurt him to turn a little tidier! With a wry smile Brittany recalled the clutter both in the storeroom and at the top of the lighthouse.

We really aren't alike at all, she thought, finding it necessary to emphasize that fact to herself. He's very slapdash, except in his writing. There Paul was careful and very, very clever.

"Brittany?"

Her heart leaped at Paul's hoarse cry. "Coming," she called, then dried her hands and hurried to the bedroom.

She found him thrashing around in the bed, crumpling and wrinkling the nice clean sheets she'd put on an hour before. "What's wrong?" she asked anxiously.

"I hurt everywhere!" he complained.

Instinctively her hand reached for his forehead, but it still felt gratifyingly cool. "Aches and pains?" she asked sympathetically.

"Some. Mostly I'm just tired of lying in this damned bed. My arms and legs feel downright sore, and I swear my tailbone is paralyzed!"

Brittany considered his complaints. "Why don't I help you out of bed?" she suggested. "You could sit here in the chair for just a little bit."

"Great." Paul sighed, flinging back the covers, and Brittany moved quickly to his side to help.

Paul leaned heavily on her as he maneuvered the short distance and fell into the armchair, panting. Then he glared down at the flannel pajamas he wore. They were Brittany's and mercifully loose and baggy enough to fit Paul, although he detested them. "Don't I look just darling?" he muttered, fingering their purple-sprigged flower design.

"Would you rather wear the pink pair?" she asked sweetly and he trained his glare on her.

Concealing a smile, Brittany bent over the bed and began straightening and smoothing the sheets. She and Paul had already been through several embarrassing moments such as the times she'd wrestled him out of one set of pajamas to wash them, then sponged off his painfully thin body before wrestling him into the alternate pair. But she'd had to. At least twice Paul had broken out in cold drenching sweats that had left him half-soaked. Nor did he have any idea where, or even if, he still owned any pajamas, having obviously preferred sleeping *au naturel*.

Brittany glanced up from the bed to find Paul watching her closely. "I guess I've given you a few thrills," he said, tight-lipped, but she could tell he really regretted the enforced intimacies.

"Think nothing of it," Brittany said casually. "I've seen it all before."

Clearly her answer surprised Paul. "That much experience?" he asked and raised one glossy black eyebrow.

"No, that many brothers," she replied.

Surprised, he burst out laughing, the sound gratifying to her ears.

"Tell me about your brothers," he said a minute later. "Or talk to me about something—anything. Anything at all."

Chapter Eleven

Four days had passed since Paul had awakened alert and lucid. Since then his recuperation had been uneventful except that he was monumentally bored; that meant he was soon getting up and down too often to suit Brittany, fetching a reference book or a pad to jot down his thoughts.

Brittany had returned to her work, but she left late and returned early. She never stayed gone very long since she feared that without her to nag him the idle Paul would overdo things and have a relapse. He was far too thin, and she feared his reserves of health and strength were dangerously depleted. At least by fetching and carrying for him Brittany could make sure Paul stayed flat on his back, ate properly and took an afternoon nap.

So she lingered and, gradually, they talked about all sorts of things until each had learned a lot more about the other than they probably would have under normal conditions.

They discussed safer topics first.

"See his gray coat, black nose and white muzzle? Those are wolf's characteristics. And the slant of this puppy's eyes? They'll be blue when they first open, then they'll probably turn pure wolf-yellow. But he's still quite a sweet puppy—oh, see him stretch and yawn!"

"Okay, I'll admit I'm learning some of the wolf's finer points," Paul agreed that afternoon. He stroked two of Ivy's plump puppies, which Brittany had brought over to visit with him, while she held a third. "I'll even admit I like these guys, now that I'm over the shock. But just for the sake of argument, do wolves really matter so much? Are they that important to the world?"

"Yes, they really are," Brittany said firmly, sitting down in the chair that was still drawn up beside Paul's bed. "Because wolves kill primarily old or worm-ridden animals this helps to keep herds of elk and moose healthy by weeding out the very ones that are liable to spread disease. Also, without a predator around herds tend to overpopulate, then their range gets overbrowsed and the excessive animals starve. That's happened at Yellowstone National Park, where the whole ecosystem has gotten out of kilter since wolves were exterminated years ago. Now there are far too many elk. Also, wolves help keep nature in proper balance because quite a number of other creatures feed on their kill. Here on Isle Svenson those are squirrels, foxes and birds.

"At Yellowstone a larger and more unique animal is presently endangered," Brittany continued earnestly. "That's the grizzly. Biologists knew that the big bears had been gradually declining for a number of years, but no one knew why until recently. Now the decrease in the grizzlies' birthrate has been linked to a lack of available protein. See, undernourished mothers won't bear their young alive. But the wolf could provide the solution to that situation, too. Indeed, it used to."

"How in the world does the wolf affect a grizzly?" Paul asked, his dark eyes watching her closely.

Paul looked a lot better today, Brittany thought. His color was good once again, and he was starting to eat everything in sight.

"Grizzlies are big and slow. Ordinarily they can't bring down elk like a wolf can. The wolf has much greater speed and it hunts in packs. Still, the grizzlies' great size does give him one advantage. Wolves will surrender their kill when a grizzly comes along. So some of the elk killed by wolves could provide the needed protein for the grizzly. Another plus is that a well-fed grizzly also becomes less of a threat to hikers and campers, of course."

"That's interesting," said Paul, running a thoughtful hand over his scraggly-looking beard. Ivy's pups had both fallen asleep in his lap, and he glanced down at them reflectively.

"You see, in nonfiction a writer is married to the facts. But in a novel you can invent anything you want. It's like playing God for three or four hundred pages. For instance, the real Dominique—the one I knew in Vietnam—was a lazy, arrogant bitch who wouldn't have spit on someone like me. I was just the colonel's lackey, and one of my least pleasant chores was driving his mistress around Saigon to see everyone from her hairdresser to her astrologer. Dominique even had a young French lover, but you can damn well bet the colonel didn't know about it."

"Was he the same Frenchman who flew off with her to Paris?" Brittany asked Paul, dangling her long legs over one arm of the chair as she listened to him, fascinated.

"No. Dominique left Vietnam with an old Frenchman. I tell you that woman had guys stashed everywhere!" Paul said, his face twisting with dislike.

"But the character based on her is coming out quite differently in your novel?"

"Yes. Although Monique, my character, is also a beautiful Eurasian, that's where all similarity ends. She does fall in love with her young American chauffeur but—"

"Don't tell me the ending, if it's sad, Paul. I hate sad endings!"

"Anyway, I'm almost through with my novel. I've written everything but that all-important last chapter. I hope while I've been lying fallow, I'm also gathering momentum for one last great push...."

"So why are you studying wolves on Isle Svenson?" Paul asked Brittany the next day. "I mean, what's happening here that's so important, wolfwise?"

"I thought you'd already guessed," Brittany said with a half laugh. "I'm a dreary ghoul who collects the bones of dead beasts."

"No, you're not," he contradicted.

"Yes, I am, too, because if you get out of that bed one more time..." Brittany let her threat go unfinished.

Paul stopped in the act of throwing back the covers. With mock seriousness he folded his hands on top of the bedspread. "Tell me what you're doing, please?" he coaxed. "You said it had a practical application, but Griff's phrase about 'wolf-moose dynamics' doesn't tell me a lot."

"'Wolf-moose dynamics'? That's basically who gets the better of whom on an isolated island where neither moose nor wolves can get away. That's why the interaction of predator and prey has been studied here for a number of years because a true picture of wolf and moose numbers, their kills and deaths, can be charted as it can't be elsewhere," Brittany explained. "Now, as a scientist I naturally gather and report data scrupulously and impersonally. But as a biologist I'm interested in preserving all endangered species. I hope my work lends support for current efforts to reintroduce the wolf into areas that were once its natural habitat. That's the practical application."

"Bring back the wolves, huh? Into what areas?" Paul asked, and Brittany was gratified to see that he had obviously been listening to her closely.

"Wyoming, Montana and Colorado," she replied.

Paul gave a low whistle. "I'm sure Right and Truth are on your side. But you'll have a helluva time convincing ranchers and farmers of that," he retorted. But now Brittany could tell he was intrigued by the sparkle in his eyes.

"I know. That's why I hope the bones I've collected can speak convincingly for me. I believe the lab people will prove that of the seven moose who died during this past winter and were consumed by wolves only one was actually killed outright by them.''

"That's amazing! I would have guessed that at least half were," Paul exclaimed. "Why the unlucky one?"

"Some herd animals are simply going to get killed," Brittany conceded. "I don't pretend that wolf nature is other than what it is, and seen through a wolf's eyes a herd animal is perfect prey: big, slow and stupid. Sometimes wolves will even kill for sport, just like people. But that's not happening on this island. Here the wolves are just barely hanging on. Yes, those Western ranchers and wool growers will lose a very few young and healthy animals to wolves. But overall, the advantages of having wolves in the world certainly outweigh the disadvantages.''

"Good luck on convincing ranchers of that," Paul said, but his voice wasn't really flippant, and the expression on his sensitive, handsome face remained thoughtful.

Indeed, several minutes passed before Paul changed the subject. Then he raised his hand, the way Brittany's third graders used to do, and made an equally familiar request: "Please, teacher, can I get up now to go to the bathroom?"

"May I ask you something personal?" Paul inquired of Brittany on the following day.

She looked up to find his gaze on her, curiosity run rampant in his deep-set black eyes.

Cautiously she considered his request. "I guess so."

"When I gathered up our trash, right before the supply boat came last week, I found a wedding invitation that you'd thrown away," he informed her. As Brittany gave a start, Paul added hastily, "I wasn't prying, it was there right on top. Anyway, I've been wondering if you did marry the guy, Howard something-or-other, or was the wedding called off?"

Oddly Paul's mention of Howard today caused not even a quiver of pain inside of Brittany. "No, I didn't get married," she answered quietly. "I got jilted. Howard called off the wedding."

Paul waited, and Brittany girded herself to continue.

"Howard had recently met somebody else. She was the daughter of a senior partner in his law firm. He finally told me about Myrna a week before the wedding. Now, may I ask you something personal?"

"I guess so." As Paul repeated her phrase his voice was just as cautious as Brittany's had been.

"I've often wondered what happened to your Peg. Dr. Foster told me only that she was in an accident." Brittany drew a breath and forged ahead. "But I haven't known what kind of accident or even where it happened."

Paul glanced down, studying his pajama sleeve. "Peg died in a car wreck," he said, his face impassive. "It was on a routine trip back to the mainland to see our relatives. Several times a year we'd visit them for a weekend and buy clothes or other supplies we needed. On this particular Saturday afternoon I took Chad to the movies and that got him out of Peg's way because she and her sister, Vicky, wanted to go to a large shopping mall about ten miles away."

Paul's voice was matter of fact, like Brittany's had been. "Peg drove Vicky's car on the trip. She'd always liked to drive, but, of course, living here on the island for so many years she rarely got a chance. Maybe her driving skills were rusty or maybe she simply panicked when a car pulled out from a side road in front of them. Anyway, Peg swerved too sharply trying to miss it, and the car flipped over and landed in a ditch. Vicky crawled out with barely a scratch, but Peg was killed instantly."

"Oh. Thanks for telling me," Brittany replied and reached over automatically to plump up the pillows on the bed that had once been Peg's. She didn't know what else to say except, "I'm sorry." But at least Paul's reaction today was much less intense than on that night when Brittany had been newly arrived. At that time every mention of Peg had obviously brought him an acute wave of pain.

* * *

Perhaps inevitably in the growing intimacy of confidences exchanged, their talk deepened. Slowly facts gave way to feelings.

"I knew something was very wrong as soon as I heard Howard's voice. I went icy cold while he stalled and stalled until I almost pulled the phone out of the wall waiting for him to tell—"

"The phone?" Paul said explosively. "You mean he didn't even have the guts to tell you face-to-face?"

"Guts aren't Howard's strong suit. Anyway, he had a long and obviously rehearsed speech about how he hadn't meant to fall in love with Myrna, but she was so cute and they had so much in common. But he hadn't meant it to happen and he was really, truly sorry—"

"He had that much right. He's about as sorry a man as I've ever heard of!"

"Paul, are you going to let me tell you this dreary story or not?" Brittany demanded, although secretly his outraged responses pleased her and helped validate her own feelings. "Anyway, you haven't heard the final extent of Howard's gall. Because he wound up this conversation by saying how he really truly hoped we could still be friends! I'm in absolute shock—I mean like walking zombie—and Howard wants us to stay friends. I barely even remember the whole next month. I just felt like the world had ended."

"I was a basket case after she died. Almost a Section Eight. Drinking. Fights. Arguments with policemen that *I* started. I didn't care, you see, except for Chad. I did care about him, but otherwise I could have hung it all up. I never knew, either, when I'd suddenly explode and start yelling or cursing people. I lost control in a way I never had before...."

"Shock carried me through those first few weeks. I kept busy writing a nice note to accompany each wedding gift I returned. By then there were over a hundred to mail back."

Paul, listening to Brittany, gave a low whistle.

"After that, I didn't get angry. Not even when I sent the ring back to Howard. I just got depressed," Brittany confided. "Most days I didn't even want to crawl out of bed. I stayed that way for weeks and months, too."

"'Depression is anger gone underground,'" Paul quoted.

"Is it?" Brittany shifted in her chair, and the frisky puppy in her lap scampered over her stomach and tried to scale her chest.

"At least that's what Dr. Freud said," Paul added, watching Brittany sympathetically. He knew her well enough now to know that she was serious, intense, sensitive and proud—the absolute worse kind of woman to be jilted since she wouldn't—couldn't—just blow off rejection. She would feel any failure keenly and take it straight to heart.

Of course, it was Paul's personal opinion that Brittany was well rid of Howard Pierson. He sounded like the kind of person who could benefit the world by stepping in front of a train. But to a relatively young and unsophisticated woman, as Brittany had been at the time, it was easy to see how she'd been swept away by a rich, handsome man with all the right social connections.

As Brittany plucked the puppy off her chest, then flashed her quick winsome smile, Paul found himself harboring the kindly hope that she was almost over Howard by now.

"Angry doesn't even hack it. Rage comes a lot closer," Paul could admit at last.

"Rage at death?" Brittany asked, listening to Paul as raptly as he'd listened to her.

"Death. Life. God. Who knows?" he said raggedly. "At least I'm finally starting to get a handle on it. Understand it. Part of the rage is purely on her behalf. Damn it all, Peg didn't deserve to die! She should have lived her full life span, seen Chad grow up and marry and make her a grandmother."

"And the other part?" Brittany probed.

"That's me. My own life. See, she was the only thing I ever had that worked. Our marriage, I mean. Nothing else has ever come together for me, not even in childhood. My dad was always off working somewhere after his job at the auto factory ended. Then, by the time I was ten, he had his first bout with cancer. It was a long, drawn-out ordeal. Next, my mother and Steve, her present husband, fell into each other's arms—and, incidentally, straight into bed—about a year before they should have. I walked in on them when I was sixteen."

"Oh! That would be especially rough for an adolescent," Brittany said, wincing.

"I tried to get away from them and ran smack into Vietnam, which, believe me, was no fun experience. Later, I wrote two books—good books, I knew—but they weren't commercial enough to be successful. So I guess I'd already built up a pretty good head of steam because here I was—am—heading into my late thirties, and nothing at all to show for it. Peg and I didn't own a house or a car. We hardly had any money in the bank. We still lived out here on a small stipend, like poor college students. But at least we had each other, and we were good together and then there was Chad, too."

Paul stopped and looked away, his face dark with brooding, but Brittany, who understood him now as she never had before, was able to finish his story. "So when you lost your wife—when the one thing you had that mattered so much and was really successful was suddenly gone—no wonder you wanted to tear down the whole world."

"With my bare hands, and set it on fire. That's just how bitter I was."

Brittany found that now it eased her to talk about what she'd gone through. And Paul was such a good and attentive listener that all those words and feelings, pressed down and long dammed up—things she couldn't tell her family or Amber or even Dr. Ingrid Jensen—she could discuss in this isolated setting with a man who also understood both love and pain.

"Yes, a big church wedding in Detroit. It was just six weeks after he was supposed to have married me. At least

Howard's parents were vastly relieved, I'm sure. They always thought I was all wrong for him," Brittany related.

Even as she talked she felt again that surprising sense of distance, of almost noninvolvement, as if this had happened long, long ago or even in a movie or book rather than being a fairly recent personal experience.

"Why did the Piersons think you were wrong for their son?" Paul asked with his usual interest.

"Oh..." Brittany gave a self-deprecating shrug. "They were important society types and I...well, I naturally didn't fit in."

"Why not?" Paul asked quietly. "What's wrong with you?"

To her further surprise, Brittany felt herself coloring under Paul's intent gaze. His face was composed, but something flickered in his eyes and that something drew forth a response she'd never planned to utter.

"Just look at me. I'm too...too big to ever be fashionable. I was also too much the outdoor type to suit their taste. You know, Paul, I've never told anyone this but once I overheard Mrs. Pierson refer to me as 'the Scandinavian milkmaid.'" Momentarily Brittany tensed as she remembered the old wound. Then she shrugged, ridding herself of it. "It was apt, I guess. I'm Scandinavian and I did grow up on a dairy farm."

But Paul's face twisted angrily at Howard's mother's words. "It's a damned put-down and you know it!" Then he described Mrs. Pierson's probable ancestry with words that made Brittany's ears burn.

"Oh, I don't care now. But then—"

"Because," Paul deliberately interrupted her, "you are an absolutely gorgeous woman!"

For the next two days Brittany floated on his compliment. Even when Paul, who was recovering more slowly than he liked, turned irascible since he was bored and unbelievably weary of being bed-bound, Brittany remained tranquil, her own mercurial disposition as smooth as glass. "An absolutely gorgeous woman!"

She fed Paul eggs, beef broth and milk-based puddings to strengthen him. Read aloud to him when his eyes grew tired. She even found a deck of cards to entertain him and let him beat her at gin rummy. And every time Brittany felt Paul looking at her she felt again that warm rush of pleasure, heard once again his astounding and extravagant compliment: "An absolutely gorgeous woman!"

But then Paul made a serious miscalculation on the first day he got out of bed.

"Is there enough hot water for me to have a long soak and scrub my dirty head?" he called to her that afternoon when she came in from the woods.

Brittany, stepping into the doorway, saw Paul drag a disdainful hand over his hair and beard.

"Paul, you sh—" Brittany stopped herself before she could utter the dreaded "shouldn't" word. She'd been saying it for days, but a glance at Paul's stiff face and set jaw announced that he was ready to stage a rebellion.

As well he might. His recuperation was coming along nicely now, and it was only her fears that had kept him from bolting straight out of bed yesterday. Because she had nursed him faithfully, and he was so grateful, Paul had been trying not to tangle with her or take exception to her opinions. But now the poor man understandably wanted a long soak in the tub instead of a sponge bath or a one-minute shower, and he wanted a shampoo. Why not? Wouldn't she?

"Yes, there's plenty of hot water," Brittany said agreeably and made herself smile.

"Great!" Paul carolled. Immediately he took a healthy bound out of bed and headed toward the bathroom.

That's when Brittany discovered that his pajama top was unbuttoned. It swung open across his chest, exposing his thick mat of jet-black chest hair. Despite its manly, robust appearance, Brittany knew it was actually baby-fine and incredibly soft. And his pajamas bottoms—hers, actually—rode low over his narrow hips, held up only by his sharply protruding hipbones. His torso was flat and Indian-brown.

Brittany suddenly found herself swallowing hard, aware of a physical attraction that was the last thing she expected. Oh sure, Paul was quite a beautifully built man, as she'd had ample opportunity to discover, but his body hadn't affected her like this before. Now, though, as he radiated renewed vitality Brittany noticed his broad shoulders and forgot about how thin he was.

"Mind if I borrow your shampoo and razor?" he called back to her.

"No, help your—" The bathroom door closed before she could finish, that's how eager he was to soap himself from head to heels. Immediately water began to roar and, over its cascade, Brittany could hear the blithe sound of Paul's carefree whistling.

"What's he going to shave?" she asked herself. Then her mind went running off on a different tangent as she envisioned his hard brown body, which would be naked by now.

Thoughts like that were too dangerous to entertain. Swiftly Brittany turned away and hurried to the kitchen, where she started making beef stew for dinner.

Ten minutes later Paul called to her again. "Brittany, I've got to have some clothes to put on."

She rinsed her hands hastily, then hurried back to the bedroom to see what he wanted to wear. Probably not pajamas, although she certainly intended to suggest that Paul lie back down and rest after the exertions of his bath and shampoo. On the other hand, she had slacks and a sweater, underwear, socks and shoes waiting if Paul reacted as she suspected.

She found him standing in the middle of the bedroom, his back to the door, wearing only a towel knotted around his waist.

Brittany's senses swirled at the sight of all that bare male skin. His legs and arms, while bony, were also long and straight. But he was exposing himself to a chill by standing in a draft.

"Paul, you shouldn't . . ." Brittany was about to suggest he wear her warm robe momentarily when he swung back around and she was stunned into silence.

Paul's beard was completely gone! Even his raffish moustache had been dramatically trimmed so his mouth was more cleanly delineated. And with his lean jawline and a just slightly dimpled chin, Paul was far more handsome than she had ever dared to dream.

"You . . . you shaved!" Brittany whispered.

"Yeah, I told you I was going to," Paul replied carelessly.

"I—" For a moment she felt absolutely lost for words. I knew he would look wonderful, but I didn't know he would look this wonderful, she found herself thinking. Then at the sight of his long bare feet, words rushed past her lips impulsively.

"My God, are you trying to kill yourself? Running around barefoot when you've been so sick," she cried shrilly. "Get back in bed right now!"

Too late she saw his astonished expression followed by an imperious lift of his black eyebrows and, once again, Brittany retreated as she had the first day she'd met him. "Please, Paul," she pleaded.

That stopped the scathing remark he was about to make. Although his eyes still looked dark with warning, his lips gradually began to curve in a rueful smile.

"Hey, calm down. It's all right, Brittany." Gently his hands went out to restrain her, for she was about to drape her heavy white robe over him.

Brittany went very, very still as they touched. Her fingers loosened until the robe slithered from her hands. She saw Paul register her exceptional stillness and silence.

Even after that, she still didn't see his warm hard hug coming. No, not until she had actually been swept up close and tight in his strong, sinewy arms—not until she was enveloped in his heady maleness and staring at his chiseled features. She felt so treacherously weak then that his bare chest and the strength of his legs supported her. Until Paul, too, simply let go and they fell backward onto the bed together.

His mouth found hers, swiftly and unerringly. The warm full lips, no longer overshadowed by his moustache, pressed

firmly yet softly against hers until Brittany's senses swam at
the spontaneous sweetness of it all.

Immediately she felt a rush of response, as surprising as
his kiss in its urgency and compulsion. Partly it was a melting, yielding sensation and partly it was reciprocation in a
caress of her own for, almost without knowing what she was
doing, Brittany wound her arms up and around Paul's neck.

Then she felt safely enfolded in both his softness and
strength. The softness was his now uncovered skin that
brushed against her hands and bare lower arms. But
strength lay in his supporting frame, in all the bones and
muscles within.

Paul smelled delicious, and quite hauntingly familiar,
since he had just used Brittany's various toiletries. The her-
bal-scented shampoo, oatmeal bath soap and wintergreen
toothpaste stimulated her sense of smell, making him seem
known and comfortably familiar. But more arousing by far
was the base aroma beneath, an innate freshness characteristic of a clean, young male.

Before Brittany could notice anything else about him, the
kiss changed suddenly and dramatically. Paul's lips parted,
and his tongue, rough and tasty, was parting her lips as well.
Tenderly he outlined the shape of her lips before slipping
inside. Sweet tenderness vanished abruptly with a series of
electric inner jolts as desire, hot and richly exciting, made
Brittany's heart leap into a newly accelerated rhythm.
Flames shot up, sweeping along her arteries and veins like
brushfire. After the emotional drought and deprivation of
her past year, those flames threatened to burn away all
remnants of her logic and common sense.

Brittany wasn't sure she really wanted to feel like this. It
was just too...too ardent and threatening. But all the fright
lay exclusively in her mind, not in her body, which still
yearned to wind around him, to envelop and consume the
urgent male power that she felt aroused and pressing now
against the juncture of her thighs.

A low whimper broke from her at the unresolved con-
flict. How could she bear—dare—to get drawn into another deep and passionate relationship? And somehow

Brittany knew that with Paul's intensity matching and possibly even exceeding her own there could simply be no other. What the combination offered was more dramatic and flamboyant, as well as more breathlessly magical, than anything she'd ever imagined. But how could she dare to hope and care so much again only to awaken on a cold empty morning and find that she'd been slammed back again into stark reality where anything too good to be true always was.

Loving and losing Howard Pierson had taken more away from her than just a mass of unfulfilled dreams. It had shaken her womanly confidence deeply, leaving her frightened and insecure because she knew now there were no miracles. She had to ask herself what this man wanted of her. The answer was that she might easily discover she'd just been used once again. Supposedly it happened to a lot of women like her, the male assumption being that big tall blondes could always look after themselves.

She went rigid against Paul at the thought, and slowly he drew back, too. But his mouth left Brittany's by slow degrees, as if reluctant to depart, and for a long moment he simply buried his hot face against her neck. At the sound of his rapid breathing and its searing warmth on her skin Brittany almost spun back out of control again.

Because Paul was completely naked now. The towel that had been knotted around his waist was lost somewhere on the bed. Brittany, aware of his every movement, felt Paul lever himself up and away from her, felt his hand grope out to find the towel. Automatically her hand searched, too, as she lay otherwise flat and unmoving. Even half paralyzed by surprise, Brittany still wanted to help Paul.

Almost together their hands closed over the nubby fabric, then their fingers brushed and tangled as he retrieved the towel at the same moment Brittany tried to hand it to him. She yielded and Paul snatched it away, then swung around on the bed to give Brittany a flashing glance of his slim olive-skinned buttocks and straight spine.

"Clothes?" he muttered, his voice clipped.

Brittany welcomed the opportunity to hide her now-flaming face. "I'll get them," she cried. She jumped up off the bed and escaped through the door, closing it firmly behind her.

My God, what had got into him? she wondered as reaction set in and her knees began to tremble. Her next thought was equally predictable: My God, what was I doing?

Earlier she had hung Paul's clothes in the living room closet, not wanting him to see them and be tempted out of bed too soon. Now her hands shook, too, as she snatched them off hangers. She knocked on the bedroom door, only to marvel at her sudden formality when she had already seen Paul unclothed on several occasions.

But apparently modesty had been reactivated in him, too. The door opened a crack and his hand shot through the opening to seize his clothes.

"I'll bring your shoes and socks now," Brittany murmured to a man she could no longer see.

"Just set 'em inside."

She obeyed. By then Paul was coughing again, and Brittany stiffened at the frightening sound. At least this wasn't his tight racking cough of previous days. Anyway, it was too late to fuss at him now.

It was also too late to restrain him from leaving, Brittany knew, nor would she try.

She retreated into the kitchen, taking refuge in ordinary chores, even welcoming a sink full of dishes, to fill the next several minutes.

"Look..."

The sound of Paul's voice made Brittany freeze even as her heart started racing madly once again.

"Yes?" she said as impersonally as she could.

"I'm grateful for everything you did for me, Brittany."

"I know," she whispered.

"I'm sorry I got carried away. I certainly chose a poor way to express my gratitude," Paul went on painfully.

Gratitude? she thought incredulously, giving her simmering beef stew an entirely unnecessary stir. Those kisses were gratitude?

"I'll never be able to thank you enough—"

"That's all right," she interrupted, her heart swelling now, bruised by pride and pain. As the emotions all rushed back over Brittany, she found it hard to think, much less talk clearly.

"I want to apologize," Paul went on, misery filling his voice. He sounded as if this conversation was about as much fun as a root canal.

"Look, Paul, let's forget it!" Brittany exclaimed, still not turning around. She just couldn't face him yet. Paul was braver at this than she.

"Yes, I think we should."

Now she heard relief in his voice. Relief and something else? No, of course not! She was mistaken about that. Paul didn't want to start anything any more than she did.

Brittany heard him start toward the front door, then he stopped again. "Thanks for helping with Ivy, too. I don't know what would have happened to us if you hadn't—"

"Paul, it's all right!"

Brittany winced at her shrill, emphatic voice. But, my God, wouldn't he ever leave and let her be alone with her embarrassment and dismay? She also needed to sort out those more subtle and complex feelings about why she'd responded to him so rapturously or why something no more serious than a few hot kisses had also scared the daylights out of her.

Paul left. As her ears measured his tread away from her Brittany's hands squeezed the soapy sponge she held convulsively.

Paul stopped in the living room to pull on his jacket, scarf and gloves. Brittany heard the door squeak open, then close with the sound of finality.

Suddenly, without warning, tears were running down her face and splashing into the dishwater.

For more than a week her mind, heart and energies had all been concentrated on healing him. Paul had been the universe around which she had orbited, and it had felt good to care about someone else again, despite her worry and fear on his behalf. At Paul's bedside she had relearned the experience of feeling needed and necessary.

Now he was gone and she was all alone once again.

"Brittany?"

She jumped because she hadn't heard Paul come inside. Three absolutely awful days had passed when they had managed to avoid each other quite successfully. Twice Brittany had heard Paul stirring around in the kitchen; indeed the sounds had awakened her, and his coughing had continued to trouble her. But she'd lain still and quiet, having discovered that he would leave just as soon as possible.

At least Paul no longer left her a mess to clean up and Brittany knew that this demonstrated both his gratitude and his regret. Perversely she even missed his previous messes. At least being mad at Paul gave her something to think about, something vibrant to feel. How still and quiet the cottage was!

She missed him.

Brittany also missed Ivy and the small half-wolves, too. The puppies' eyes should open any day now, and she wished she could be around when they did.

She also missed poking around the lighthouse. Missed climbing the spiral stairs up to the lantern room and savoring the spectacular view once she was there.

Sometimes Brittany daydreamed, wondering what Paul would do if she walked boldly over to the lighthouse, called his name and asked to see Ivy and her pups....

Now he was here, standing right behind her as she sat at the kitchen table eating a sandwich for supper, the exact same thing she'd had for lunch.

"Look, Brittany, I think we need to talk." Paul's voice sounded a little desperate.

She could almost feel him pushing against her silent resistance, wanting to be friends again, only she still couldn't manage that. Hastily Brittany reached for the map she'd planned to study while she ate. "I don't think we do, Paul. Everything's fine with me. Isn't it with you?"

Ignoring her bland question he dropped down into the chair directly opposite her.

Brittany couldn't help admiring his forthrightness. She glanced up and then she just couldn't seem to look away. Paul had continued to shave and his face looked so much younger without a dark bush covering his cheeks and chin. A lock of black hair falling over his forehead emphasized the youthful look. He seemed fit and very handsome, and Brittany thought he'd improved even more since she'd seen him last.

"No, everything isn't fine with me," Paul said, contradicting his physical appearance. "I've missed seeing you, Brittany, and I'm sorry I offended you. I feel as if I've lost my best friend! Honestly I don't know what came over me or why I—"

"Paul, please!" she cut in painfully. Just mentioning that scene in the bedroom still made Brittany's insides ache. She didn't know why. She still didn't really know why.

"Look, I think I know why you're disturbed," Paul continued, ignoring her plea. "Why we both are," he corrected.

Brittany couldn't resist staring at him in surprise. Maybe Paul actually did know something that as yet she hadn't figured out. But his eyes, as restless and changeable as ever, offered no clues.

"For myself, I know good and well I don't want to get involved with anyone," Paul said emphatically. "Maybe some day but definitely not now. It hasn't been long enough since Peg died. And I have a couple of other very pressing matters as you know, like my kid and that book I still can't seem to finish. I really wasn't trying to start up something with you, and I hope you'll feel better now that you know it."

Paul's words didn't make Brittany feel any better. Rather, they made her feel infinitely worse. Indeed, it was as if she'd always known he would make this particular and meaningful speech, that's why she'd been braced for it. Any and all compliments he'd paid her ("You are an absolutely gorgeous woman!") were actually meaningless.

"You surely don't want to get involved with anyone, either, do you, Brittany?" Paul pressed.

She stared back down at the top of the table, her hand groping almost blindly toward the detailed map of Isle Svenson as if her salvation lay there somewhere. She had honestly meant to study it and try to determine the few remaining areas of the island that she hadn't searched for a wolf's den. Only her thoughts had gone meandering off on a tangent, the way they always did these days.

"No, of course I don't want to get involved with anyone," Brittany responded automatically. "I want to finish my study here, write my thesis, get my master's."

"You planned to get married once," Paul pointed out.

"I know, but I've come to my senses now. What do I want with marriage?" Brittany retorted hotly.

A husband? A home and kids? How ridiculous to think an independent single woman would want a lot more work and bother or a lot of people underfoot. What Brittany couldn't understand was why her throat had suddenly knotted up as if something she'd just swallowed was choking her. Lies perhaps?

Instead of dwelling on those feelings she began grimly to spread out her map. "Look, you could do me a big favor, Paul," she said, changing the subject deliberately. "Would you please think back to the places where you once saw wolves on this island. Anywhere you saw them. Finding a den is the single, most important thing to me now. I need to be able to verify new wolf births."

Paul sighed, then reached for the map. "All right," he said grudgingly. "The first time I saw a wolf was on an overcast day. I remember because it almost blended into the mist. Ivy and I were . . . here, I think. Or maybe it was further along . . . say, about here. . . ."

Brittany fumbled for a pen to mark each spot that Paul indicated.

Chapter Twelve

Brittany's boots crunched through the thin layer of snow and sank into the damp soil below. Surely this was the place that Paul had marked on her map.

So she stopped, bent down and waited quietly, hoping against hope that this really was where Paul had once seen a large silvery wolf.

It looked like a wolves' den, all right. A solid earthen embankment lay before her that could easily have been tunneled through to create a chamber where five or six baby wolves would be stirring about and yipping right now. At least Brittany devoutly hoped that new wolves had been born this spring; hoped, too, that the wolf packs on the island, which were estimated to be two, had not lost too many of their members since the wolf population here on Isle Svenson was already quite precariously balanced.

Alas, it wasn't only elderly moose carcasses that Brittany had found. Indeed, as the deeper snows from the long winter had melted, the sun also uncovered the bones of three wolves who had died. One had succumbed from a broken leg, the injury probably acquired in a fight. But Brittany wasn't at all sure that the other two hadn't simply starved. Although their bones when analyzed back at the College of the Upper Peninsula should tell the story, one thing was already apparent: The moose were thriving and the wolves were not. So much for the myth of vicious, rapacious predator and tragic, helpless prey. Young vigorous animals were just not readily killed. Male moose didn't have their elaborate racks of antlers solely for decoration. And mother moose could also fight off attacks to their offspring.

When humans felt threatened they defended themselves by more subtle means. With a sigh Brittany shifted her position since her leg muscles were starting to cramp from cold. Slowly she raised her head, wishing the thin wintry sun could strike her face. Spring was flirting with them again, but now she was too wary to believe its promise.

Paul probably was, too, although Brittany couldn't very well speak for someone she hadn't seen in a whole week. Yes, Paul definitely blew warm, then cold, just like the Great Lakes' weather.

Yesterday he'd even tried to leave the island, and without a word to her, either. The sound of his runabout had awakened Brittany as Paul took it out into Lake Superior, and she had pulled her pillow over her ears in anger.

"You fool!" she'd muttered to Paul fiercely.

There was still entirely too much ice for him to dare leave the island in so small a craft, a fact Paul had obviously soon conceded. Because less than ten minutes after Brittany had covered her face and even shed a furious tear or two she had heard the motor of Paul's boat come putt-putting back.

Of course, Paul wouldn't have gone very far away or stayed gone many hours, Brittany realized belatedly. Not with Ivy and her puppies needing his solicitous care.

I really understood him much too well, Brittany thought despondently, knowing why Paul was spooked and behaving as he had. Hadn't he admitted he was afraid to get involved with her? And didn't she feel exactly the same way? So why was she taking his attitude personally? Brittany wondered and could arrive at no good answer. Because she still felt rejected and resentful.

Unconsciously a sigh escaped her. Oh God, what a mess! What a really awful mess! Just when it seemed that their relationship had smoothed out, becoming warm, comfortable and friendly, she and Paul had suddenly found themselves kissing hungrily, clutched in each other's arms.

Had two people ever made a worse mistake? Brittany didn't think so as she slipped down even deeper in conifer cover, hoping to conceal herself from any sharp-eyed wolves. Although she'd spent every day lately checking out each site Paul had marked, so far Brittany had drawn a blank. This place, too, for all its favorable appearance at the side of a brush-covered hill, looked as if it would come up another big fat zero.

For just a moment, though, Brittany wistfully visualized how a wolf's den would appear. Although wolves sometimes used the dens built by foxes, badgers or other animals they also dug their own, often more than one. They took that precaution in case one den was discovered; they could then move their young into the other.

A tunnel, sometimes as long as thirty feet, always led inside to the birthing chamber where the baby wolves lived for their first three weeks. The tunnel was also carefully constructed to slope upward, which prevented rain from seeping into that all-important chamber.

A wolf litter might vary from five to fourteen, although six was average. Also, the pups might be quite different in color. So-called gray wolves had been known to have brown and even solid black pups.

Lord, I would settle for any color at all, if I could just see them! Brittany thought passionately.

How long had she been here now, watching and waiting? An hour? Two? Brittany peeked at her watch and was aghast to see that only fifteen minutes had passed. Of course, this waiting game when you were highly skeptical of results was about as exciting as watching paint dry, to use Paul's expression.

She muffled another sigh and bent down to knead her cramped thighs. If she didn't stand up soon and stretch she might have to contend with strained, sore muscles tonight. Maybe she would have been better off, after all, to have sat on the cold damp ground and braved pleurisy or galloping grippe.

And then, just at that boring, frustrating moment when Brittany felt infinitely discouraged and weary, a large silvery animal and then a second smaller one came silently out of their den.

"Paul! Paul, are you up here? I've found a wolf's den! On the side of the hill! It was the last place you checked off for me. And I've already seen the male—he's a big, husky magnificent guy. His mate came out, too, for just a minute. She's flat-bellied—not pregnant—so I think she's got pups stashed inside..."

Brittany's excited flow of chatter stopped and disappointment streaked through her when she heard no reply.

"Paul?" she called again, then, "Ivy!"

"Woof!" barked Ivy and a couple of staccato yelps came from her pups. Then Ivy appeared at the door of the storeroom where she and her family now dwelled. But Paul was gone.

Maybe he was at the cottage. Brittany was still so excited by the discovery of the wolf's den that she literally had to share the news with him or burst. Maybe her conduct wasn't very professional, but hadn't Dr. Foster warned her not to count on finding a wolf's den? On Isle Svenson they'd seemed particularly well concealed, he'd stressed. But now Brittany had gotten lucky, thanks to Paul.

She left the lighthouse and dashed along the path that led to the back of the cottage. She leaped the steps and came skidding through the storm door, then the inner door as well.

Later Brittany would realize that by taking the back path and being so preoccupied, so excited and elated, she had failed to see the sleek white-and-teak cruiser tied up at the dock. Of course, in her delight and eagerness to find Paul, she could probably have missed seeing anything smaller than the Queen Mary.

As Brittany rushed into the deserted kitchen she saw a few dishes in the sink to encourage her. He was here! Excited all over again, she flung open the door that led to the rustic living room. "Paul, guess wh—" she began.

Abruptly the next words froze on her lips. Paralyzed and speechless Brittany stared at the couple across the room who turned in surprise at her precipitous entry.

Paul stared straight back at Brittany, his black eyes wide and his arms wrapped tightly around a shapely, pretty brunette. She still embraced Paul, too. But even that wasn't the worst, because when Brittany had first tumbled through the door the two of them had been kissing.

For weeks Paul had written scarcely a useful line on his long overdue novel, and today scarcely promised to be any better. That's why he'd finally tossed in the towel and sent out an SOS to Vanessa Davidson.

His present unhappy state wasn't at all like that mind-numb daze that had followed in the wake of Peg's death. It certainly wasn't the same as the writer's block born out of anger, resentment and—yes—curiosity, too, where Brittany was concerned.

Now Paul felt awake and alive but immensely aggravated and frustrated, too. There was an ache inside him from lack and a longing for he-knew-not-exactly-what. Being naturally introspective, aware of himself and in tune with his emotions, Paul could spot a definite difference.

It felt as if, during his illness, something more significant than the merely physical had quietly healed inside him. He remembered something else now, remembered crying out to Peg's ghost to "Go away!"

Poof! Peg's ghost had promptly departed, since even in spirit form she was just as agreeable and cooperative as she'd been in life. Only then Paul had felt guilty for sending Peg off when he still wasn't over missing her. He felt guilty because Brittany was unhappy, although Paul didn't know what was bothering her—just that undoubtedly it was his fault. So he felt guilty, too, because he had initiated their embrace when he'd reached out and held her, kissed her, and suddenly wanted her so much.

Paul didn't know why he'd done it, either, except that at the time nothing in his life had ever felt quite so instinctive or so utterly, completely natural.

But, God, he was sick to death of feeling guilty! And he hadn't even started yet on those more logical and reasonable causes for present remorse, like leaving his son stuck with relatives and disappointing the New York editor who had hung in with him for so long.

No wonder he never answered his mother's letters, Paul thought savagely. Didn't he have her to thank for instilling this overly developed sense of responsibility and guilt in him? Maybe someday he'd get around to telling Gina just what he thought about it, too.

Maybe someday he'd also tell Brittany what he thought about her rebuff to his latest attempt at friendliness. Just thinking of it made Paul grind his teeth in impotent rage, but all the while he hurt inside, too, a strange, completely alien sort of hurt.

Brittany. A thousand recent memories from his illness threatened to swamp him. Now that his more dominant memories of aches, coughs and fever were fading, the quieter memories of that time returned. Paul recalled the coolness of her hands stroking his hot forehead and the silkiness of her hair when strands of it drooped down—usually at night—and brushed his face. He remembered a scent uniquely her own, as well as the reassuring murmur of her voice and that grave blueness of her eyes.

He remembered her sponging him off and how once, only half conscious, he'd reached out quite boldly and touched her breast. Even now Paul's palm seemed to tingle at the memory. He hadn't seen the breast, not swathed as it was by a layer of flannel nightgown, but his hand still remembered its imprint and his mind could supply lavish mental images guaranteed to drive him slowly crazy.

Dammit, he'd told her the exact honest truth. He didn't want to get involved with anyone now because there were too many problems. Vast urgent problems of his livelihood, now next to nil, loomed up in Paul's mind as well as the needs of his motherless child.

Yes, the timing for romance was definitely all wrong, even if he'd had the heart for it. Paul suspected that he didn't, not with a difficult, proud, often-prickly woman who had been jilted just a year ago and still obviously carried wounds from the experience. Brittany would naturally find trust and faith in men rather hard to come by.

The longer you lived, the more of life's scars you acquired, Paul reflected. That's what had been so great about his relationship with Peg. They'd started fresh, back when love was a brand-new discovery; when hope, trust and optimism in the future and in each other came as easily to them as breathing.

Certainly there had been little risk for Paul in such an innocent and unconditional love as Peg's. Or in one so—dare he say it—traditional. But there was a great deal of risk involved with someone like Brittany. Not only was she older, with more experience and more scars. She would also have definite expectations that Paul wasn't sure he could meet, as well as a viable career. Unlike Peg, Brittany would not be inclined to put his work first, nor should she.

Actually, Paul found a career-oriented woman interesting and even exciting at this stage in his life. But he'd have a hell of a lot to learn about shared labor and equal opportunity. Things he'd missed learning since Peg had always encouraged him to go right on living in his ivory tower, in more ways than one.

Oh, the hell with it! Paul thought suddenly, his mind feeling weary and his emotions still a riddle. Right now he needed change, excitement and company other than Brittany's cool silences or Ivy's pups' yelps.

Yesterday he had tried to take out his small boat, thinking that a morning spent over on Catt Island would help break his monotonous routine. He could get his hair trimmed, eat lunch at Sally's Cafe and visit with the locals. But very quickly Paul had encountered enough ice in Superior to turn him back.

By today he felt absolutely desperate for human companionship and conversation. So what the hell was stopping him? Nothing but false pride. Abruptly he turned and hurried downstairs to his radio. Then he was rapidly broadcasting his own personal SOS. "This is the Isle Svenson Lighthouse calling Davidson Island. Come in, please, Trent or Vanessa."

The Davidsons not only came on the radio promptly. Since it was almost noon on Friday, when they frequently started their weekends, they came right over, enveloping Paul in warmth, friendship and good company. While their terrier, Boots, raced around and around Paul, barking a frenzied welcome, and small Jassie—Trent's nickname for their infant daughter, Jessica—jabbered nonstop and tried to pull Paul's hair, Trent punched Paul affectionately on the shoulder.

Vanessa, though, had yet to greet Paul in her own inimitable style, since she had her hands full carrying a hamper of food to the kitchen. Next, she relieved Trent of the picnic basket, slung over the same brawny arm that held his daughter.

"We forgot Jassie's diaper bag," Vanessa reminded her husband.

"I'll go back for it," Trent replied and tried to hand Jassie over to Paul. But the black-haired, blue-eyed child was definitely a Daddy's girl. As she started to wail, Trent swept her right back in resignation. "Okay, Jassie, come along."

Barking, Boots followed them out and that left Paul all alone with Vanessa, who was a lush and exotically dark beauty. Although many men had coveted Trent's wife, Paul had always only pretended to, being quite happy with his own. But now, when Vanessa hurled herself into Paul's arms, he—who had always enjoyed women—certainly wasn't going to push her away.

Anyway, even though their relationship was purely platonic, Paul always enjoyed smelling Vanessa's perfume.

"Poor baby!" she said, hugging Paul fiercely around his waist. "Having a tough day, are you?"

"This has been one of the worst," Paul replied honestly.

"I'm so glad you called us. Life can get rough," Vanessa noted, leaning back to peer up into Paul's face.

Vanessa probably understood his feelings even better than Trent, Paul realized, because she had been widowed once herself and severely depressed.

As understanding flowed between them and their arms tightened, Vanessa leaned up to plant a light kiss on Paul's lips.

She would probably have kissed him, anyway, for Vanessa was still very much the Southern belle, despite Trent having transplanted her so successfully to Michigan. Southern belles just tended to do a lot of hugging and kissing, thank goodness! Paul thought appreciatively.

But just try to convince a hard-headed, wintry Swede of that.

Because no sooner had Paul gratefully murmured, "I adore you" to his best friend's sweet wife than he suddenly found himself jerked away from Vanessa by a surprisingly strong hand. Found himself staring straight across into Brittany's now glacial eyes that gave a whole new meaning to the color ice-blue.

"You SOB!" Brittany snapped, only she used the actual words, and right after that she kicked Paul in the ankle just as hard as she could.

Brittany wasn't sure exactly what she'd said to him. She wasn't entirely sure what she'd done, either. But since her toes throbbed even in her sturdy boots and the sound of Paul's yell still echoed in her ears she thought she'd probably delivered a good kick.

When the red haze of rage had engulfed her, all Brittany could think of was that Paul was another glib, devious liar.

And just who was that petite and delicate-looking brunette wedged in his arms, the one who'd exclaimed, "Goodness gracious!" in a sickening drawl, consternation on her picture-pretty face.

The little witch is lucky I didn't pull out her hair strand by strand, Brittany thought savagely as she sailed through the front door and dashed down the steps. She reached the stone walk without knowing where she was headed, her vision obscured as crystal tears began to shimmer through the blood-red haze. So Paul didn't want to get involved, did he? With her, that's what he'd meant—the lying cheat!

But now she had made the consummate mistake of falling in love with him, Brittany realized.

"Hey!"

Abruptly Brittany found herself halted by a big, black-headed man with blue eyes who stood like a tank in her path. She blinked, recognizing Dr. Trent Davidson whom she'd met once before when he'd brought Paul's telegram out here. Now Trent carried an amazingly pretty baby of perhaps six or seven months who bore a striking resemblance to the brunette beauty inside.

One of Trent's large hands shot out and stopped Brittany's headlong flight, then he steadied her as her legs started to tremble.

"Hello, Brittany," he said pleasantly. "It's nice to see you again. Have you met my wife yet? Or is Paul, that fiend, still trying to make her his love-slave?" Trent finished with a laugh. Then his face changed as he noticed Brittany's own rage-clouded face, her tear-filled eyes and—finally—her dawning and daunting embarrassment.

That was Vanessa Davidson inside? Oh, my God! Brittany thought and closed her eyes, feeling wretched.

Paul had told Brittany quite a lot about the Davidsons when he'd been recovering from flu. His voice speaking of Vanessa had always been affectionate, even admiring, but it had held utterly no tones of the sort to make a woman pathologically jealous.

Now Brittany could only pray that the ground would open up and swallow her alive.

They were all so very nice about it, which only made her feel worse, deepening Brittany's already acute sense of shame and embarrassment. Even Paul, limping noticeably on the ankle she'd kicked with deadly precision, started acting nice to her after the first ten minutes when he'd been too enraged to speak.

As yet Brittany hadn't found the strength to look Paul in the eye. It was awful enough to realize she loved him, without also having to face the fact that she'd tried to maim him.

But Vanessa and Trent both acted as if it were perfectly normal for a grown, mature woman to jerk Paul around, screech insults about his mother, and then haul off and kick him. Indeed, Brittany wondered if any other two people on earth could have pulled it off, especially as Vanessa nonchalantly dismissed Brittany's stammered apology.

"Why, it was just a misunderstanding," Vanessa reassured Brittany, deftly diapering her daughter at the same time.

"I'm glad we'll finally get to visit with you, Brittany," Trent chimed in, ignoring Brittany's fiery face. "Just the other day I wondered if you'd found either of the island's wolf packs. You have? Today! That's wonderful."

"Honey, guess what?" Vanessa swung back to look at her husband. "Paul said that Ivy's pups are half-wolves. Or so Brittany says. Is that true, Brittany?"

"I think so. I haven't seen them recently," Brittany mumbled miserably from the depths of the chair where Trent had seated her.

"Can we go see them, Paul?" Vanessa asked.

"Sure. You lead the way, I'll limp along behind." Paul stopped speaking, aiming another wish-I-could-strangle-you glare in Brittany's direction.

Vanessa swept Jassie up in her arms. "Want to see some bow-wows, sugar?" she asked and the baby chortled.

Brittany found herself carried along with the three Davidsons who talked constantly while Jassie jabbered away in unison. These were undoubtedly the most verbal people Brittany had ever met. Of course, Southerners like Vanessa were known for being loquacious, but had Trent always been such a talker, too, or was he inspired by his wife?

They exclaimed even more over the plump, floppy-eared half-wolf pups whose slanted eyes, so characteristic of wolves, were wide open now. "That baby blue should gradually change to a yellow wolf's gaze," Brittany pointed out.

"I'd like to adopt one of those pups," Trent exclaimed, restraining Jassie who ooed and cooed at the other small beings.

"But would it make a good pet, honey, with Jassie crawling all about?" Vanessa said to her husband.

"Ask the expert," Trent suggested with a wave to Brittany.

Now she felt Vanessa's anxious gaze. "Wolves have been raised successfully in captivity, and many have become quite tame," Brittany informed them, still filled with anguished discomfort. "But some wolves retain a tendency to snap and bite, I've heard. Ivy's pups may not since they're half domesticated dog but I couldn't swear to it. Personally I think wild animals belong in the forest. These, of course, being only half-wolves, present a special problem."

"Chad's determined to have one," Paul cut in, and Brittany felt relieved that he had been able to walk unaided to the lighthouse.

"Before I take a wolf-dog off your hands I think I'd better see how Chad gets along with his," Trent decided. Then they returned to the cottage again to eat the lunch that Vanessa had brought. Although Brittany tried to excuse herself, the Davidsons insisted she stay.

During the meal they talked and kept on talking. Even Paul, normally talkative himself, could scarcely get a word in edgewise. At least Brittany found both Trent and Vanessa interesting as they described various developments in their respective careers. Also, their descriptions of the doings on their particular island were entertaining, especially when they discussed trying to bring their elderly housekeeper, Mrs. Pushka, into the present century when she thought computers and microwaves were direct works of the devil.

Vanessa and Trent tossed off quips, fed each other lines and utilized those gestures common to couples who were closely attuned and deeply in love. Brittany, having seen the way the Davidsons' eyes met, realized that this made her kick at Paul all the more ludicrous.

Finally the meal ended. Although Brittany was sure the food had been delicious she was unable to recall a thing she had eaten. Silently she retreated to the kitchen with Vanessa for clean up while the men went off to look at Paul's boat. It was making a strange racket, Paul had complained, and Trent wanted to check it out.

There weren't many dishes since they'd eaten off paper plates. "I'll wash, Brittany. I'm sure you're sick of doing dishes," Vanessa said warmly. "And unless you otherwise insist, I'll rest my mouth, too. Goodness, isn't it tiresome to be around people like us who talk all the time?"

"It wasn't today," Brittany answered grimly, reaching for a dish towel that hung nearby.

"Well, I could tell you were mortified—"

"I made a complete ass of myself," Brittany said in bitter self-condemnation.

"Oh, honey, we all have at one time or another. That's why Trent and I understand. You can't believe what total jackasses we were once. Why, we almost never got together!" Vanessa exclaimed.

"Oh?" Brittany asked, inviting Vanessa to continue.

But the beautiful, brown-eyed woman was too shrewd for that. "Tell me, Brittany, how long have you been out here? How much longer do you plan to stay? And when did you and Paul start falling in love?"

In the cold, dimly lighted boat house where water lapped rhythmically at the dock and Paul's boat bobbled up and down on its gentle waves, he was only midway through a long and vehement tirade to which Trent continued to listen patiently.

"I tell you that blond woman is trouble with legs! She's been absolutely infuriating from the first day she got here. She's either ice cold or blazing mad and she's got complexes and compulsions like you wouldn't believe. The kiss of death to any normal guy. I swear I'd sooner tangle with a wildcat than with a Valkyrie like Brittany Hag—"

"Wait a minute, Paul," Trent cut in mildly. "What did you just call her?"

"A Valkyrie. Oh, you know. One of those legendary blond goddesses who fly on horseback over the battlefields and wear breastplates and horned helmets. By God, I'm the one in need of a helmet, because with Brittany it's always a battlefield!"

"Oh," said Trent. "Didn't the Valkyrie choose men to carry off to Viking heaven—Valhalla?"

"That's about it. I guess I sound kind of morbid, don't I, Trent?"

"You think of flying off to paradise with a blond goddess? Somehow I don't exactly find that picture morbid." Trent laughed, fiddling with a screw that fit in the small craft's engine.

Paul fell silent for a minute. "Maybe not. But, God knows, I don't have anything to offer a woman except probably everything she doesn't want or need, including a lonely little kid who misses a mother. Anyway, Brittany got used to all the finer things chasing around with Howard Pierson of the Detroit Piersons. Ever heard of that rich, slick bastard?"

"I've heard of him," Trent replied. "An attorney, isn't he?"

"Yeah. He left Brittany waiting at the altar last year. That's why she's madder than hell at men. Next time she'll want someone even smarter, richer and better-looking to really rub Howard's nose in the mud," Paul continued, sunk in gloom.

"Did she say that?" Trent asked curiously, reinserting the same screw he'd removed.

"No. But that's bound to be the way she feels. Ripe for revenge. 'Hell hath no fury like a woman scorned.' Why, if we weren't stuck all alone out here she'd never give me a second glance," Paul said disconsolately. Then he added, "Who could blame her? She's a beautiful girl, don't you think?"

"Beautiful? I wouldn't quite say that, though I like her looks. She's fresh and wholesome, but I'm still partial to brunettes." Carefully Trent set down the wrench he had yet to use. "Listen, Paul. First, Brittany isn't a girl, she's a grown woman. Second, you've been straight with her so she understands your situation. Third, if she used to be a schoolteacher she probably likes kids, too. Fourth-or-whatever, it's significant that she nursed you through a bad bout of flu—"

"That's just because she couldn't figure out how to call the Coast Guard," Paul said even more morosely.

"Okay, buddy, I can tell you don't want to feel any better, so let's go back to the house. Maybe you can provoke Brittany into kicking you again," Trent finished with a sigh.

"I don't want her to kick me again! I want—" Abruptly Paul stopped. Then he added fiercely, "But I definitely don't want to get involved with the contrary woman."

"That's perfectly obvious. She doesn't want to get involved with you, either. Congratulations on how well it's working." As Trent clapped a hand on Paul's shoulder, he also steered him toward the door of the boat house.

"Hey!" Paul stopped with a blink. "What's wrong with my boat?"

"Not a thing I could find," Trent said cheerfully. "Maybe you heard that noise because you really wanted to turn around and come back."

Brittany's guard was lowered by degrees and mostly because Vanessa washed dishes just the way she herself did, carefully yet quickly. Brittany had, in fact, decided that despite Vanessa's appearance she was quite an intelligent and perceptive woman.

"Paul feels very guilty about Peg. That came out while he was so sick," Brittany heard herself saying.

"I think Paul did feel guilty about the way he and Peg lived," Vanessa agreed. "But he shouldn't have. Peg was perfectly happy baking bread and teaching Chad his ABCs. Anyway, what's so bad about living here? Trent and I chose to because we like the beauty and isolation of our island and being close to nature."

"You don't think that maybe Paul...uh, ran around on Peg?" Brittany asked.

"*Paul?*" Vanessa's voice was incredulous. "No way! Why, he was an absolute model of marital fidelity."

"Then why did he say once that he'd been a lousy husband?" Brittany persisted.

"He was talking about not providing Peg with a house and car, mink and diamonds, stocks and bonds. Guys always worry about stuff like that." Vanessa shrugged. "But Paul never forgot Peg's birthday or their wedding anniversary. I know because Peg used to show me her presents— inexpensive things, I'll admit, like lingerie or costume jewelry. Still, they showed Paul remembered and they showed he cared."

"He flirts, though," Brittany said in dark censure.

"He sure does!" Vanessa laughed as she handed over the last dish for Brittany to dry. "Paul Johnson not only makes eyes at women, he makes remarks, too. He always has, but no one ever takes him seriously."

Except me, Brittany thought in chagrin, then she turned back at Vanessa. "Didn't Peg object to his flirting?"

"No. She thought it was funny. She always said Paul might have been born American but his heart was pure Italian." Deftly Vanessa wrung out her sponge. "Peg was a very secure and confident woman."

But I'm not, Brittany thought to herself. In fact, I'm anything but! Especially where Paul is concerned, because one day he's here and the next he's gone. He still blows hot, then cold, and there's nothing Vanessa can say that will change that.

Nevertheless, Brittany was grateful for the insights she'd gleaned, as well as for the new friends she'd obviously acquired in the Davidsons.

It was quite a lot to discover in one day that she—who hadn't thought she wanted to be involved, either—had fallen madly in love with Paul and was ferociously jealous as a result. Not to mention so appallingly insecure.

Nor did Brittany know what to say to Paul after the Davidsons had left them, in a flurry of hugs and laughter. At least the warmth of Vanessa and Trent, Jassie and Boots still lingered.

Paul lingered, too, even though he kept walking through the cottage, picking up and then setting down one item after another. Finally he walked to the door of the bedroom where Brittany sat on the edge of the bed, taking off her heavy boots.

"Look—"

It was Paul's usual opening line, and Brittany regarded him warily even as she stood up and rushed into brusque speech. "I'm sorry I kicked you, Paul. I've, uh, been trying to handle a lot of different feelings lately. But I am sorry I've been such a tartar."

"No, you're a Valkyrie," Paul contradicted, managing a faint smile.

"I'm a what?" Brittany asked, exactly as Trent had done.

"Think about it," Paul said, then his smile gradually widened as he walked over to her.

Brittany stood frozen, standing between her boots in her stocking feet.

"I told you I didn't want to get involved with anyone," Paul began ruefully. "That wasn't just a line, either. I really meant it."

"I knew you meant it," Brittany said nervously because Paul kept moving steadily closer. In a minute she'd be cornered.

"For what it's worth, it hasn't worked, Brittany. Even though the timing's all wrong I've gotten involved with you, anyway. Trent had fun pointing that out. I know I'm scared of being close and feeling committed again. But I guess there's one thing that scares me even more."

"What's that?" Brittany asked breathlessly. All at once the present air supply didn't seem sufficient for both of them.

"Losing somebody I really care about again. I know I don't want to lose you, Brittany, now that I've found you."

Then it was all right. She could breathe again, and everything in her world steadied...well, almost all. "Paul, you're way ahead of me," Brittany said shakily, but since his soft dark hair had tumbled over his forehead again, she couldn't resist gently pushing it back. "Right now I'm still afraid to get close to someone again."

"It's not like we have to decide something tomorrow," Paul pointed out.

"That's true," Brittany agreed with relief.

"In fact, I think we ought to agree that we aren't going to pressure each other or—or—"

"I agree!" Brittany said fervently.

"Still, I don't see any reason not to enjoy our physical proximity," Paul added, a decided gleam shooting through his dark eyes.

Brittany decided to quash that gleam while she still had enough resolve and fortitude to do so. "Paul, I'm not prepared to sleep with you," she said bluntly.

"Oh." Disappointment and relief were both evident on his face. "You're right. Let's take things slow and easy and get to know each other better."

Then he leaned down and kissed her gently and sweetly. Their lips clung until the kiss heated, threatening to change into one of those passionate and heart-stopping ones that had so shaken them before. Paul moved back from Brittany then.

As he lifted his head he stared down at her intently, a look that quickened her pulse and risked her still-jumping heart with accelerated rhythms once again. "Let me tell you just one more thing, Ms. Hagen," Paul said huskily.

"What?" she breathed.

"If you ever dare to kick me again you will see the world upside down, from across my knee!"

Chapter Thirteen

It might have all worked out just as they'd planned except for that one unpredictable element, the weather.

A mere three days after Brittany and Paul had agreed to take things slow and easy snow came swirling down again out of the north.

When Brittany arose that morning she knew the gathering clouds looked threatening, but between two very happy developments, her work going well and the sheer happiness of sharing cozy evenings again with Paul, she felt like snapping her fingers at the steel-gray sky. Certainly she wasn't going to let a few dismal snowflakes peppering down prevent her from observing the wolves. So she headed into the forest that day as usual.

This proved to be Brittany's best day, because the five wild wolf pups that she'd been watching so excitedly ever since they'd first appeared at the opening of the den now came gamboling out to play. With their floppy ears, fluffy coats and puppylike movements Brittany thought they were simply adorable, especially when the pups cocked their heads, bemused, to stare at the unfamiliar phenomenon of snow flitting down. Then they chased the flakes or batted at them with small paws.

And Brittany was managing to record all these delightful antics on film!

Fascinated, intrigued and mesmerized she squeezed off one photograph after another with her zoom lens, then decided to risk using the video camera in her pack. She edged only a little closer for she didn't want her scent to reveal her presence to the wolves lest they disappear overnight.

Of course, a few past observers of wolf behavior had carefully acclimated their wolves to the human scent. But it was Brittany's opinion that having wolves gradually lose their fear of human beings could prove disastrous for the animals since not all of her species were benign.

As her video camera whirred, recording numerous feet of film, Brittany thought of how pleased Dr. Foster would be with the material she was gathering. But she was having to stop every few minutes now to keep the lens of the video camera free of falling snow.

Brittany was even able to foresee her work being used in a nature film of some kind. Surely popular images of the "big, bad, wicked wolf" would be hard to sustain once people actually saw the beauty, intelligence and family affection demonstrated by these members of the wolf pack. Surely exterminating these appealing and adorable baby wolves would then be considered about as civilized as gunning down a litter of puppies or slaughtering baby lambs.

Or so Brittany hoped and prayed as she automatically brushed snow off her face and focused her camera on the wolf family at home here in the northern woods that were their natural habitat.

Finally, she had to turn off the camera. The thick swirling snow was now sticking to the ground, and the pups and their parents retreated back into the den.

It was time she went home, too, Brittany thought, glancing at her watch.

She gave a start when she saw the time. Oh, it can't be that late, Brittany thought, for long hours had passed like minutes. All the while she'd been sitting here entirely oblivious to cold and cramped muscles, to hunger and thirst, too.

Halfway through the woods, Brittany stopped to put on the snowshoes she needed now. She also crammed down half the sandwich she'd brought for lunch and then had forgotten to eat. She was nearing the edge of the woods when she heard Paul's distant voice calling her name.

"Brittany!"

She started to reply but realized Paul would never hear her softer, higher voice this far away so she simply rushed on, using her energy to get out of the woods before her trails and landmarks became obliterated. Brittany hurried on until she was winded, even panting when she broke out of the trees not far from where Paul, with Ivy on a leash, stood calling her name. Between them lay a thick curtain of rapidly falling snow.

"Here, Paul!" Brittany cried and just a moment later he and the whining Ivy were beside her.

"Thank God, you're out of there!" Paul seized Brittany's shoulders to give her a swift hard kiss. His usually warm lips felt cold, and she doubted that her own were any warmer. "Let's go. There's a late-in-the-season blizzard brewing and Ivy wants to get back to her puppies."

Brittany groaned. Would this long cold winter ever end?

"Trent called us on the radio about a half-hour ago," Paul added. "He wanted to be sure we knew since it doesn't usually snow in May."

"What should we do?" Brittany asked. Accustomed as she was to blizzards she had never experienced one on a small island before.

"I've got to check out some things down at the boat house. You'd better collect enough clothes and blankets for yourself, as well as some food for both of us. Plan to stay at the lighthouse for the duration," he warned.

What a lot of bother! Brittany thought first. Then as his last words sank in, her heart knocked against her ribcage.

Did she dare stay all alone with Paul for who-knew-how-many hours? Anticipation warred with her normally prudent nature. Then, as Brittany's eyes met Paul's again, she knew that the best place to endure a blizzard was curled up beside the person you loved.

They parted at the cottage. Brittany dashed inside and bundled up sweaters and blankets as well as a complete change of clothes.

In the kitchen she looked around desperately, trying to consider what she could possibly cook readily on a two-burner hot plate. The box of food she gathered together quickly was still a hefty one and, added to her bundle of clothes and blankets, made too large a load for her to carry.

Paul returned in time to help her. Rapidly he closed up the cottage while Brittany struggled back into her parka and gloves. "Come on," Paul said, seizing the box of groceries, while Brittany hastily finished tying a thick scarf around her neck.

She grabbed her bundle and they plunged back out into a world now froth-white with swirling snow. Instinctively they linked arms as they fought their way toward the lighthouse against an almost gale-force wind. Dire memories returned to Brittany of her nightmarish trek through the snow when Paul had been so ill and she'd had to half-carry, half-drag him to shelter. Thank God he was well now and able to help coordinate this emergency!

They skidded inside the lighthouse, then Paul slammed and bolted the outer storm door as well as the inner door beyond until they were sealed inside, safe in a haven of peace, warmth and quiet. All alone together....

But before either of them could relax there were things for both to do. While Brittany unpacked provisions, Paul got on the shortwave radio. Since Chad was still at school he talked to his sister-in-law, Vicky, on the mainland, explaining that he might be out of touch temporarily until the storm blew itself out. Vicky promised to assure Chad that Paul was okay; she would also inform Griff Foster that Brittany was now safely inside the lighthouse. Then Paul called Trent back with essentially the same message.

Brittany, for her part, was trying to fix a hot meal since she not only felt half-starved, her bit of sandwich having quickly disappeared, but she suspected that Paul probably hadn't stopped for lunch, either. In recent days, ever since their truce, he'd been writing ferociously, trying to finish his novel.

Meanwhile Ivy watched with interest this flurry of activity in her ordinarily quiet domain. Although most of her pups were engaged in their favorite activity, nursing, Ivy barked an occasional warning to Brittany or Paul when she thought they were getting too close to her little ones.

Paul set out fresh dog food and water for Ivy. Then he came over to sniff hopefully at the contents of the two pots that Brittany was stirring.

"Just more soup," she told him apologetically, "and a throw-it-together-fast chicken dish since it might be our last chance for a hot meal for a while."

"Smells great to me," Paul said. "But I don't expect we'll lose electricity or heat. At least we never have before."

Unconsciously Brittany relaxed at that news.

"Hey, let's go up to the lantern room to eat," Paul suggested. "I'll light a couple of candles and rustle us up a bottle of wine."

That sounded so romantic that Brittany's inner alarm rang. But could she honestly suggest they dine in this drab little room with seven dogs? Anyway, she had once liked things romantic.

Even with their dinner on paper plates and bowls, Brittany had to climb up the numerous spiral steps twice to bring everything they needed. But by then Paul had things well organized. His desk had been cleared and covered with a red-checkered tablecloth Brittany had found in the store-room. Candles flickered and Paul had already opened the wine to allow it to breathe.

"This is nice," Brittany reflected as Paul helped her into the room's only armchair.

"Yes, it's definitely the way to have a picnic," he replied, settling on the typewriter chair that he'd moved opposite Brittany's.

"No ants or mosquitoes," she agreed.

Paul poured the wine into two Styrofoam cups, and he and Brittany touched cups in a silent toast. Then they fell on their food, famished.

"Good!" Paul exclaimed between hungry bites. "Is it chicken stew or chicken and dumplings?"

"Both, I guess. It's chicken stew into which I dropped some refrigerated biscuit dough," Brittany confessed.

"Don't tell that to anybody else," he advised, his eyes amused. "They'll give it a four-star rating and you'll win a bake-off. More wine?"

"Please." Brittany smiled, holding out her cup.

Even when they'd finally finished eating they lingered, sipping wine and describing their day's events. At last, though, Brittany looked down at the remains of their meal and sighed.

They tidied up together, which made the routine chores almost fun, then played for a time with Ivy's puppies, comparing their weight and prowess. Afterward, Brittany declared that, storm or not, she wanted a shower and went into the closet-sized bathroom that served the lighthouse.

When she came out and climbed back up to the lantern room she felt far more comfortable in her clean clothes and with her hair brushed and loose. She had rejected bringing over a nightgown and robe as being too obviously seductive. Anyway, should the absolute dire worst happen, blizzardwise, Brittany didn't want to be found frozen tight to her nightie alongside a man to whom she wasn't married.

Just having that thought told Brittany how really conscious she was of being all alone with Paul.

If he was experiencing similar tension it didn't show. Or maybe, because he'd been married for so many years, he just handled it better. Paul looked and acted far more relaxed than Brittany. He was even sprawled nonchalantly atop a pallet on the floor.

He'd built the pallet from the blankets Brittany had gathered up so hastily at the cottage. Now with a pillow beneath his black head and his shoes kicked off he was a lean and handsome figure as he listened to a portable cassette player softly spinning out New Age instrumental music featuring many harps.

Candles still flickered, the only illumination in the large, round room of snow-blurred windows.

Since Paul was already on the pallet, Brittany sat down on the edge of his narrow bed and took off her own shoes.

"Hey, I've got a great idea," Paul called up to her from where he lay. His full lips beneath the moustache had a sultry curve to them, and his black eyes held an avid gleam.

Brittany could recognize trouble when she saw it. On the other hand, trouble was also quite exciting, making her skin tingle all over. "What's your great idea?" she asked, feeling her heart boom louder and louder as her body gradually warmed. Heat both from the wine she'd drunk earlier as well as that look in Paul's eyes began to fan out along her trunk and the limbs of her body.

"C'mere," Paul said softly, then opened his arms to Brittany.

She swallowed hard, her mouth suddenly dry. But as the object of his relentless and desirous gaze her whole body began to feel flushed.

She longed to bridge the short distance to Paul and simply curl up in his arms. But letting a man make love to you could have quite serious ramifications, Brittany had learned, and they weren't necessarily the ones your mother had warned you about. Paul Johnson not only had restless, changeable eyes but he had a tendency to change his mind as well.

On the other hand, he knew she was no ready conquest, no easy, convenient pushover. Had he thought otherwise Paul would never have taken the trouble to make up a pallet on the floor.

Also, some warm affection and tender kisses shared with Paul could be very sweet.

"C'mon," he urged her again. "I won't bite. In fact, I won't do a thing that you don't want me to do."

That breathless feeling stole back over Brittany. The warmth that had earlier spread like oil, suffusing her skin, now began to penetrate and seep in like a deep-heat rub. She started to feel that heat in the most sensitive recesses of her body. "That might be the problem," Brittany said unsteadily.

"What might be?" Paul asked, looking at her now from between half-closed eyelids.

That look, accompanied by a slow perusal ranging deliberately over her, was more effective than his earlier request to come had been. Swiftly Brittany arose and found herself kneeling down next to Paul.

His hands spanned the short gulf between them, drawing her down until they went sprawling across the pallet. Brittany's hair spilled over Paul's chest, and his fingers began stroking it while she listened to the regular steady beat of his heart.

"So what's the problem?" he asked gently, his voice softly seductive against her ear while the hairs of his moustache tickled its delicate curves.

"We, uh, might want more than is wise," Brittany admitted.

"I already do. Now let's test your resistance," Paul suggested before he kissed her with lips as hot and sultry as the expression in his eyes.

It was a long, slow, deliberate kiss. At first, Paul only used his lips, deepening the pressure very gradually. Then, as Brittany's mouth parted spontaneously, his tongue pushed inside.

Paul's hand cradled her chin as he kissed her. His other hand slipped around to Brittany's back, stroking slowly at first. Then he lowered his arm and used it to draw her closer, molding her tightly against him.

To feel the contours of that hard, male body beneath her was like stoking a fire with fresh kindling. As the warmth blazed up anew, hot and high within Brittany, she felt her eyes close languidly. Her eyelids felt too heavy, and she wanted to feel, not to think, to hear but not to see.

Paul murmured soft endearments, his lips pressed against the tender flesh of Brittany's throat. He whispered that she was soft, lush, lovely. That he wanted her. That, indeed, she drove him half out of his mind from wanting her. Some of his words, ending with kisses or emphasized by new and passionate caresses, were so intimate that at any other time or setting she would have turned scarlet.

She relaxed, melting against him, just listening and feeling, as they kissed ardently again and again until Brittany knew Paul had no intention of stopping. Knew that the past three evenings when they'd simply talked for hours and even danced in sock feet to the music spinning from his cassette recorder—those evenings mild and innocent—had nevertheless been a prelude to this. To the wonder and delight she felt wedged tightly in Paul's arms.

Slowly he turned, using his deceptively wiry strength to slide Brittany gently down until she felt the pallet beneath her hips and the pillow under her head.

Her eyes opened then, looking straight up into his jet-black, triumphantly blazing ones. She knew he must see the surprise on her face—how had he been so sure she'd yield? Paul laughed gently, cuddling her closer.

"Don't be too sure of yourself," Brittany warned, her own voice catching since it came from deep in her throat. "I could get up from here any time and end all this."

"I'm suitably impressed by the threat," Paul answered respectfully, although his warm, warm hands were gliding beneath her sweater. "Will you?"

Then he kissed Brittany again without waiting for her reply, and her eyes closed again as virtually every thought but Paul was wiped from her mind.

"Well?" he teased.

"I think I've forgotten what we were talking about," Brittany heard herself say raggedly.

"That's wonderful."

She hadn't really forgotten, of course, although she could now that his hands were curving so warmly over her breasts. They simply rested there for several minutes, his fingers stroking sensually. Then Paul reached around to her back again and unhooked Brittany's bra. His own breathing was unsteady as he slowly drew her sweater up and over her head.

Brittany's bra followed, then Paul brushed back her hair that he had left in disarray.

"You're beautiful, Brittany. More exquisite than I ever dreamed—and, believe me, I dreamed plenty!" Paul admitted just before his hands and mouth paid homage to all he'd extolled.

Brittany let her hands glide up around Paul's neck, then burrow into the black softness of his hair. As they kissed again, fervently, she knew that this night could only end with them close and warm together, sharing the same bed.

She felt surprised that she was letting this happen. Just a year ago she'd planned to marry another man. In fact, Brittany knew she had arrived on this island less than healed only to find a man whose own grief was even rawer, newer and deeper than her own. Yes, by all logic, it was too soon for this to happen.

But that was her head talking, not her heart. Because from the moment Paul first kissed her that night, nothing else in Brittany's love life seemed to have had much consequence.

Indeed, there was such a quality of inevitability to this that Brittany even wondered if she had been jockeyed into place, plunked down here a few short weeks ago just so they could meet. Then when she'd been stranded and alone with Paul while he was so sick, all her natural defenses against men in general and him in particular got waylaid somewhere. Now, as the final coup, they were marooned together in the lighthouse.

Had some mischievous sprite—some god or goddess, perhaps—playfully thrust them together? Maybe even one of those thunderous Norse deities that Paul seemed to know about?

Even as she smiled, thinking such fanciful things, Brittany's own hands were tugging off Paul's sweater.

The sensation when their naked chests met had no frame of reference; it was completely unlike anything she'd ever felt. His mat of dark silky chest hair blanketed her sensitive breasts completely while his mouth played lip-and-tongue games with hers once again.

Then Paul reached for the zipper on Brittany's slacks.

She allowed him to remove all of her clothes first although, in truth, she was almost as eager to see him unclothed again. But she knew Paul's curiosity naturally was greater than hers. He'd had no earlier covert peeks at her.

But, unfortunately, this was also a moment when Brittany felt particularly insecure. A moment when she wished desperately she'd been constructed on a less robust frame and draped with not quite so much flesh.

But Paul's fingertips—then his lips—marvelled at the curves of her body. At least, thank God, she was very smooth and firm.

"How beautiful you are!" he breathed, then placed his mouth on the dimple at her calf.

For the first time in her life Brittany voiced her insecurity. "I wish I weren't quite so large."

Momentarily Paul drew back, and Brittany saw the passion stamped on his face. "Not large," he contradicted, his own voice as breathless now as Brittany's had ever been. "Voluptuous!"

"Voluptuous," Brittany repeated. What a wonderful word to describe her and how clever of him to have thought of it.

"Unfortunately I'm too skinny," Paul murmured as he reached for his belt. "I didn't used to be this thin."

"I'll feed you well and fatten you up," Brittany whispered back. But, to her eyes, Paul was beautiful, too, and always had been—brown, long-limbed and so boldly masculine.

"Let's get in the bed," he whispered, easing Brittany up off the pallet on which it appeared neither one of them was destined to sleep.

Brittany slid into the narrow bed and Paul followed. Oh yes, so much better, she thought ecstatically. Now they had it all—a mattress that was firm yet pliable, and covers draped over them to keep out the chill. Then as Paul's body settled against hers and he began to initiate bold forays, Brittany thought, Yes—oh yes, now we will have it all.

She yielded completely then to his hands and lips, to the dimly lighted room of flickering candles and the completely silent, white, enchanted world of swirling, dancing snowflakes beyond....

Although Paul lay sleeping, Brittany was still awake. She couldn't yet part with so vital and momentous a happening. Tomorrow it would just be a memory, but right now it was still alive. And anything as wonderful as what she'd just shared with Paul ought to be preserved as long as possible. It should stand alone, framed outside of ordinary time, since it belonged to a realm rarely touched by ordinary human beings. Paul had introduced her to this realm that was sheer magic and wonder and love.

He fascinated her. He had from the very beginning. Why, she'd arrived on this island already quite intrigued by Paul Johnson.

Now he was the consummate lover—that one-and-only that every woman always sought but rarely found. The man masterfully adept at understanding her mind and heart as well as her body. And what a man he was! With her Paul had turned aggressively masculine, potent and vigorous. How had he also managed to convey such tremendous tenderness and sensitivity that finally surmounted even physical glory?

Yet somehow he had, easing Brittany through those often awkward moments when two people, who had never made love, did so for the very first time.

Making love—yes, that's what they had done—for it was as different from sex as night from day.

Paul had understood her body, and he also had the maturity and patience to wait until Brittany's responses caught up with his. Until, together, they had flown straight to the sun and exploded like comets in a shower of fiery sparks.

Brittany still wasn't sure she was entirely back together again. Fragmented parts of her seemed to spin yet in the cosmos or drift languidly from star to star. But she didn't want to sleep. She wanted to relish this afterglow. Savor the marvelous feeling of Paul's body curled up against hers and his arms still linked around her. Savor, too, the evenness of his breaths that kept lifting and dropping a strand of hair on her temple. Up, down and up, down... Unexpectedly she slept.

"Brittany?" Paul asked in the dark hushed quiet as he felt her stir. His hands went to her instinctively, but as one found the perfection of her breast and the other touched a delectable knee, he started to smile. Even in the dark his aim was good.

"Umm-hum?" she murmured.

"I just woke up," Paul whispered, dropping a kiss on her forehead.

"Me, too. What time is it?"

"Very late," Paul said enigmatically. "Or else it's very early."

"Doesn't matter," Brittany said and snuggled closer.

"Are you warm enough? Do you have enough room?"

She turned, buried her face in his chest and laughed aloud, softly. "I'm perfect."

"Yes, you sure are."

That only made her laugh more. "That wasn't what I meant!" she exclaimed.

"But you are," he protested, "and I love you."

"I love you, too."

Then they were locked in each other's arms and moving together ecstatically once again.

* _ * *

Although Brittany had gone back to sleep Paul was wide awake now, his brain fairly humming. He was still amazed by the extent of Brittany's innocence.

That wasn't at all what he'd expected. Oh, she wasn't technically a virgin. What normal person of her age still was? But neither had she been fully a woman, not in the deepest, most sensuous meaning of the word.

What sort of clumsy fool was her ex-fiance? Paul wondered before dismissing Howard with contempt. Good thing the inept guy had money. He'd need it to keep a woman around.

Maybe I don't have much in the way of worldly goods, Paul ruminated, but at least I've had the pleasure of watching this beautiful and intelligent woman bloom in my arms. And she did! Both times I saw her surprise and felt her excitement and that made it all the more exciting for me.

Now if I could just write the ending to that damned book of mine! I might earn a few coins from that. I'd sure like to buy us a house—it doesn't have to be anything big or expensive—just someplace close to woods and water. And I'd be willing to live there forever with Brittany and Chad—Ivy, too, of course, and a puppy or two. . . .

As the satisfying scenes unfolded in his mind Paul leaned down to lightly kiss Brittany's satin shoulder just inches away.

At that exact moment literary lightning struck and sheer inspiration dawned.

The next thing Paul knew he had dressed automatically and just a minute after that he drew up his chair to his typewriter.

About an hour later he paused to go downstairs and fix a cup of instant coffee. Ivy came over, sniffing at her empty bowl, and Paul rubbed her head absently before dumping dog food and water into her dishes. Then carrying his coffee, Paul hurried back up the spiral staircase and returned to work.

* * *

That monotonous clattering had been going on forever, it seemed. Slowly Brittany came awake to a dull, drab light snaking in through the great expanse of windows.

She smiled drowsily, flexed her muscles and touched her toes, until that repetitious clatter began to bother her. Then, frowning, she turned her head to discover Paul pounding his typewriter with such intense concentration that she doubted if he even knew she was here.

Brittany smiled again. Oh, it felt good to see Paul working so intently at his writing. She was glad it was apparently going well.

What time was it? Nine o'clock! Why, she hadn't slept so late in years. Was it still snowing? Yes, earth, sky and water were all given over to a blinding barrage of fat white flakes, she saw as she eased out of bed and reached for her clothes. But while she dressed, Brittany decided that she would probably never again hate blizzards.

Several hours later, when less snow was falling, Paul was still writing nonstop, gripped by feverish creativity. Brittany, though, was beginning to feel caged and restless. She paced the storeroom downstairs, not wanting to disturb Paul.

"I think you inspired me," he'd said, kissing Brittany's arm earlier that morning when she'd set a bowl of warm cereal by his elbow. "Do you mind my writing?"

"Not a bit," she assured him. "Keep going." So he did. But as Brittany tiptoed back upstairs at one o'clock to bring Paul's lunch of soup and a melted cheese sandwich this keeper of the flame routine was already growing old. How had Peg managed it day in and day out for all those years?

According to Vanessa Davidson, Peg hadn't minded. "She really believed in that book," Vanessa had told Brittany.

"I think he's a good writer, too. But I wouldn't go traipsing meekly up and down all those stairs just to be sure he ate," Brittany had retorted. "Paul's a big boy, and he can take care of himself. I've got other things to do with my life."

Yet here she was, falling automatically into the same dumb routine, Brittany thought, finishing her own sandwich and crumpling her paper napkin. The very same dumb, servile routine she'd performed so adoringly for Howard. She hadn't minded then, but she did now. She hoped that represented progress.

Next, Brittany played with Ivy's puppies, then she took another shower. Dressed again she dared another peek outside. Snowing still . . .

So Brittany went back upstairs and watched as Paul continued to pound away furiously. He needs a computer, she thought when she realized that he was retyping a particularly messy page, and made a mental note to discuss it with him later. Then she glanced through Paul's assortment of paperback books. What she needed to do was find an engrossing book to read.

Instead, her eyes went to that tall stack of white pages on Paul's desk. That was the book she really wanted to read. Slowly Brittany got up and walked over, not knowing what Paul's response to her request might be.

He was too engrossed to display artistic reticence. "Sure, go ahead," he told Brittany absently, then paused just long enough to tug her face down to his, which was darkened by a day's growth of beard.

Their lips met warmly yet briefly. Then Paul returned to work, and Brittany stretched out on the bed she'd made up neatly and began to read *Saigon Falls Today*.

After the title page came the dedication "To Peg." Brittany certainly couldn't argue with that when she thought of all those steps Peg had climbed. Curiously Brittany turned another page, arrived at Chapter One and began to read.

An hour later she looked up and stared over incredulously at Paul.

Nothing he had written before had prepared Brittany for this. His book was wonderful—and awful. It was filled in places with bitter gallows humor and brightened at others by surprising touches of human behavior at its funniest or best.

The descriptions, of the time, the place and the people were so vivid that whole scenes leaped to life before her eyes.

It was exciting. Poignant, too. Most of all, it hurled along at such a breakneck pace that she absolutely couldn't put it down. Even as Brittany glanced up occasionally at its author, a man she loved and had thought she knew pretty well, she was automatically groping for yet another page.

All the rest of that day Paul wrote and Brittany read. It was nearly dusk again before he stopped typing and looked up at her in a daze of exhaustion. She stood poised by his side, waiting, and fairly snatched that last page from his hand.

"Boy!" Paul rubbed both hands across his face. "I've worked so long and hard I feel numb. I think I'll lie down for just a minute."

"Yes, do that. I'll feed Ivy," Brittany replied absently, but inside she felt thunderstruck. She finished the page, said, "Whew!" and glanced up. But Paul didn't hear her. He was already deeply and soundly asleep.

While she'd been reading so voraciously the snow had stopped and the sun had come back out, Brittany discovered. In fact, as warmer breezes blew in now from the south, the thick mounds of snow were already starting to sag and melt. Soon it would start dripping.

Brittany took Ivy out for air and exercise. Then she went back inside the lighthouse to gather her clothes and blankets. Since Paul still slept on, Brittany tossed a blanket over him.

She fought her way through still-high drifts back to the cottage and managed, by cursing and tugging, to wrest open the snow-jammed door.

The inside temperature felt freezing, so Brittany kept on her parka as she turned up the heat and built a fire in the fireplace. Then she waited, shivering, for the cottage to warm.

Later she sat for hours, watching the flickering orange flames that usually hypnotized her. But despite those darting, dancing tongues of fire tonight Brittany could think of little except Paul's very amazingly good book. Now she understood why an intelligent, educated woman such as Peg had climbed all those stairs. Maybe one man in a million was doing something significant enough to justify such sacrifice; Paul just happened to have been the exceptional one. But did she really want that for herself? Brittany wondered. Already she knew the answer.

Paul's book had added still another dimension to their various differences. Already Brittany feared that his novel might divide them, if only by the incredible difference it would create in Paul's life if it was just half as good as she thought it was.

An unexpected crash of snow just a few feet away caused Brittany to spin around in surprise. Then she relaxed as she saw the still quivering limb of a tree that had just dropped its heavy white burden almost directly on top of her.

All around Brittany the deep snow that had blanketed the silent thick woods for so long continued to melt. In the five days that she had been living here in her tent, working eighteen-hour days, she had gradually grown used to its incessant *drip, drip, drip*. But those crashes of snow off the trees, many of them happening in the dead of night, still had the power to startle and scare her, making her jerk up in her sleeping bag, her mind numb with fear.

Nor were snow crashes, of course, the only thing that had scared her silly in recent days.

That was why she was here, rushing the season and freezing her fanny because despite the continued warming trend it was still damned cold. In fact, this island was probably the coldest spot in America right now, just because it took the deep icy waters of Lake Superior so long to finally warm up. But since Brittany had decided it was time she got on with her own work and her own life, here she was.

She had realized that Paul's life was much too uncertain at present to allow herself to become more involved with him.

So on that evening after she'd left Paul asleep in the lighthouse following his marathon writing session, Brittany went to bed early and rose in time to catch the first weather reports on her FM radio next morning. When warmer days had been predicted for the next fortnight, she packed all the things she'd need, beginning with her lightweight tent. Naturally she included those canned goods she'd brought for her field work until her backpack was crammed full and achingly heavy.

Of course, she had left Paul a note in the kitchen—a very nice note, actually, which she'd agonized over writing. It praised his novel and predicted wonderful things as a result. It admitted that she'd found joy the night they'd spent together at the lighthouse. "But, frankly, my study remains my single most important consideration," she'd concluded. "Maybe I'm just not ready for a real relationship, at least not one of the sort that you would require."

Knowing Paul, Brittany had little doubt of what his reaction would be: He was going to get madder than hell, turn absolutely livid and blow sky high. But anger would be better than pain.

She certainly didn't want to hurt Paul. In fact, Brittany's heart gave more than one twinge as, staggering under her heavy load, she had left the cottage at dawn just in time to see the first electric light snap on in the lighthouse. And by the time she'd reached the woods tears were freezing on her face.

But the truth of her note remained. She simply didn't dare to get in any deeper with him, and she knew that this was her final chance to pull free.

After five days, though, Brittany wondered if Paul was still stomping around in a towering rage, muttering imprecations about wringing her neck or battering down her tent or turning her over his knee.

As much as her heart ached, her long hours of work had proved worthwhile for Brittany continued to enjoy an almost-close-up view of the seemingly healthy wolf pups, although they now numbered four. Why did one or two usually die during denning? As yet no one knew.

For that matter, why did only the dominant male and female in the wolf pack breed and produce young? Were the smaller and weaker wolves content to live a celibate life? If that was nature's way of insuring survival of the fittest it also contributed to dropping wolf numbers perilously low.

Brittany had observed a number of other family members—aunts and uncles—who, along with the pups' parents, comprised this particular pack. They had all turned up on two different evenings.

That all the adult wolves doted on the family youngsters was obvious by the meat they brought along to help feed them. There were never any orphans in a wolf pack, for even if something should happen to the pups' parents the other wolves stopped by regularly to check on the offspring and would raise them, if necessary.

The affection the wolves displayed for one another, licking their loved ones' faces, made Brittany's heart throb. Made her remember the tenderness as well as the passion of Paul's kisses.

One of the extended family members, a male, kept limping slightly, to Brittany's distress. She hoped he was healing from an injury rather than being diseased. She noted his condition in her field journal, of course, and shot film of "Uncle Albert," as she'd nicknamed him, for documentation.

Each night that she'd been out here the adult wolves went hunting, except for the pups' mother who stayed home to baby-sit. Most nights of hunting in a wolf's life proved futile; a dozen moose would escape for each one finally caught, so the wolves' howls reverberated throughout the night. This evening promised to be no exception. Brittany, who had been teaching herself to mimic their cry, sometimes howled along. Last night she had actually drawn one wolf fairly close to her tent and had observed it through infrared binoculars that made it possible for her to see in the dark. But apparently, at closer range, Brittany's howls were less than convincing for the wolf soon melted back into the night.

Now, as mama and the pups turned into the den while the others trotted off to scare moose, Brittany returned to the dubious comfort of her tent and braced for another dismally cold night in the wild.

Supper first. In a clearing where she'd set up her small camp stove Brittany heated a can of beef stew and made herself a cup of herb tea. First, she choked down most of the gluey-tasting stew, then cleaned her dish with a slice of bread that she popped into her mouth.

Dessert was an apple that, despite its crisp red outer appearance, tasted old and mealy inside. Brittany ate half of it, then pitched the rest away. But she drank all of her tea to warm her in preparation for the worst ordeal of all; a spit bath.

Despite having heated the water she would use in her small wash pail, it chilled rapidly in the crisp evening air, even in Brittany's sheltered tent with the flap securely zipped. As Brittany sat crouched, wielding her washcloth grimly and trying to ignore the chatter of her teeth, her inner voice of sanity spoke up. It reminded her that, by now, she was heartily sick of the tent, the frigid nights, icy sandwiches and tepid spit baths.

Why do you keep subjecting yourself to this miserable ordeal? sanity inquired. Or are you just naturally crazy?

For three days Brittany had rejected that same practical voice of wisdom in favor of her proud determination to stay free and unencumbered, to prove both to Paul and to herself that she needed no man. But, unfortunately for her resolve, there was one she still wanted. Now, shivering uncontrollably, Brittany was finally disposed to listen.

Just a couple of miles away is a man who said he loves you, the same man you love, too. Why, you could be lying in a warm bed, held tight in his arms right now!

Oh sure, falling in love is risky, but what on earth could be worse than this? Anyway, why do you always insist on believing a worst-case scenario? What's Paul ever done to make you think he really wants a domestic slave? As for his novel, you may be regarded as a good critic in certain circles, but you're not a New York editor. You don't even know if his book will even be found acceptable, much less cause any real stir in the publishing world. Why, for all you know Paul might have merely a moderate success and things could just rock along nicely for both of you—and for young Chad, too.

But how will you ever find out if you don't take a risk?

All right, Brittany replied to the voice that only she could hear. *Maybe I will . . . tomorrow.*

By the time she'd finished arguing with herself she had struggled into her warmest pajamas—the ones with feet in them—and lay curled up tight in her insulated sleeping bag. Although it was supposed to feel toasty-warm inside it just felt clammy and *cold*. God, she was miserable!

For the next three hours Brittany tossed and turned. She couldn't fall asleep, and there was nothing to do but listen to the wolves sing as well as the other night noises.

CRASH!

She jerked up, her muscles tensed for fight-or-flight. But it was just more snow falling off another tree.

Just what was she trying to prove with this endurance contest?

Suddenly, without even making a conscious decision, she sat up and switched on her flashlight. Then she located her lantern and set it glowing as she reached for her wool slacks, her warm socks and boots and finally her heavy parka.

"All right!" she declared aloud, through teeth that clattered anew. "I'll go back. I'll find out if Paul actually meant what he said about loving me. I'll see for myself if he's still coming on to me then backing off, running hot and cold. And if he's really ready to take a chance on us then I will, too!"

Chapter Fourteen

Paul, Ivy and the puppies were gone!

To Brittany's astonishment the lighthouse was not only deserted, it had actually been emptied of Paul's clothes and toiletries, his typewriter and file case. Ivy's dishes and toys, her collar and the leash Paul rarely kept on her were also missing.

Although Brittany hadn't gone to the cottage yet she could see that it was blacked out and seemingly deserted as well.

Panic began to stir in her midsection, making her feel sick. Where could Paul have gone? she wondered as she raced back down the spiral staircase of the lighthouse. Why had he left?

But there were no answers. That he had actually run off and left her all alone was something Brittany still couldn't quite believe. Oh sure, she'd expected Paul to be angry at her. Fuming even. Okay, downright furious. But not gone.

Why, it wasn't even safe to leave a poor woman stuck in the woods on a deserted island. Hadn't Paul Johnson thought about that? Since Brittany had just risked life and limb, returning alone in the dark over snowy and ill-marked paths, which was admittedly a foolish thing to do, she couldn't help feeling galled by his cavalier attitude.

Oh my God, what if something has happened to Paul? she suddenly thought, her mind flooded by wild and terrible images. Maybe he'd fallen off his boat and drowned. Maybe he'd gotten sick again and since she wasn't there to care for him, his condition had worsened rapidly and he'd died. If he were dead as a result of her negligence Brittany knew she would never forgive herself. Just thinking about it made her stumble on the stone path to the cottage.

Then she got a grip on herself. By God, he'd better be dead, she decided, hearing her heart pound so deafeningly in her ears. After scaring her like this, if Paul Johnson wasn't dead she'd kill him!

If she discovered that he'd packed up and left her over a stupid note that he ought to have known she didn't mean in the first place then he wasn't worthy to walk the earth beside her, and she'd certainly tell him....

Her thoughts going haywire again, Brittany raced up onto the porch of the darkened cottage.

The doors were locked but, of course, she still had her key, which she used to let herself inside. Then, as the interior door closed behind her, she leaned back, waiting for her eyes to adjust to total darkness. She still banged her shin painfully as she groped for a tabletop lamp.

The cottage seemed just as deserted as the lighthouse had been when Brittany made her way to the back. A few dishes had been left unwashed in the sink. So Paul had reverted to his old bad habits, she couldn't help observing.

She was still half out of her mind with worry and fear when she opened the door to the larger bedroom. She stepped inside, only to trip immediately and quite noisily over a suitcase.

But in that instant before she'd stumbled Brittany saw the mounded figure in the bed and heard the welcome sound of

Paul's now-familiar breathing, heavy with sleep. Of course, the racket she made changed that.

As Brittany struggled to regain her balance, Paul bolted up in bed. "Who's there?" he demanded.

The sound of his vigorous voice increased her relief. "Who do you think?" she asked crossly, girding herself for a battle as she stepped over his suitcase. She stopped a foot away, in a patch of white moonlight that streamed in from a window. Paul had not closed the drapes, as she always did, but had left them open to a view of stars and moon.

He sat up fully now, pushing a pillow behind his back and laughing a little in relief, too. "Lady, it's about time you came home," he said softly. "Trent and I were planning to beat the bushes for you tomorrow."

Paul didn't sound as angry as she'd expected. He certainly didn't seem livid. Brittany, caught off guard, looked across to the pale oval of his face. "You, ah, aren't mad at me?" she asked.

"Moderately," Paul replied, although his laugh belied his words. "But your timing's good. I finally got over being mad at you today and just plain started missing you. Anyway, I figured that when you cooled off you'd come back to me."

"That sure of yourself, huh?" she said, her words faintly edged with sarcasm.

"No, I was that sure of you, Brittany, and your own particular integrity."

Now how could she fight with that? And, anyway, she didn't want to fight with Paul. She wanted to be held tightly in the haven of his arms, wanted to close out the world and switch off her busy little mind and simply love him in the way she'd always longed to love someone. Suddenly Brittany felt shaky again, this time from longing.

"Come join me," he called softly.

But her busy little mind couldn't let go just yet of all its churning questions. "Paul, I don't understand. Why are all your things gone? Where are Ivy and the puppies?"

"Everything and everyone's fine," he soothed. "You've missed some excitement, but we'll talk about it later."

Automatically Brittany shrugged out of her parka. Then, for the first time in her life, she let it drop to the floor and simply lie there. Her gloves and scarf followed. But questions still stirred.

"Why are you sleeping in my bed?" Brittany asked bewilderedly.

"I missed you," Paul said simply, "and the bed still holds your scent. I love you, Brittany."

Her throat choked up, her heart throbbed with a pleasure so intense it felt close to pain. "I love you, too, Paul," she whispered as her hands moved spontaneously to her turtleneck sweater.

"Come closer," he urged softly. "Yes, stop right there where I can see you better. Now take off your clothes, my lovely, voluptuous Valkyrie. Let me watch you."

His voice was hypnotic. And the pale moonlight streaming over her created a madness all its own. Instinctively Brittany reached for the bottom of her sweater and drew it up over her head.

She heard the breath he sucked in. "You're gorgeous, Brittany!"

She uttered a triumphant little laugh of her own. Although Brittany had never done a languid striptease in her life, right now the idea appealed to her, too. How natural it felt to undress for Paul. She dropped her sweater on top of her parka, then moving tantalizingly slowly she reached for the zipper to her slacks. It glided down easily.

As she stepped out of the slacks and stood in her body-clinging, insulated underwear, Brittany felt a new confidence, even in her body. She'd definitely lost a few inches lately—maybe some pounds as well—thanks to all of her outdoor exercise as well as her roller-coaster emotions where this particular man was concerned.

Paul moved forward, and now the magic moonlight silhouetted him, too. He was bare chested, his hair mussed, and Brittany thought he looked absolutely wonderful. Then she saw a change in his appearance so dramatic that it almost made her gasp. His moustache was gone!

For a paralyzing moment he seemed a stranger. "Why did you shave?" she asked, still spell-struck.

"Maybe, oh, because I have something important to ask you. And you'd better see exactly what you'd get," he said whimsically.

"What are you talking about?" Brittany asked, her hands still not moving.

"Or maybe it's a warning." Undercurrents swirled in Paul's tenor voice. "Because I have very, very serious intentions where you're concerned."

"What sort?" Brittany asked, her pulse leaping in response, although her head kept telling her not to hope so much. But she did, anyway.

"Serious and honorable ones." Even as he spoke Paul threw back the covers on the bed. Brittany saw his white shorts and the long length of his legs. "I'm talking marriage and instant motherhood. Do they scare you?"

Were his words real? Or was this all a dream? Brittany drew a ragged breath, but the remaining tightness around her chest suddenly, miraculously eased. "Quite a lot. But my answer's yes!"

Later she would sort out what was reality and what she had merely imagined. Later she might wake and cry in disappointment to find she'd imagined it all. But right now there was only this magic time with Paul.

"Good! Now come closer..." Then Paul began telling her just how she looked to him. "You're so beautiful," he breathed as Brittany stood before him still in her underwear. "Ripe and absolutely luscious!"

Brittany went up on her toes in sheer delight. "You make me sound like an apple, or a pear," she chided playfully, but she liked the way that husky note in his voice was making her feel.

"That's because you make me so hungry," he shot back. "And any time you'd like to continue undressing..."

Slowly she peeled her long-sleeved chemise down, baring her breasts and waist.

"Um, yes, now I see that 'pair' I'm most interested in!"

"What a terrible pun!" Brittany said with a mock groan, but the rest of her underwear was already gliding slowly down her body.

"No more puns," Paul said, his voice going taut. "You're too glorious and I need you too much."

"I need you, too," she heard herself echo.

"Good! Now come here, my goddess, my exciting Valkyrie."

She glided forward, sank down and fell straight into Paul's warm waiting arms. As their lips crushed together Brittany felt a sudden driving sense of excitement so powerful it was like a great turbine motor propelling a vast machine. Sound, movements, rhythm.

His lips, making love to her mouth, were sweetly delicious. His skin felt hot, but the hair that matted it was silky soft, rubbing tantalizingly against her limbs. Her hands stroked his chest, his shoulders and neck as she caressed him gently.

Paul explored Brittany's body as avidly as though he'd never made love to her before, until tender pain speared through her again, making her ache with longing, and her hands on him tightened.

Paul pulled her closer, slowly eased her thighs apart with the touch of his knee, then pressed his aroused lower body against her. The contact, as thrilling as it was brazen, left her moaning softly and as their loveplay continued, desire flared and exploded inside of Brittany.

She had simply never known that a woman could want a man so much. She surprised herself, writhing in his arms, crying his name, dizzied by the pleasure of being with him again.

Pure unbridled passion surged, ending patience and no longer needing words. When Paul moved to possess her, Brittany's hands were already drawing him down. His pants of breath were echoed in her own ecstatic gasps. Glorious, tempestuous delight lifted them off their moonlight-drenched bed and swept them away to a paradise that neither had ever known.

"Is this heaven?" Brittany managed to whisper a short time later.

"Maybe," Paul whispered back, "or Valhalla."

Then, while the heavenly spell still lay upon them, Paul stroked Brittany's face tenderly and shared his big news.

"I've sold my novel and I have to leave for New York tomorrow."

As Paul related the events to Brittany everything had happened very quickly. For even as she had left the cottage to go camp in the woods, Paul had that very morning been talking to Trent over his shortwave radio.

Neither saw any reason to delay mailing Paul's book to New York. So since Trent took his cruiser over to Catt Island almost daily because Vanessa worked part-time as a meteorologist there, the Davidsons had swung by Isle Svenson to take Paul along as well. On Catt Island Paul had had his novel photocopied, then he sent it away Express Mail.

The book landed on his editor's desk the following day. Since Arlene Arnold had been waiting for more than two years to read the rest of Paul's novel she took it home with her for the weekend and found, as Brittany had, that she couldn't put it down.

By Monday afternoon a ham-radio operator in New York City had gotten through to Paul at the lighthouse to inform him that his book would indeed be published. Since paperback rights would be auctioned and book clubs would obviously want to bid on the book, too, Paul was advised to come to New York as soon as possible.

"I have no idea what kind of money is involved," Paul added excitedly, "except that it's going to be a lot." Paul had immediately gone on the radio to call friends and family, telling them his news. Trent and Vanessa dropped everything and came rushing back. It was Trent who had bundled up Ivy and her puppies and taken them all the way to Copper Harbor, Michigan, where Steve and Gina were waiting for the dogs. Meanwhile Paul and Vanessa were packing up his belongings, which would be stored on Davidson Island until Paul wanted them.

"I've talked to Griff, too, of course," Paul continued explaining to Brittany. "The college will have to rustle up another caretaker. Do you want to keep staying here or—"

Although Brittany's head was whirling from Paul's news, her own priorities were clear. "I have to stay here, Paul."

"That's what I figured. Trent and Vanessa will check on you every day, and they've promised to come visit you often."

"That's good. But what about Chad?" Brittany inquired.

Paul hesitated. "A six-year-old doesn't really understand what this means to me. Right now I think Chad's pretty frosted. I wish I could take him with me but, of course, he's still in school."

"I'll go back to the mainland in a couple of weeks to confer with Dr. Foster," Brittany said quietly. "I could stop by and see Chad then, if you like."

"Please."

The following morning Paul left quite early, and after that things happened even more rapidly than before.

"Brittany! I hoped I could catch you while I was still in New York."

"Paul, how wonderful to hear your voice. I just got back to the college and my dusty apartment today. Dr. Foster has filled me in on all your exciting doings. Of course, I'd already seen a few news clippings."

"How about that!"

"The largest advance ever paid for an American novel, they said."

"Yes. Now Hollywood's interested, too. I'm flying to the West Coast this afternoon to discuss the movie rights. And a TV producer may even be interested in buying my first two books. Listen, I'm sorry I've only written you a couple of postcards.''

"You've been busy. I understand."

"Brittany, have you seen Chad yet?"

"I met him earlier this afternoon, at the Fosters' home, and he's just as dear as you said he was. He absolutely loves his new puppy. He ought to be back at Vicky's house by now."

"I'd better call him. Look, I wish I could say more, but I'm phoning from Arlene's office...."

"I understand, Paul."

"Chad, this is Brittany. Since your daddy is in California right now I thought you might like to go see that movie...oh, you'd rather wait for him to get back, huh? Well, would you and Wolfman like to take a boat ride? Oh, I see. He throws up every time. Yes. Sure, I can walk you guys down to the mall. He does need a leash, I agree."

"Ms. Hagen, we've never met but I'm Gina Olszewski, Paul Zachary Johnson's mother. I believe I've repaired a navy cap of yours that got torn. Yes, Paul sent it to me before he ever left the island. Say, have you heard his latest news? He's in Mexico. Yes, some television producer who's filming a series down there wanted to talk to him. It's too involved to go into over the phone, but I'd be glad to tell you all about it. Could you come to dinner tomorrow night? My husband and I would love to meet you, and Steve says that Ivy's been absolutely pining away...."

"Hello, amigo! How did you track me down over here at Amber's?"

"Believe me, it wasn't easy, Brittany. Don't you ever stay home?"

"Look who's talking! Now you're going on TV talk shows, I hear?"

"A couple. Oh, maybe three or four. Everything's so whirlwind and confusing I can't keep track. What's happening in Michigan?"

"I'm fine. Chad and Wolfman are, too. Hey, I met your mother and Steve the other night."

"God help you."

"Seriously, Paul, I had a lovely time, and I think they're very nice people. Your mother knitted my navy cap back together until I can't even tell that Ivy ever chewed a hole in it."

"Gina does a couple of things really well. Nagging is the other one."

"Paul, you ought to be ashamed of yourself. You can't believe how proud she is of you!"

"A cover on *People* magazine gets her every time."

"You looked very intelligent and literary. But I still haven't gotten used to you without your moustache. It's like you're a . . . a whole different man."

"I feel like one! Look, I'm sorry I haven't called or written more but—*what*? Excuse me, Brittany. As usual, I'm not alone. Since you're at Amber's I guess you can't speak freely, either. Tell you what, I'll call you tomorrow night . . . Oh, hell, I forgot. There's a party tomorrow that I should attend—"

"Sure, Paul. Good night."

"Thank goodness I caught you, Paul."

"Yes, I'm still here at the Beverly Hills Hotel. Is something wrong, Brittany?"

"It's Chad. He's . . ."

"What's wrong with Chad?"

"He's all right, Paul! I didn't mean to scare you—"

"Well, you did. My God, I almost had a heart attack."

"There is a bit of trouble, Paul. Today Chad simply came unglued. He started—wait a minute, Paul. Calm down, I'm trying to tell you. He had quite a temper tantrum. He started yelling and crying and kicking the furniture. Vicky and I had a hard time getting him calmed down. Then he just cried and cried. He says you have time for everything and everyone but him and...I know, I know. I'm not blaming you, Paul! Vicky isn't, either. We understand, but we're both grown-ups. Chad's just a little boy who wants his daddy.''

"What can I do for him, Brittany?"

"Since school is out, Vicky and I think Chad ought to fly out and join you in California immediately, if you can possibly spare the time...."

"I'll make time! Just put him on a plane."

"Guess who, Brittany? Yes, it's Chad. Today Daddy and I went to Disneyland and tomorrow we're going to Knott's Berry Farm and then on Saturday we're going to the beach at the Pacific Ocean where some people Daddy knows have a big ol' bungalow. Is Wolfman okay?"

"Wolfman is just fine, Chad."

"Good. That's why I wanted to leave him with you 'cause Dickie might forget to feed him. Out here we mostly eat from Room Service. Today they brought me waffles with strawberries for breakfast and yesterday I ate pancakes..."

"Yes, Mom, of course I knew Paul Zachary Johnson. We were the only two people on the island so naturally we got acquainted. Yes, that TV show was right, he is a widower and—yes, I did meet the child and he's a cute little boy of six...it's 'Chad.' Mom, please stop with the wedding bells. I don't care what sort of rumor you heard from Amber's mother, we're just friends and...Mom, that was before he got rich and renowned and every slick chick from New York to California got him in her gun sights. Mom, will you please do me a favor and forget you ever made me that wedding gown..."

"Hello, Brittany."

"This better not be who I think it is!"

"Hey, I don't blame you for being sarcastic. You're entitled to say a lot of things and, believe me, I know I deserve them. But it just isn't working out with Myrna, and I can't help remembering how good you and I were once. So I told your mother I was already divorced, that's why she gave me your phone number. Brittany, are you still there? Are you listening to me? Baby, won't you say anything?''

"Drop dead, Howard."

"Brittany, this is Dr. Ingrid Jensen. What's this health card I've found on my desk? Are you going back to the island?''

"Just as fast as I can, Dr. Ingrid."

"I'm not supposed to sign this thing without examining you.''

"Have a heart, Dr. Ingrid! You saw me just three months ago.''

"I don't know..."

"All I want to do is get back to isolation. I've got three dogs I'm playing nursemaid to and that's all the company I want, except for moose and wolves, birds and squirrels.''

"Brittany, are you all right?"

"I'm fine, Dr. Ingrid."

"I've wondered because... oh, actually, I've heard some talk that you and the hometown's hotshot celebrity are—or were—an item.''

"Past tense, I'm sure, Dr. Ingrid."

Paul got up out of bed and walked over to look out a dark window. He and Chad were presently staying at the sprawling Arizona ranch of noted television producer Stan Drake. It was a modest little spread that had cost maybe six million bucks. Right now, Chad was asleep in a bunk bed down the hall.

"Let's blow Lotusland for a few days," Stan had urged Paul. "I've got my kids for the weekend, so let's take 'em all out to my Arizona ranch.''

Paul wasn't exactly in a position to say no, not to a producer who was going to film an entire TV series based on Paul's first book about shipwrecks. Also, Chad was wild to visit "a real Western ranch," and Stan actually did raise cattle and horses. Mostly, of course, he cut lucrative TV deals around his huge oval swimming pool.

Hey, when do I get to do what I want for a change? Paul thought now, staring up into a night so filled with stars that he felt like he could almost reach out and touch them. Suddenly he remembered the last time he'd looked at moonlight and stars and an intense homesickness assailed him with such tender ferocity that his throat abruptly tightened.

When did he get to go home to Brittany?

At just that moment Paul heard the forlorn cry of a coyote far off in the hills—a hair-raising, spine-chilling wail from this smaller "cousin" to Brittany's beloved wolves. Then another coyote answered the first, almost as Paul's thumping heart answered his question: Now!

Then for the very first time—though certainly not the last—Paul listened in appreciation to the rising, falling song of America's wild free animals. That undoubtedly was George and Martha, and now Charles and Evelyn were chiming in.

"Gina's gonna have a fit that she's missed you, Paul. She went off with Griff and Ruth somewhere, but they'll all be back in a couple of hours. Can't you wait?"

"Not now, Steve. But I'll be back again in a day or two. Tell Mom that Chad's over at Vicky's for the next couple of nights. That ought to be long enough to regale his cousins with stories of Disneyland and everything else he saw. So Brittany is keeping Ivy as well as Wolfman?"

"Yes, a good thing, too. Until Brittany came, Ivy had almost quit eating, she was so lonely. Brittany's also got Scooter."

"Who the hell is Scooter?" Paul demanded.

"That's Ivy's runt. I found takers for all the other half-wolf pups but not Scooter. He's a sweet little dog. I think Brittany must be a sucker for orphans and strays." Steve laughed heartily and reached down to pat the healthy, gleaming shepherd at his knee.

"Steve, how did you get interested in German shepherds?" Paul asked his stepfather curiously, since he had never known.

"Why, it was my first wife who got me involved. She loved dogs more than anything, 'cept maybe me. Since we were married twelve years before she got sick Betty had time to lower my resistance. Later, while she lingered those four years more, not even knowing me half the time, I just kept tending her dogs for her. That's what kept me going till I met Gina...." Abruptly Steve stopped. "Sorry, Paul. I know you've never understood about that—"

"I do now," Paul said and clapped his stepfather on the shoulder for the very first time. "Hey, give Mom my love."

"Amber! Thank God, you finally got home. Listen, this is Paul Johnson. Where the hell is Brittany? I've been trying to find her everywhere."

"She's gone back to the island where she has meaningful work to do," Amber said coolly. "I think she got tired of sitting by a phone that rarely rang because a certain famous writer didn't have time to call her or—"

"Oh hell, Amber. Are you saying Brittany is at Isle Svenson right now?"

"You're the big genius, Paul. You figure it out."

Paul barely managed to catch the last ferry from Copper Harbor to Catt Island. Then, by arriving almost at dusk, he had to pay an arm and a leg to charter a boat for Isle Svenson. He was grudgingly counting out bills to the be-whiskered boatman when it suddenly occurred to Paul that he was still handling money just as he used to, pinching every penny and trying to be frugal. But he didn't have to live that way anymore. Impulsively Paul surprised the boatman with a generous tip.

That tip also got him out to the island in ten minutes flat. But as Paul watched the familiar shoreline draw nearer he didn't have eyes for the waves crashing on the rocks or the thick forests beyond, now lovely with spring. He just glanced at the tall white lighthouse and homey, familiar cottage. Then he concentrated exclusively on that tall, distant figure, walking down the beach, all alone except for three lively dogs at her heels.

Even at this distance she looked unbelievably feminine and shapely to Paul's longing eyes. She stopped and looked up as the boat drew nearer, obviously surprised to have callers arrive at this time of evening. Then he saw her natural, fresh-faced blond beauty. Saw a certain air of innocence, highlighted by her light bright hair, combined with an elegant sophistication in the sleek black sweater she wore over jeans. Of course, he'd always had a thing for a pretty blond woman wearing stark black.

Would Brittany be glad to see him, too? Suddenly, as the boat turned in to dock, Paul found himself bathed in the cold sweat of apprehension. He had never meant to neglect Brittany, as he knew he had, but these last few weeks had been so absolutely, incredibly unbelievable—

Would she believe that? New York and Hollywood both seemed practically unreal to him now—how must they seem to her?

Suddenly Paul was reminded, too, that Brittany had been jilted once. Oh God! She'd probably felt jilted again when he'd faded so completely from her life.

Brittany had quite a temper, too, when she was good and mad. That he had no difficulty in recalling. She would be either freezing cold or boiling furious with him. Suddenly Paul began to fear not only for his future but for his scalp as well.

Still, he mustn't be too apologetic and abject, either. Not with a Valkyrie who would utterly despise a wimp. God, what on earth was he going to say to her?

Brittany didn't even recognize him at first, that's how dramatically his appearance had changed. She had just been out walking the dogs as she did every evening, making quite a long stroll of it while she tried to unwind and not worry about anything in particular.

This time, with Paul—or, rather, without him—she really had been all right. Okay with what had happened and with all that might happen yet. Well, at least most of the time she was all right. Brittany's work filled her days. Miracle of miracles she'd even found a second wolf's den on the island. Its pack consisted of only four adult males and three small cubs.

Long hours of work in the field had kept her hands busy and her mind occupied. Long hours of writing had filled her evenings as she compiled statistics, recorded field notes and noted other information for the various scientific papers she'd write. Hers was a drudge's schedule, of course, but it suited Brittany perfectly at present.

Later, after she returned from the island, she'd think about family, friends and having a social life again. Maybe one day she'd even be able to think about meeting men again, but that wouldn't happen for a while.

It was only during these walks on the shore at dusk, or sometimes in the middle of the long dark nights, that thoughts of Paul possessed her mind again. Then suddenly Brittany's body would react, her midsection aching as if she'd just been punched hard in the stomach. Then tears would rush to her eyes as she thought of never, ever lying in his arms again, of never being able to reach out and touch him. She would cry bitterly then, thinking of some other woman sitting at his dinner table, reading the pages he wrote and raising dear, lovable little Chad. At moments like that Brittany felt almost overwhelmed and crushed by pain.

But then—usually at the very worst of such painful moments—some part of her heart would defiantly deny the evidence. "No! Paul is not Howard Pierson, a shallow, fickle, flighty man," it said. "And he's much more, too, than those people know who can only call him a 'natural-born writer' and a 'towering talent.' He will be back one day!"

Sometimes, though, that belief was very hard to hold on to. It seemed so...mythical. But she was into mythology these days. Brittany had even filled one rainy Sunday reading a child's book on the Norse gods and goddesses that she found on a shelf in the cottage. It didn't discuss the deities in any depth, of course. Still, she had found Odin a particularly interesting god.

Not only did he oversee war and its battles, but he was also the god of wisdom and poetry. Odin sat high in a watchtower, where nothing escaped his gaze.

Odin's wife was Frigga, goddess of the sky. Although she presided over the home, she also shared a rare equality with Odin, including dominion of heaven. Then there were the Valkyrie—Odin's willing maidens—ready and eager to do his bidding. Brittany wondered just how Frigga had felt about those women!

Then she had smiled over the illustration of a Valkyrie on horseback. Darned if it didn't look just a little bit like her. And she liked the way the book ended with the gods and goddesses riding over the rainbow to their enchanted palaces.

Now, in the dusky twilight, Brittany strained to see a very real man alighting from the chartered boat. But he was virtually unrecognizable. Well-built and clean shaven with short, dark, well-groomed hair he wore an expensive business suit, white shirt and tie. He carried a small flight bag.

Brittany's first startled thought was that maybe Paul had sent a lawyer or some other personal representative out here to talk to her. Oh, surely, Paul didn't fear that Brittany might file a breach-of-promise suit.

But that didn't seem to be the case, either, because now the boat was pulling away from the dock instead of waiting for the man to conduct his business.

Then a dog's simple love penetrated the disguise. Suddenly Ivy began barking ecstatically, then she was off and running like a streak straight toward the stranger on the dock. Chad's dog, Wolfman—a follower if ever there was one—also gave a bark and went loping after Ivy. But small Scooter, Brittany's very own little wolf-dog, merely stopped closer to her side, as if both offering and seeking protection from this stranger.

Brittany reached down to automatically soothe Scooter who had started to growl softly. But now her heart was racing toward the danger zone as she watched the reunion down the shore.

So Paul had come back. But he looked so changed and different that Brittany warned herself not to get her hopes up. Not to expect anything—no, not anything at all.

He's got class, I'll give him that, she found herself thinking admiringly. Paul doesn't send anyone else to do his dirty work, and he doesn't do it by phone or radio, either.

When she straightened up she saw that he was walking toward her. Then Brittany shivered, feeling so afraid...so desperately, damned afraid! Defiantly she crossed her arms across her chest and stood just as straight and tall as she could, but she still couldn't think of any way to protect herself adequately.

Now Paul was close enough that she could see his eyes. Black eyes that brimmed with tenderness as he glanced again at the adoring, delighted Ivy. At least Paul was still a sensitive guy, Brittany was glad to see. But as those same black eyes met Brittany's... Uh-oh! Restless and changeable eyes? No, not quite, but exactly what was their expression? It seemed to combine fear and defiance, too, or was it—?

She was simply too nervous to tell.

Paul didn't try to come over and kiss her, not even a careless, meaningless Hollywood kiss. In fairness, Brittany guessed her stance appeared a bit too formidable to encourage familiarities.

"Well, look at you in your pretty suit and with your pretty hair!" she said brightly. She spoke first, since Paul still hadn't. "I think Room Service must have been very good to you."

"What?" Paul said, perplexed, his hand still resting on Ivy's head.

"You've gained weight."

"Maybe I've put on all the pounds you've lost," Paul replied, flashing such a devastating smile that it threatened to melt her into a puddle at his feet.

"I've lost a bit," Brittany said, trying to keep this very, very casual. "Exercise and hard work. I've been on the go a lot myself...."

"Brittany."

He said just her name, but she stopped rattling. Somehow he'd always had this quieting, gentling effect on her when she might otherwise start sounding half-hysterical. "Yes?" she whispered.

"I'm sorry I've neglected you. I never meant to. But it's really been such a zoo!"

"I know." Again her voice was just a whisper.

"Do you? Important people everywhere, telling me where to go, what to do and then what I should say when I got there—"

"And you've loved every minute of it," she said flatly.

"You're right!" He grinned. "It's made up for quite a lot, and I loved the whole crazy circus until I woke up yesterday. Maybe I woke up in more ways than one. Brittany, I want to buy an island of my own out here. And I'll grow a beard and moustache again so no one will recognize me, and I'll tell anybody who dares come looking for me that I'm just the handyman and garbage hauler since I can do those jobs convincingly. What do you think of that?"

"Sounds good to me." She shrugged, understanding the anonymity Paul might now desire. "Personally I've always liked you with a moustache and beard." Of course, she could also have learned to like him if he'd had two pointed heads.

Paul laughed, the sound carefree. "Since when did you like all that hair on my face?" She shrugged again, and Paul added quietly, "At least that's what I'd like to do after I've married you—"

Then Brittany was very proud of herself because she didn't start crying or make a fool of herself. Indeed, she stood as aloof and proud as any Viking woman in the annals of history. "That's not necessary, Paul," she replied coolly. "I'd never hold you to a...a thought you expressed once before all the hoopla began."

"—in that church in Little Stavanger, Minnesota, with all of your family and mine present," Paul continued evenly, just as if Brittany hadn't interrupted him. "I don't see any reason to wait, either, since I believe you already have an appropriate dress."

She drew a breath. There really was oxygen, she just couldn't seem to find any. "Paul, I've told quite a number of people—Amber and my mother and Dr. Ingrid Jensen— that I consider us a thing of the past." Only why did her heart start twisting and turning like a puppet in the wind as it tried to protest?

She saw hot anger flare in Paul's eyes now. Great. All she wanted was a nice quiet safe place to sit and lick her wounds. Instead they were going to have a rousing fight just like their early days, though never had she had less heart for fighting!

Then she watched Paul struggle for control, and win. Indeed, he grinned at her mischievously again. "Then you're going to have to call them all up and eat crow. Because I definitely still intend to marry you. Incidentally that wasn't any understanding. It was a carved-in-stone promise."

"Pretty sure of yourself, aren't you?" Brittany asked, her arms tightening across her chest, but now her voice started to quiver just a trifle.

"I'm sure of you. But in case you're worried I don't plan for our relationship to interfere with your work. I know it's important and you want to get your master's. You won't be burdened with household duties. We'll hire an old troll or two, and they can handle the day-to-day stuff. Incidentally I intend also to respect and appreciate all wolves. So when will we get married?" He paused thoughtfully, waiting for her reply.

"You really are sure of yourself!" But now Brittany's voice was getting all choked up because Paul had sounded so firm, so definite, so—so committed.

"No. Frankly I'm standing here shaking in my shoes. The last thing I ever expected in my life was to fall in love with you when I did. But I fell as hard as any man ever does from the moment I first saw you with that cap blowing off your head and your glorious blond hair in the wind. Don't tell me I've lost you when I love you so very much, Brittany!''

Now she did have to struggle not to cry, that hard cold lump of fear and pain in her midsection dissolving like a sugar cube in the rain. But one small sore sticking point still remained.

''I saw pictures of you, Paul, with some very beautiful women,'' Brittany said, dashing away her tears.

''Bathing beauties with bubble brains and silicone boobs?'' he retorted. ''Did you happen to read the captions on those pictures? They're just actresses who'll star—''

''You've always liked women,'' she accused. ''Somehow I can't imagine you living now without a handmaiden or two.'' Oh God, why was she doing this? Why was she trying to drive Paul away? And yet she had to say these things to him because she had to be sure.

But apparently nothing could ruffle Paul tonight. ''I think any handmaidens of mine will undoubtedly be our own daughters. I'd like two or three kids to add to Chad, if that's okay with you.''

Brittany was almost completely speechless now. ''Why me?'' was all she could manage to say, but she knew he must hear her unspoken question: ''Why—when you can have almost any woman in the world?''

''Because I'm very particular,'' Paul answered steadily. ''My wife has to be the sort of woman who truly cares about an unhappy little boy or a lonely dog. If she's the kind who takes in orphans and strays maybe she can even put up with me. She's also got to have character and be strong enough to handle adversity or fame.''

Character. He'd always liked that in wives, she thought.

''Finally, she has to be someone who loves me and whom I can love with all my heart... as I do, Brittany. As I always will.''

''Promise?'' She could barely say the word.

''I promise.''

Then she came rushing into his arms again, after so long and empty a time, and was caught tightly against him. As she looked up into the dark blaze of Paul's eyes, just a second before he kissed her, Brittany whispered a truth of her own.

"I convinced everybody that it was all over between us—"

"That's all right. I'm magnanimous enough to forgive you."

"Except one person."

"Yourself?" Paul guessed, gently stroking first her hair and then her face.

Brittany nodded. "You and your mixed messages. Just when I was convinced I'd never see you again you'd send me a navy cap or—or ask my opinion on what to do for your child. Or drop all the glitter just to take Chad to Disneyland and make him happy again. So some part of me always knew a man like you doesn't say things he doesn't mean or make promises rashly or—or break my heart—"

"Never! And now I'm home to stay." Paul tilted Brittany's chin up then and kissed her with such yearning and such passion that she could only wilt against him until she caught her second wind and began hugging and kissing him, too.

"I do love you, too, Paul Zachary Johnson!" she said fiercely, her hands winding tightly around his neck. "Oh, whatever took you so long to come home?"

* * * * *

Silhouette Special Edition

presents

★ LOVE AND GLORY ★

from
Lindsay McKenna

Introducing a gripping new series celebrating our men—and women—in uniform. Meet the Trayherns, a military family as proud and colorful as the American flag, a family fighting the shadow of dishonor, a family determined to triumph—with **LOVE AND GLORY!**

June: A QUESTION OF HONOR (SE #529) leads the fast-paced excitement. When Coast Guard officer Noah Trayhern offers Kit Anderson a safe house, he unwittingly endangers his own guarded emotions.

July: NO SURRENDER (SE #535) Navy pilot Alyssa Trayhern's assignment with arrogant jet jockey Clay Cantrell threatens her career—and her heart—with a crash landing!

August: RETURN OF A HERO (SE #541) Strike up the band to welcome home a man whose top-secret reappearance will make headline news . . . with a delicate, daring woman by his side.

Silhouette Intimate Moments®

AWARD OF EXCELLENCE

NORA ROBERTS
brings you the first
Award of Excellence title
Gabriel's Angel
coming in August from
Silhouette Intimate Moments

They were on a collision course with love....

Laura Malone was alone, scared—and pregnant. She was running for the sake of her child. Gabriel Bradley had his own problems. He had neither the need nor the inclination to get involved in someone else's.

But Laura was like no other woman ... and she needed him. Soon Gabe was willing to risk all for the heaven of her arms.

The Award of Excellence is given to one specially selected title per month. Look for the second Award of Excellence title, coming out in September from Silhouette Romance—**SUTTON'S WAY**
by Diana Palmer

Im 300-1

You'll flip . . . your pages won't!
Read paperbacks *hands-free* with

Book Mate • I

The perfect "mate" for all your romance paperbacks

Traveling • Vacationing • At Work • In Bed • Studying • Cooking • Eating

Perfect size for all standard paperbacks, this wonderful invention makes reading a pure pleasure! Ingenious design holds paperback books OPEN and FLAT so even wind can't ruffle pages — leaves your hands free to do other things. Reinforced, wipe-clean vinyl-covered holder flexes to let you turn pages without undoing the strap . . . supports paperbacks so well, they have the strength of hardcovers!

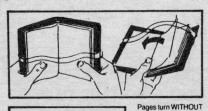

Pages turn WITHOUT opening the strap.

SEE-THROUGH STRAP

Reinforced back stays flat.

Built in bookmark

BOOK MARK

BACK COVER HOLDING STRIP

10 x 7¼ . opened
Snaps closed for easy carrying. too

Silhouette Intimate Moments

NOW APPEARING!

LIEUTENANT GABRIEL RODRIGUEZ
in
Something of Heaven

From his first appearance in Marilyn Pappano's popular *Guilt by Association*, Lieutenant Gabriel Rodriguez captured readers' hearts. Your letters poured in, asking to see this dynamic man reappear—this time as the hero of his own book. This month, all your wishes come true in *Something of Heaven* (IM #294), Marilyn Pappano's latest romantic tour de force.

Gabriel longs to win back the love of Rachel Martinez, who once filled his arms and brought beauty to his lonely nights. Then he drove her away, unable to face the power of his feelings and the cruelty of fate. That same fate has given him a second chance with Rachel, but to take advantage of it, he will have to trust her with his darkest secret: somewhere in the world, Gabriel may have a son. Long before he knew Rachel, there was another woman, a woman who repaid his love with lies—and ran away to bear their child alone. Rachel is the only one who can find that child for him, but if he asks her, will he lose her love forever or, together, will they find *Something of Heaven*?

This month only, read *Something of Heaven* and follow Gabriel on the road to happiness.

The heat wave coming your way has arrived . . .

⊙ SILHOUETTE SUMMER *Sizzlers*

Whether in the sun or on the run, take a mini-vacation with these three original stories in one compact volume written by three top romance authors—

Nora Roberts
Parris Afton Bonds
Kathleen Korbel

Indulge yourself in steamy romantic summertime reading—

Summer was never so sizzling!

Available NOW!

SIZ-1B